O_
GEORGE
AND
ALLECTUS

In memory of Diana,
with whom I first saw the Roman town of Silchester

*What eyes are seeing,
what faces faded
eyes of ashes....?*

OF GEORGE AND ALLECTUS

A NOVEL

JOHN AUBIN

© John Aubin 2024

Published by John Aubin Books

All rights reserved. No part of this book may be reproduced, adapted, stored in a retrieval system or transmitted by any means, electronic, mechanical, photocopying, or otherwise without the prior written permission of the author.

The rights of John Aubin to be identified as the author of this work have been asserted in accordance with the Copyright, Designs and Patents Act 1988.

A CIP catalogue record for this book is available from the British Library.

ISBN 978-1-7396959-4-1

Book layout by Clare Brayshaw

Cover photograph: The Roman amphitheatre at Silchester

Prepared and printed by:

York Publishing Services Ltd
64 Hallfield Road
Layerthorpe
York
YO31 7ZQ

Tel: 01904 431213

Website: www.yps-publishing.co.uk

1

The way was heavy, sloughed with fallen leaf, sodden and oozing into black puddles. He kicked out careless feet, scuffing the leaves, splashing his trouser legs with muddied water. Coming to a junction of paths, he took the one he knew best. It rose to a drier place on a low ridge, known as Holy Water Clump, beyond which a line of dark trees marked the edge of Woolmer Forest. Behind him to the west, lit by the autumn sunlight, lay tracts of woodland and open moor, and even further beyond could be seen squares of ploughed fields, with the spire of Blackmoor Church piercing the skyline.

There was a sign here where the path entered the deep woods, hammered to a trunk by a single nail and already hanging sideways. Some boy will have that off soon, the man thought; a souvenir to show his mates, to be displayed in some hideaway they have set up in the woods.

The sign was of metal, painted white, and in black letters upon it was written:

DANGER.
Brimstone Inclosure. Firing Ranges.
This land is owned by the War Office. Entry is forbidden when the Red Flag is hoisted.

Although the red flag did hang down limply upon its pole, he ignored it. These were his woods, not theirs. He laughed. It was a dry, crackling laugh, which he cut off as soon as he made it. It sounded mad. He did not wish to think he was mad. Yet he could not deny those inner pressures that seemed to rule him now at time.

He knew that soldiers were all about him. But not those the sign and the flag warned about. Those were not the riflemen either with whom he had once fought: they were all dead years ago, thousands of miles from here, sprawled amongst the rocks and long grasses of the battlefield where he too had nearly died. No, it was those soldiers of a much earlier age whom he wanted to find and see. He knew they had once marched here into a great battle.

To him, they were alive again. He could feel them rustling past him, hear their boots on the gravelled soil, hear the sharp rattles of their armour and their distant shouts, their trumpets calling shrilly, sense the shadows of their spears slicing the air, hear the thuds of bolts in flesh and bone, the screams, the roars of pain and anger......

He could not free himself from those sounds. They went on and on in his aching brain. And here in these woods they were at their most intense. It was why he had come today. It was time to confront these soldiers of the past, not just to hear them in his head but to see them too, to look upon them not as shadows, but as flesh. How he longed to see their faces and gaze out upon their battle standards; to know he had been *right*.

He took out the small, round disc from his pocket and gazed at the bearded head of the usurper Allectus moulded upon it, the brow, jaw and jutting nose of a man who looked tough, dominant, brutal even. It was this man's army that he sought.

He pushed his way amongst the trees, pulling aside the branches and the briars with his one arm, peering into the dense undergrowth, wondering what lay ahead of him, what was going to happen this day.

Some way behind on the footpath hurried a young woman, bent forward, a cloak about her shoulders, black tresses of hair spilling out from her bonnet.

2

The long strands of yellow grass fringed his eyes. The rocks he lay behind were burnt dark-red in the sun. Heat shimmered on the air like veils of rippling water. It was water he wanted most of all. A sharp crack and puff of white smoke in front of him, then a shrill cry behind.

Voices, more cries. Some heavy shots of returning fire were sounding close by.

'Stretcher bearers! Drag 'im in, lads! Keep yer heads down now!'

A sudden boom reverberating from the rocky ground as a 9-pounder fired its heavy case shot.

Across his front, two loose horses of the mounted infantry came at a canter, their reins dangling, terrified, foam at their mouths. He turned his head to look rearwards, not easy from his prone position. He could make out General Colley in his white pith helmet and blue patrol jacket at the centre of the plateau by a pile of rocks. Colonel Ashburnham wearing the dark-green of the Rifles stood beside him. They were talking animatedly, both using their arms vigorously to emphasise points.

To one side of them stood the two field guns, their crews bent low over the barrels. One artilleryman was stretched out close by, crumpled onto the grass. Even as he watched, another fell close by, grasping at his side. The sound of the Boer's shot hung flatly on the air. A crack against the rock by his own head and the ricocheting whirr of the bullet made him turn sharply back. His head, in its brown-stained helmet, was protected by the rock, but not his limbs. He clutched his Martini-Henry rifle in his right hand, pushing it out before him. How could he fire in reply without exposing himself instantly to a bullet? Those devilish 'Bo-ahs' were marksmen of the first order. He felt his flesh flinching every time he moved.

It had been a hopeful morning. Some movement at last. It was what the soldiers had wanted after days cooped up in camp. Five companies of the 3rd/60th – some three hundred riflemen – commanded by General Colley himself, were to march in light order from their camp at Mount Prospect to meet up with supply wagons coming up the road from the fort at Newcastle. The 60th Rifles would then escort them back to the camp. The Boers had been harassing the road in recent days, but it was thought they would not dare attack such a strong column, which included, in addition to the companies of riflemen, mounted infantry and artillery as well.

But the Boers had done so. At a distance that was only five miles or so from the camp, they had flung forward their fast moving, mounted commandos to surround Colley's column and force it to deploy onto the bleak, treeless upland known to the Boers as Schuinshoogte (the slanting heights). Here they had been able to keep the British soldiers pinned down by accurate rifle fire.

Below Schuinshoogte, flowed the muddy Ingogo river, which the column had forded only two hours before on leaving the camp at Mount Prospect. In the distance to the north, the distinctive flat summit of Majuba mountain was outlined against a sky even now darkening with rain clouds, presaging another rain storm. It was early February, but in northern Natal this was the hot, summer season when the rains could be heavy and frequent.

The General had underestimated the enemy once again. He had already lost one battle, in which the 3rd/60th, at first to their chagrin, but as it turned out, thankfully, had been little involved. Eighty British soldiers had been killed in that battle ten days ago, and over a hundred wounded.

Colonel Ashburnham had commented to a staff officer at the time that General Colley was not fit 'to command a corporal's guard' – or so the rumour had gone around the camp. That was not something which helped Rifleman George Maple, pinned down by Boer rifle fire, one little bit at this moment.

George Maple had been in the army only some eighteen months. He had joined the 3rd battalion of the 60th Rifles at their Winchester depot in a state of some desperation in the summer of 1878. He had volunteered for twelve years, the last six of which would be spent in the reserve, which seemed to make the twelve years easier to accept. There was time to reconsider after the ale had left his head, yet he was still determined. He was taken with three other recruits in a cart into Winchester to begin his training.

What had he left behind? His father, who worked in Alton as a stableman at the Swan Hotel, he remembered mainly as a heavy, hairy arm that clouted him about the head. Then, when George was only five or so, the stableman was kicked in the head by one of his own horses, dying a week later. The coroner's report stated he had been drunk, 'a dangerous state around spirited horses.' His mother, George had scarcely known at all. He retained just a sense of her skin against his face and a faint scent of roses. He had been brought up by his aunt, who made sure he went to his schooling. She told him his mother had gone away with a soldier, but George didn't know at the time what that meant. She never came back.

He was studious. He enjoyed his lessons, and learnt to hold his own with the other town boys, who often taunted him on the way to and from the school-mistress' house. When he turned fifteen, his aunt had said that was enough schooling for him: he must work now and learn to provide for himself. He got a job as a general labourer in the town, and then, when it was known he could read and write and knew his numbers well, he obtained a post in a bank to train as a clerk, which work he did, propped up all day on a high stool in a dreary office with high, shuttered windows, for nearly three years.

One day, he came home to his aunt's house to find it locked up. His aunt must still be out. She sometimes went to see a friend in Farnham: perhaps she had been held up and would arrive soon. But it grew dark and no one came. He was frightened. He broke a rear window to get in. There was only a small loaf and some lard which he could eat. He drank water from the outside tap. He went into work the next day and told them what had happened. The bank manager, a kindly man, said he would try to help. He returned a little later and took George into his study. 'Your aunt is in the police cells,' he told her. 'She was arrested for stealing.'

Some weeks later, after George had struggled on in the house on his own, getting his meals out in ale houses, the oh-so-kindly bank manager told him that 'he had to let him go': the work he did was no longer needed. It was clear to George, however, that he did not want to keep on a member of staff with criminal connections: this would not impress people seeking to place their money with his bank. George's aunt had since been sentenced by the magistrates to two years in Reading Gaol for passing counterfeit money: all the sordid details of her liaisons with a gang in Farnham were reported in the local paper. He did not go to see her, nor did she make any request for him to do so.

On his last day at the bank, the manager sent for him in his office and introduced him to a tall gentleman with a thin, shrewd face and high-domed, balding head, who wore a black suit made of an expensive fabric, and had a high white collar with a black cravat about his neck. A top hat and gloves lay on the table by his side. The gentleman's name, he was told, was Lord Selborne, and he was the Lord Chancellor of all England. The manager spoke the last words in a hushed and reverent tone.

Lord Selborne had heard of George's story from the manager, and, as an act of great condescension for a man of such eminence, wished to speak with him.

'This is your chance, boy,' the manager said out of the corner of his mouth, pushing him into the room. 'Don't make a mess of it.'

So, greatly wondering, George shook hands with the stranger, whose long, bony fingers wrapped themselves around his own broad, stubby hand for a moment, before withdrawing into the white cuffs that half-hid them. Lord Selborne looked into George's face for a long moment, seeing a slimly-built youth of medium height, shabbily dressed in a much worn suit, with untidy light-brown hair and bitten nails, but who stood up straight and had an enquiring look, with eyes that did not look away, but were focused and sharp.

Yes, he thought, there is a quality in this lad. I can probably help him. It would be a tragedy to have him cast adrift, perhaps to fall in with bad companions, such as, I understand, his guardian has done. Lord Selborne believed in a liberal philanthropy, which included helping those less fortunate in life, who, through no fault of their own, had strayed from the path that might lead them on to the better fulfilment of their abilities, whatever their background and class.

And so it was agreed. George was to travel down to Lord Selborne's home at Blackmoor, some eight miles distant, in three days' time to be interviewed by the secretary to his lordship. Depending on that interview, the secretary – a Mr. Whiteley, a former schoolmaster now in Lord Selborne's employ – would have the final say, one way or the other.

Or so Lord Selborne had stated emphatically, while pulling on his gloves and preparing to make his departure, the bank manager fawning about him. If successful, George would be placed entirely in the secretary's hands for direction. Mr. Whiteley had long expressed the need for an assistant, particular with his lordship's huge library to catalogue, and George appeared to have the necessary numeracy, literacy and penmanship to fulfil the role. The post would be on a trial basis at first, until his competence and diligence were established. It might also involve some outdoors work to assist Blackmoor's regular garden staff, should the need be there.

So, on a bright April morning in 1873, with all his clothes and other possessions – few as they were – packed into an old, battered portmanteau, George boarded the carrier's cart in Alton's Market Square which had been instructed to bring him to Blackmoor House, and set out along the Hampshire lanes most optimistically, yet fearfully too, to begin his new life.

3

It was now nearly three of the afternoon on the 8th February 1881, and Rfn. George Maple had been pinned down by Boer fire behind his sheltering rock for nearly three hours. He had fired off all the rounds in his pouches in the general direction of the enemy. No obvious target had presented itself and he had had no orders to move his position. No one came with more ammunition. What was the General planning? There seemed to be no plan. Not even the 9-pounders fired now. They had been silenced by the Boer fire.

George was growing increasingly desperate with thirst. He chewed on some dried beef, but that only made his craving worse. His water flask, which he had unhooked from his belt and cast down at his side, had been hit and drained by a ricocheting Boer bullet, which had come close to hitting him too. A rifleman of his company, with whom he had been friends, had tried to advance to a more forward group of rocks, but had been instantly shot in the head. He lay now crumpled on his side, his bloody brains still oozing onto the grass, attracting a trail of black ants. His canteen lay beside him, tantalisingly close to George's reach.

He tensed his body. A sudden exchange of fire to his left seemed to present the necessary distraction. He tried to rise to grab the canteen, but his legs, long motionless, would not react at first to his will. He stumbled and half fell over his comrade's body. The canteen, when he pulled at it, was caught up by its strap over the dead man's arm. He tugged harder, exposed now, desperate to get back under cover.

The first bullet caught him in the right arm, high up by the shoulder, the second scored the right side of his head, tearing off most of his ear. He felt no pain at first, just the great shock to his body, which pitched him flat onto the grass. He had the sense to lie still, his hands around his injured head, expecting another shot – the death shot – but none came. Eventually he was able to crawl back to the shelter of his rock. Then the pain began to beat against him in waves. He lay in agony, slipping in and out of consciousness, until the shadows began to fall over the battlefield and the firing died away. Sudden rain, borne in by the approaching storm, swept the plateau in bursts.

In the darkness, they brought him in, careful hands trying not to hurt him further as they half-dragged, half-carried him to the centre of the plateau from where Colley had commanded. The General was still there, his drawn, bearded face like that of a ghost, whitened by the constant lightning. Colonel Ashburnham's booming voice could be heard somewhere nearby. He was giving orders. Thunder rumbled constantly, like the artillery of a greater army locked in battle beyond the horizon.

All about George were other wounded soldiers laid out in their suffering on the wet grass. Some of the lighter injured were still on their feet, hobbling about trying to help the few medical orderlies with the worst of the wounded. Canvas sheets had been found and were being laid over some of the prostrate men in a vain attempt to keep the rain from them, which was now falling in torrents. An occasional cry and groan could be heard, but mostly silence reigned, only the commands of the officers and the serjeants rising above the drumming of the rain. The silence probably owed much to the general sense of disbelief that such a disaster could have happened, and was yet unfolding. A rag tag force of civilian

Boers had outfought a famed regiment of the British Army. It was inconceivable.

Then the word began to be whispered around: the wounded were to be left here on the field, while the able-bodied remainder of the force, with the surviving horses and the guns, sought to get through the encircling Boers back to the protection of Mount Prospect camp. Help would be sent in the morning. The Boers would then surely agree to a truce. This news did now produce some anguished – even angry – shouts from the injured.

'For God's sake, sir,' one man called out to a passing officer, 'Don't leave us behind. At least get us water or we die.'

'I'll see what I can do,' he mumbled desperately, head down, looking and feeling ashamed, 'Bear up for now.'

And all about him, those wounded who could yet move were even sucking at the grass, and at the cloth of their uniforms, to send a few drops of moisture down their throats. Some cupped their hands to the rain and splashed water onto their faces, but most lay still in their pain – many, it would prove, forever.

4

George had been interviewed by Mr. Whiteley in a small backroom of Blackmoor House – the grandest house he had ever looked upon, let alone entered – and then, as it was approaching twelve, was taken to have his midday meal with the house servants. He had been introduced to them in the kitchens by the bearded Whiteley, who wore steel-rimmed pince-nez glasses and had a high-pitched voice. The housekeeper, a Mrs. Broughton, had taken George under her wing.

'When are yer to start?'

'I don't know,' he replied. 'I've only just been interviewed. They haven't said anything. I think it went well enough.'

'Well, that's good, I'm sure. You'd best sit down then.'

She pointed towards a well-scrubbed table at which others were seated, staring up at him. He felt awkward standing there in his best dark jacket and high, winged collar. Once seated at the end of the table, he found himself opposite a pretty housemaid in a white frilled cap and apron. She looked sharply away when his eyes met hers.

He was given a bowl of a meat stew to eat. It was delicious and he finished it quickly.

'Hungry were yer? There's bread as well.'

Mrs. Broughton cut him a thick hunk from the end of a crusty loaf and spread some butter on it.

'Get that in yer'.

Apart from some curious looks, they ignored him after that. He did not feel it was his place to open any conversation.

He rose to his feet, feeling the need to relieve himself. 'Is there a johnny here?' he asked.

'A what?!' It was Mrs. Broughton's shrill voice.

'You know, a khazi, a lavvy...'

'Outside in the yard,' a gruff voice said, adding in more friendly tones. 'On the left by the cart shed.' He was a bearded man in a grey-striped shirt, wearing braces. He had large hands, with tufts of hair at the knuckles.

'Take yer plate to the sink,' Mrs. Broughton said. 'Wash it over and leave it on the drainin' board.'

'Of course. Thank you.' I must be as polite as possible, George was thinking. Likely I will have to live with these people, from now until....He did not know. His future seemed to shelve away from him.

Beyond the kitchen door was a large courtyard with a cobbled surface. It was surrounded by buildings, a long barn, a cart shed and stables. Two archways opened from the courtyard to the driveway at the front of the house.

Stumbling uncertainly from the kitchen door, George could see a horse's head looking out at him from a stable door. He found the lavatory. It was the latest design of water closet, with a white ceramic handle on a long dangling chain. A pile of torn squares of newspaper stood on the tiled shelf of a small window, high up in one wall. A candle in a metal holder was placed there also, ready for any nocturnal visit. All very up to date, George thought, pulling the handle with a great clang and seeing the water rush down. He was used to privies set over pits. His aunt's had been at the bottom of the garden behind a green painted door. His first job in the morning had been to empty the chamber pots there.

When he returned to the kitchen ante-room, it was to find Mr. Whiteley now present, standing over the table and talking to one of those seated. The large wall clock behind his head showed close on one of the afternoon. George hovered waiting, not knowing whether he should seat himself again or remain standing.

'At last, Mr. Whiteley looked up at him. 'Are you ready?'

'Yes, sir.'

'Straighten your collar.'

He fumbled at his throat and adjusted collar and necktie.

'That's better'.

He followed Mr. Whiteley out of the room and along a long, dark passageway that opened into the main hall of the house. Here, George felt enclosed by dark oaken panelling, upon which were hung rows of framed heraldic crests, and, above these, portraits of sternly-visaged gentlemen and ladies. A broad stairway led upwards, overlooked by a large stained glass window shaped like one in a church, its light casting splinters of colours onto the wood-lined walls.

Mr. Whitley opened a heavy, cross-framed door and peered inside. 'My Lord....?'

'Come in. Come in.' George remembered the pleasing tones of Lord Selborne.

He followed Mr. Whiteley into the room, and immediately gasped at what he saw. Row after row of books, most in rich, golden bindings, stretched away on bookshelves that rose high on all sides of the room towards a vaulted ceiling. Sunlight poured in through upper windows. At the centre of the room a number of tables and dark-green leather-upholstered chairs were placed. At one of these Lord Selborne was seated, a book open on the table before him. He rose now to greet them, an arm thrust out towards George.

'Welcome again, young man. Mr. Whiteley has spoken very well of you.'

George shook his hand, aware of his pounding heart. 'I am pleased, my Lord,' he managed to say.

'Good. Good. Please be seated.'

Mr. Whiteley took a chair beside his master, while George sat down opposite them. He tried to read the title of the book on the table, but all he could make out was the word 'Antiquities'.

'Mr. Whiteley has given me a good testimony of your suitability for the post as his assistant,' Lord Selborne said. 'So I am very pleased to appoint you, if you will be satisfied by the terms. It will be subject to a probationary period of six months, and during that time be at a payment of two shillings a day, to be raised to 2s 6d if your work proves satisfactory. Will that be acceptable to you?'

Lord Selborne leant forward as he asked the question. His eyes are piercing black, thought George. He seems to look right through me. That is less than I earned at the bank, but I cannot turn it down. I would be mad to.

'Thank you, my Lord. I shall be most gratified to accept the position on those terms.' He did not normally use words like that, but they seemed to float into his mouth out of nowhere.

'Well, that is excellent,' exclaimed Lord Selborne, clapping his bony hands together. 'For you too, Whiteley. You will have your assistant at last.'

'Indeed, my Lord.' Mr. Whiteley's face had yet to lose its severe expression. George's heart sunk a little as he looked upon him. He suspected this man would prove difficult to please. He would rather his future lay more directly in the hands of Lord Selborne than his secretary. But at least the job was his. He would give it his very best. And he had a roof over his head.

'You will have a room in the house, but one you must share,' Lord Selborne said, confirming that last point. 'And your meals will be provided as part of your service. Is there anything more you wish to ask me, young man?'

George thought rapidly. He had no real idea yet what his job would involve. 'I think you mentioned before, my Lord, that I might be required to undertake other work as well. I think you said outdoors. What would that consist of, if I may enquire?'

Lord Selborne looked a little surprised. 'Why, whatever becomes necessary according to the season,' he replied. 'This estate is new: Blackmoor House was only completed a year ago – we had workmen still fitting out the kitchens in January this year – and there is much work still to do in the gardens and the woods. I am short of outdoors staff at present. You will not mind clipping a hedge, I think, or mowing some grass, or cutting a tree. It will be good for you – the exercise, I mean. Young men must develop their bodies as well as their minds, do you not agree?'

'Indeed, my Lord,' replied George gravely. The prospect did not alarm him at all, indeed he welcomed it. He had spent too much of his life already cooped up all day in a dark, stuffy office, where little daylight ever filtered through the narrow, dirty windows. The green park he had seen while being driven up to Blackmoor House had looked a most welcome place, where he could get good air into his lungs and make much better use of his body, rather than peering at ledgers and books all the time.

'Well, I'll leave you here with Mr. Whiteley then, so you may make a start. You have eaten, I believe?'

'Yes, indeed, my Lord.'

'Mr. Whiteley will later take you to your quarters, so you can begin to learn the house and settle in.'

'Thank you, my Lord. And for giving me this chance.'

Lord Selborne grunted, waving an arm airily. 'You have made it for yourself, my boy. I wish you success in your employment here. I have every expectation of receiving good reports about you.'

And, so saying, he rose and made his exit, leaving George to stare across at the expressionless Mr. Whiteley, whose only animation seemed to lie in the lenses of his pince-nez, reflecting the shifting light from the library's upper windows.

5

For Rfn. George Maple, the night after the battle was a dreadful one. He lay in terrible pain. A bandage had been wound about the right side of his head, but with the rain soaking it the whole sodden, bloodied mass of the bandage had fallen down below his chin. He tried to push it back with his left hand and hold it there, but it soon dropped down again, so he tugged it right off, exposing the still bleeding wounds to his skull and ear.

His head hurt: sound rattled against him like the sharp tapping of a devil's drum. His injured right arm, he could not move at all, not even the fingers. He could feel the bones grating upon each other as he tried to settle himself more comfortable on the hard ground, and then the agony came to him again, consuming him completely. Blood had soaked his tunic breast and his sleeve, but seemed to have stopped now most thankfully, so a major vessel has not been cut. There was little he could do to help himself – only endure.

Sheets of lightning lit the scene intermittently, followed by monstrous peals of thunder that seemed to shake the very earth, reverberating amongst the mountains as if rocks were being thrown about by giants. The man next to him lay still: his low moans had ceased suddenly. George whispered, 'Tommy, Tommy.' He had been in his tent: they had been friends. Tommy had come from Alton too; had joined up earlier than he and fought the Zulus when that war began. Now he was dead.

The dead lay all about – black, frozen shapes amongst the rocks, seared white under the sudden flares of lightning. Many more bodies lay further out – and probably other wounded too – where the forward skirmishing line had been. It had not been possible to bring those men in. Nothing would rouse most of them now – no dawn bugle call, no serjeant's shout, no mother's love long misted by time, not even this frenzied storm with its great bolts of lightning. Did not some say electricity could wake the dead?

Would the night and the storm never end? George sucked at the ends of the blanket that had been thrown over him by one of the few brave unwounded who had stayed on to help. The rain at least gave him some water to trickle in his throat, even if furred with wool.

Amazingly, through the heavy drumming of the rain and the crashes of thunder, George heard the thudding of a horse's hooves coming closer: was this the Boers coming to finish them off? But no, a rider – a British soldier, no less – cocooned in a bulky greatcoat and with wicker panniers either side of his horse's neck, came into the narrow clearing amongst the rocks where the dead and the barely-living lay.

Turning his head as well as he could, and unable to rise, George saw by the light of lightning flickering against the black horizon that the rider was Lieutenant Wilkinson, the regiment's adjutant. He had brought medical supplies in the panniers: they held canteens of water and one at least of spirits, as well as several loaves of bread, plus more bandages and other comforts. The lieutenant had returned to the field of his own volition. There was no one else with him, not even his orderly.

Lieutenant Wilkinson dismounted and came over to the wounded, some like Rfn. Maple stretched out on the ground, others leaning against rocks, a few even pillowed by dead horses.

'The Boers have gone,' he told them. 'Taking shelter very likely. The army will return tomorrow. We'll get proper help to you then. Those of you who are in a bad way will go down country to hospital. I promise you, my lads. So be steadfast. Remember, you're English!'

'I'm a Scot, sir,' a wounded man croaked. He was sitting up, leaning on one arm.

'Ah, McGregor. I know you. Well, remember you're a Scotsman then.'

'I will, sir. I will.'

With the contents of the panniers already being distributed, Lieutenant Wilkinson remounted and disappeared into the rain and the blackness. Another sudden flash of lightning and there was no sight of him, no sound now of his horse, no one to witness what was to happen.

Reaching the Ingogo ford for the fourth time that day, Lieutenant Wilkinson forced his horse into the strong current of the swollen river. His horse stumbled seeking its footing. A wall of water hit the lieutenant's body, encumbered by his soaked greatcoat. He was swept out of the saddle, rolling and turning and tumbling in the water, until his head smashed up against rocks. Next day, his body was found three miles downstream. Earlier, seven men of General Colley's retreating column had been drowned at the ford too. The Battle of Ingogo had proved an unwarranted disaster, redeemed only by courage and sacrifice. It had not killed Rfn. George Maple, but it was to change him forever.

When a fresh force of British troops, now under a flag of truce and including hospital wagons, returned to the Ingogo plateau the next day, the injured who had survived the night, including Rfn. Maple, were cared for at last, and the dead buried. The truce was respected by the Boers, who had their own wounded and dead to carry away, albeit a very much smaller number.

6

George soon found his employment at Blackmoor House most congenial, as indeed were his surroundings. The house – as Lord Selborne had told him – had been built very recently, indeed the landscaping of the gardens closest to the house had been completed only last year. Thus, everything looked very new – the sharply-cut, light-grey stone of the house's exterior, raised along its great length into many sharply-angled gables and pinnacled towers, the freshness of the paintwork, the wooden fittings and the furniture of the rooms, the sparkling chandeliers, the rich colours of the curtains and the carpets – so it seemed a particular pleasure to be present at all, let alone be paid to work here. In places workmen were still to be seen, adding the last touches to stonework and tiling. High to one side of the great entry porch at the front of the house, the stone-carved coat of arms of the Selborne family was even now being fixed into place.

George was to learn from fellow staff members that Lord Selborne had hosted a party in the village to celebrate the completion of his house late last year. It had been held in the schoolroom, which, together with a most splendid church and numbers of stone-walled houses, he had built ahead of the completion of his own great house, such was his munificence to his Blackmoor villagers.

Previously, there had been only one humble farmhouse here, some near-derelict cottages, and land that was in the main unprofitable moorland. The replanted estate – some

2,000 acres of it – had already begun to flourish, and there were further jobs for local workers tending it, planting clumps of noble trees, and turning it by degrees into the park by which it was now to be known. There were stone-flagged terraces close to the house, an artificial lake and island, greenhouses, where the fuschias were the pride of Lady Selborne, while the rhododendrons about the main driveway were already being noted in the county for the depths of their colours.

George learnt he was not required to put on a uniform, as his service was unlike that of the maids and footmen. He continued to wear the clothes he had arrived in, which seemed to satisfy for the present, although both his jacket and trousers were showing clear signs of wear. He soon worked his way in with the other servants; would chat with the maids, although they had little attention for him, being invariably busy; learnt to steer clear of the butler who would often appear from his cellars, red-eyed and unsteady; showed a careful respect to the house steward when he returned from a period away at Lord Selborne's London home; could be cheeky with Mrs. Broughton, who seemed to relish a sparring match with the men, but seldom the women; and got on particularly well with the footmen and the gardeners. His small room, high in an attic, approached by a narrow winding stair, he shared with a footman, a few years older than himself, by name Harold Wilkins. The only fault George could find with Harold was that he snored. He had to sleep with a pillow pressed over his head.

Harold gave him much information about the other staff, some of it, George thought, probably scurrilous. 'Don't try your luck with the maids,' he told him, 'or that will get you dismissed for sure. The old man's very strict on that, hobnobs with bishops and that sort of thing, very eager to see you aren't corrupted by any dalliance with the opposite...' – he mouthed the word behind his hand – '....sex. Oh, and by the way, never talk to any of his lordship's daughters unless they address you first. He watches over them like a hawk.'

George, in fact, was already well aware of these daughters. There were at least four of them, he thought. They were hard to keep track of. The young ladies would come into the library occasionally and sit there, usually reading the daily newspaper, or a magazine, rather than one of the very many books that filled the walls. One, he soon learnt to recognise, as she came most often. Once she had asked him to find a volume for her, treating him offhandedly as any servant, not even saying thank you when he brought her the book. He did not know her name. He remembered what Harold had told him. It was not his business to ask.

Mr. Whiteley proved to be a more congenial manager than George had at first thought. He put his stiff, rather forbidding manner down to an inherent shyness. When he had worked with him for a while, Mr. Whiteley became a little less formal, more relaxed in his manner. He ceased to hang over George all the time, checking his work, as if he expected him to make a mess of it. Mr. Whiteley was content now to leave him to his own devices, confident he knew his tasks and how they should be carried out, while he retired to his office to attend to the other work his master gave him, which he did not share with George at all.

George's main job was to catalogue the library fully. So far only a small part of that task had been completed – by Mr. Whiteley, himself, when he had been free of his other, more immediately important work for his lordship. Indeed, there were still several piles of books heaped on the floor that had yet to be allotted a place on the shelves.

Each book in the library was given a catalogue card, written with the book's title and author, publisher, edition, and publication date, plus its reference number, according to the pre-lettered and numbered bookcase and shelf upon which it was placed. The card had to be written in both black and red inks, the title in red block letters, and most of the other details in ordinary lower-case script, some of it in red, some black. Conformity must be maintained at all times. George had practised writing the cards until Mr. Whiteley had been satisfied he was fully appraised of his system. Even so, there were some works he had to hold over until Mr. Whiteley could check them and advise him of how exactly to catalogue them. George had not realised that so many books came with such variations of titles, sub-titles, authors, editors, illustrators, and editions.

The catalogue cards were kept in long drawers, which were themselves within a wooden cabinet especially designed to hold them, each drawer labelled by the first letter of the title (excluding definite and indefinite articles); separate drawers held cards arranged by authors' names. To complete the work of cataloguing each book, basic details were recorded as well in foolscap-sized, hard-boarded registers.

It was exacting work for George. He had to take the greatest care with each card; good penmanship was vital. After a time he began to enjoy the work, and soon was completing two score of cards, or even more, a day, but with many thousands of books to go the full task was daunting. After two months of such work, he had only cleared half of one bookcase, and the shelves stretched away dauntingly on both sides of the library, many with upper tiers that could only be reached by ladder. It crossed his mind to wonder what would happen when he completed the job, even if that were many months – even years – away? Would Lord Selborne then dispose of his services, or would there be other work for him? But for the present he did not worry too much about that imponderable.

Long hours were spent by Mr. Whiteley in Lord Selborne's study, which occupied a corner room at the far end of the house, with broad bay windows overlooking the park. George had been there just the once, taking some papers that Mr. Whiteley had left behind on his desk and which he now sent for by a written note given to a footman. It was an enormous room for a study, with a huge desk at its centre and yet more bookshelves. Sets of stags' antlers hung on the wall between the shelves, and the floor near the great stone fireplace was covered by the pelts of two tigers, their snarling heads still attached. Glass-topped display cases occupied a further wall, but George was not able to view what they contained. Instead, he delivered the papers to the desk of a harassed-looking Lord Selborne, and at once retreated. Mr. Whiteley called out, 'Thank you, George', and that was all.

He came to enjoy being called out from time to time to assist the gardeners. A particular job was the clearing and replanting of a copse, damaged by a gale, that stood across the park at some distance from the southern front of the house, where from the terrace only the tops of the copse's surviving trees could be seen.

George first worked in the copse during very hot weather in June. He had to help lift sawn branches, and even one complete trunk, into timber wagons, drawn by oxen, which entered the park by the drive from the South Lodge. He soon found he had muscles where he had not known they existed. That night he groaned so much as he turned in bed that for a change it was him keeping Harold awake. The work lasted for another day when his muscles were so sore he was scarcely able to pick up his knife and fork at dinner.

'What have you been up to?' one of the housemaids queried, and they giggled amongst themselves.

But, as soon as he was back in the library with a heap of books to be catalogued on the table before him, he began to yearn for the green leaves of the woods and the tall grass of the hay meadows, wishing he had the chance to be out in the sunshine again. His young life was spilling away, his body unused. Sensations consumed him at times. He had to lock them away as his shameful secret. This was an age when little was discussed, but much guessed at, then tucked away to be recalled at leisure. He grew more interested in the prettiest of the housemaids, the one he had sat opposite at his first meal here. But she continued to ignore him, maintaining a haughty silence. She was a ladies maid. Her mistress was Lady Selborne herself, who George seldom saw – just occasionally walking on the lawn, with a daughter or two beside her, parasols raised to fend off the sunlight threatening their milk-white skins.

In September, Mr. Whiteley – his Christian name of Alfred was known to George now, although he did not dare to use it – went away for a week's leave. Now George was called in by Lord Selborne himself. He went to the study, as summoned, and sat down, poised and alert, ready for his master's command. It was simple work. Just the dictation of three letters, which George was to write out in his best hand and present back to his lordship.

Lord Selborne took the opportunity to ask him how he liked his work, and whether he had settled into the house to his satisfaction and found the company of the other servants congenial.

'Yes, my Lord. I enjoy my work and all are friendly.'

'Excellent, George. Mr. Whiteley has spoken very well of you; indeed, he has sung your praises.'

'I am very pleased to hear that, my Lord.'

'Your probationary period is up very soon, if I calculate it correctly. So let us say now you have passed satisfactorily. I will raise your remuneration with immediate effect.'

'Thank you, my Lord. I am very grateful.'

'What have you liked most in your work?'

George spoke with confidence, for it was the truth. 'Strangely perhaps, my Lord, it was the work I did outdoors. I like to be out in the elements to work on the land.'

'Indeed. Not so much the library task then.'

'It interests me, my Lord. The books take my attention.'

'Have your read any?'

'I did not think I was entitled.'

'Why, of course, you are. Did not Mr. Whiteley inform you of that? If not, he was remiss. Is there anything you would like particularly to read?'

'I have just catalogued a work by White, my Lord. On the natural history of Selborne village and its antiquities, if I recall its title correctly. I would like to look at that further. Its plates interest me particularly.'

'Oh, the Reverend Gilbert White's work. It is a first edition, published last century, so take the greatest care of it. Only view it in the library.'

'Of course, my Lord. Thank you. I shall do that.'

'Is it the nature observations or the antiquities that interest you most?'

'Both, my Lord. But the antiquities, I know little of. I did not proceed far in my learning of such things at school, my Lord.'

''Well, you shall look at these then.' Lord Selborne rose to his feet and ushered George towards the glazed-topped cabinets that he had noticed previously.

'When this house was being built,' Lord Selborne said, bending over one of the cabinets while George stood diffidently beside him, 'a number of items were found: those you see here are they. Most are of the Roman era: you've heard of the Romans?'

'Yes, my Lord. I believe so. They were great soldiers.'

'Indeed, they were. They may have had a station here at Blackmoor; certainly one of their roads passed close by. For you see, they left their pots here, and some other pieces too, which were found when building the house and laying out the gardens. The finest item that was turned up is this many-coloured jug.'

Lord Selborne opened the glass lid of the cabinet and took out the jug in question. He gave it to George to hold, who felt an immediate tingling in his fingers, such as he had experienced once from a piece of amber a showman had rubbed before him at Alton Fair. The man had then passed it over his head, where it had lifted his hair in a wave, causing spectators much amusement.

'How old is this, my Lord?' he asked.

'Certainly of the time the Romans were here. Let's see. That's some fifteen hundred years ago. I have been told by experts the colouring is of enamel, a clever art for them at that time. And here is the pot, within which the jug had been placed.'

He indicated a large earthenware vessel with a broken rim. 'And see, there were bronze items found too; one that is called a *patera* was likely used in worship of their gods. There were a hundred or so coins also, of which those here are but a few examples. And in the next case, see, some iron axe heads, and some bronze spear heads. It looks like there may have been a battle somewhere nearby, and these relics were later collected from the field and buried here.'

George was enthralled, in particular by the tale of the battle. 'Do you think there is more to be found, my Lord? Or did the house builders find it all?'

'A good question, George. It shows you think laterally, not just about what has been, but that which might yet come. Excellent. To answer, yes indeed, some more pieces were found in the digging of the lake that you can see from the window here.'

Lord Selborne led him to the large window that filled the room with sunlight, pushing aside the curtain so it was fully drawn. Looking out, George caught sight of a distant glint of water, surrounded by beds of green reeds. He could just make out a higher square of land that formed an island close to the far edge of the lake, upon which a stone obelisk stood. In fact, he had been close to that place with the gardeners only recently to help with the scything of the grass bordering the reeds.

'You are looking at the island, I think,' said Lord Selborne. 'You are most percipient, my boy. Some of the finer objects I have were found exactly there. I ordered the island to be made when the lake was dug to preserve that piece of land for future study. Perhaps there is more there, or indeed beyond the far bank, but we have never looked. The whole area was once covered by a farmhouse and its yard, all of which had to be demolished, opening up the ground for the first time for generations.'

His whole face reflected his enthusiasm for the subject. 'We might yet find one of their buildings – a house perhaps with mosaic floors. Only time and good luck will tell.'

Neither George Maple or his master could have had any idea then how soon the next discovery would come.

7

One bright and sunny autumn day, late in October, George was just finishing his midday luncheon of bread and soup with other of the servants, adding cold chicken to his bread from the leftovers of the family's meal the night before, when the outside door from the yard to the kitchens was suddenly opened, and Mr. Lock – the head gardener – in some excitement stood there.

'Where is the master?' he called out to the room, not wishing to enter because of his muddied boots, and aware of Mrs. Broughton's sharp eyes fastening on him.

'I know not,' she said, then looked across at George. 'You have seen him this morning, I think.'

'Yes, I have,' George answered, wondering what Mr. Lock could want with is lordship that was so urgent. Lord Selborne had only returned from London that morning, and had spent most of his time since with Mr. Whiteley in his library office discussing aspects of his Parliamentary business. George had needed to interrupt them, begging their pardons, for he had required a fresh supply of the catalogue cards kept in the office. His lordship had waved him in and out with an impatient thrust of his arm. He had seemed in an ill mood.

'I saw him last in the library,' he said. 'But he may be elsewhere by now.'

'Go and find him, young feller,' said Mr. Lock.

George knew the man well. He had worked alongside him during some of his outdoors work. He was known to everyone as 'Mister Lock' – a man approaching his retirement after a life of hard labour: he lived with his wife in a cottage on the edge of the park.

'What's up, Mr. Lock?' he asked.

'The master will want to see what we've found. At the new copse. Coins. Lots of them. Little green things, some black, maybe silver. Thousands, I'd say.'

George's heart leapt with excitement. He took a last bite of his meal and hastened away.

He found his lordship still with Mr. Whiteley in the office. They were standing, poring over a document. George burst in without knocking. Both men looked up with annoyance on their faces, but George forestalled their reprimand by spluttering out his news. He was so excited he was stammering, something previously unknown to him.

Lord Selborne said to Mr. Whiteley, 'We'll talk further later.' Then immediately, with no word to George, left the study and strode out into the main hall, passed through two reception rooms where George had scarce dared to tread before, but now he entered close behind his master. Astonished maids, busy brushing and dusting, turned their heads to watch. Lord Selborne fumbled with the main garden door, then opened it, leaving it swinging wide. George followed. Across the lawns, Lord Selborne strode, with George almost running to keep up. In the far distance, perhaps as much as half mile away, he could see a number of men gathered at the thinly-treed copse where he had worked a few days ago. It was set forward a little distantce from other woods behind. Mr. Lock had returned, and there were three others with him whom George recognised, all from the estate.

'So what is this I hear about?' Lord Selborne barked out, coming up to them at last, slightly out of breath. 'Why have I been called out?'

Mr. Lock reached out, pointing at the ground. A young sapling lay close to his feet. Nearby, the earth had been opened up to make the hole in which to root it. Amongst the earth that had been dug out, George saw a few broken pieces of dark-coloured pottery – curved pieces perhaps from the rim of a vessel. And then he spotted a number of round, green objects as well scattered amongst the earth. Taking a step forward alongside Lord Selborne, he could now make out the shoulders of a large earthenware urn in the hole, some two feet below the surface. Many more coins were spilling from its mouth.

Trying to restrain his excitement, and not daring to call out any comment until his lordship had spoken, George saw that the hole had been extended at one side, revealing the shoulder and part of the lip of a second urn. It too was filled with coins in a tight cluster at its rim, some of which, despite their black tarnish, showed glints of silver in the sunlight.

'Good God!' Lord Selborne exclaimed. As a devout Christian – indeed he demanded the attendance of his staff on Sundays at the church he had had built in Blackmoor village – only most rarely did he call upon the Almighty in what might be termed his common speech. Lord Selborne, Lord Chancellor to Mr. Gladstone's Liberal Government, was clearly overwhelmed by the discovery.

'You were right to have sent for me,' he said, recovering himself. 'Now, first, tidy up what you have dug out. We don't want to lose any of those coins in the earth. Does anyone have a container? Oh, that's good – a metal work tray. Take that coil of twine out, and the other bits and pieces, and place the loose coins in there. Here, George, you help me.'

He bent over to pick up the loose coins from the soil, with George beside him doing the same. This great man, so formal, with all his responsibilities and all his wealth, who moves in the very highest circles, is now just one with us, George thought. He is as excited as anyone else. The past, not the present, has levelled us all.

But not for long. Soon Lord Selborne straightened himself, while placing – George noted – one or two coins in his jacket pocket. He decided to keep one for himself also, to be able to examine it at his leisure later on, and he slipped it into the watch pocket at his waist while backs were turned.

'Now, make the hole much bigger,' Lord Selborne said to his workers. 'Let's make sure we get those two pots out complete with their contents, without damaging them further. There might yet be other pots as well, or who knows what else, so keep a sharp lookout. One of you, send to the stables for a cart to be harnessed up with one of the ponies. It can come here over the grass. And bring some sacks too. These pots may break up when we try to lift them and all the bits must be kept together.'

And so in good time – an hour or so must have passed and Lord Selborne still watched over the proceedings – the two urns were excavated to their full extent, and the walls of the hole cut further back, but without revealing any further treasures. The urns proved bulbous in shape, the second unearthed very similar to the first, both being just over a foot tall and almost as wide as they were high. All the loose coins, from the second vessel, as well as the first, were now in the metal tray. All, that is, except the one George had picked up. It seemed to burn in his pocket. He should add it to the rest, he knew, but he didn't. He could not really say why. Perhaps he felt it would be a talisman for him. One coin would not be missed, surely. His lordship had taken one or two as well, but then, of course, they were all his property anyhow to do with as he wished.

Following the pony cart traversing the lawns, now came Lady Selborne with two of her daughters at her side. By this time George had learnt the daughters' names: the tall one holding Lady Selborne's arm was Sophia – Lady Sophia, as she should be correctly addressed. It was she who came to the library quite regularly these days, and was now more considerate of him when requesting his assistance, even friendly at times, if that were conceivable between one so high born and a lowly staff member. He remained very wary of her, however, summoning Mr. Whiteley to assist her with any more difficult enquiry for which he could only have expressed an uncertain opinion.

The other daughter present was Lady Laura, whose engagement to marry had recently been announced. George recognised her from the blonde ringlets protruding from her hat with its tilted brim. All the staff at Blackmoor – Mrs. Broughton, in particular – had been most excited by the wedding news. She was to marry an Earl, no less. There was to be a great gathering at Blackmoor House in early December to celebrate not only this engagement, but that of the Lady Mary as well, which too had been announced only the other day. Soon Blackmoor House would be emptying of his lordship's daughters, with just Lady Sophia and the fourth daughter, Lady Sarah, remaining, these two also likely to be plucked away before long by eager suitors.

The whole county, it was said in the servants' hall, had been invited to the grand gathering in December, which was to be a ball also. It was thought some distinguished political associates of the Lord Selborne might attend as well, perhaps even Mr. Gladstone, himself. George had been asked to help out, as this was to be the biggest occasion the new Blackmoor House had ever hosted, for which, it was said, his lordship was even to hire in servants from elsewhere, much to the house steward's concern. George had been told he must assist that evening, and had already received his first training from the senior of the footmen. His job would be to help meet the carriages as they arrived, to open doors, to take coats and cloaks and gloves, and fulfil all else regarding the immediate needs of the guests.

He was very relieved not to have been asked to wait upon table, which was a particular skill that could not be learned in a trice and must be much practised. He knew he would be little good at it. There was a good chance of making a bad error: a cold confection dropped upon a fine lady's décolletage, for instance, would likely end his service altogether, or at least have him placed somewhere out of sight where he could do no further damage, which was not what he wished at all.

Harold Wilkins, his room companion, of much the same height and build as he, was to fit him out in his second-best suit of formal footman's wear – white shirt, grey waistcoat, black jacket and tails, with black trousers and shoes. At least, so Harold told him, while measuring the jacket for its length against his body, he should be grateful the knee breeches and stockings that his lordship had earlier favoured had now been discontinued.

'Those breeches,' Harold said, 'had no flies, you see. It took ages to open them up to get your pistol out. More than one accident in that time, I've seen, I can tell you!'

But all that lay several weeks in the future. For the present, here was Lady Selborne, in company with two of her daughters, crossing the long meadow grass in their trailing dresses to examine the exciting find that was taking so much of her husband's attention. Lord Selborne greeted his wife and daughters enthusiastically, his normal calm reserve, particularly in the presence of his servants, for once cast to one side.

'How good of you to come, my dears.' He took out the coins he had placed in his pocket and gave one to each daughter to marvel over. 'Another major Roman find,' he said. 'We are becoming used to them now.'

There was a smudge of dirt on his nose and cheek, which his wife dabbed at solicitously with a lace handkerchief from her dress pocket. He tried to pull his head away, aware of the eyes on him, but she persisted in her ministrations. 'Are you quite warm enough, Roundell?'

'Warm, my dear? I am like a furnace!'

Seeing, Mr. Lock was now manoeuvring the cart with its patient pony as close to the hole as possible, Lord Selborne broke away from his wife's attentions to supervise the raising of the first of the urns. 'Carefully, carefully now: as many of you as possible get your hands on it. George, wrap your arms underneath. We don't want it bursting open.'

Soon the heavy vessel was placed on the boards of the cart, and then the second was raised too and placed beside it.' The pony stood in the shafts quiescently.

'Now two of you at the pony's head. I want the smallest – the lightest – man on board supporting the urns, just in case of a sharp movement. George, that had better be you.'

'Where are they to go to?' Sophia asked.

'A good question,' Lord Selborne said. Clearly, he had not thought of this yet. 'They will be too muddy and too cumbersome to go in the house at present, so how about the workshed at the far end of the servants' yard? Do we have the key?'

'I do, m'lud,' came Mr. Lock's gruff voice. 'I keeps my winter pots there and some other pieces. There is a workbench there and a basin and water tap too.'

'That's the place then!' Lord Selborne exclaimed., 'It sounds perfect. I will need to work there with these coins, until all can be cleaned and taken indoors.'

The pony and cart had already moved forward with George on his knees aboard, his arms flung out around the urns. One of the gardeners was leading the pony by its head.

'I'll be there just now!' Lord Selborne shouted after them.
'Right ho, m'lud.'
'Shall we fill in the hole, m'lud?' one of the workmen asked.
'Yes, there seems nothing further to be done here for the moment.' Then, as an aside, more to himself than anyone else, 'Although, of course, you can't be sure without digging the whole bally place up, and I shan't be doing that.'

'And put the sapling in,' he called out to the gardeners, beginning to walk away with his wife and daughters. He turned back with a laugh. 'Call it the money tree. Indeed, call the whole place, the 'Money Copse'.'

'Father, I can see a face and some lettering on this coin,' said Lady Sophia, looking earnestly upon the coin in her hand.

'Show it to me.' He gazed down at the small, green coin lying in the cup of his daughter's soft hand. 'That's one of Allectus. Look, you can make out the lettering 'ALLE' and I'd recognise the cruel profile of that man anywhere.'

'Who was Allectus, father?'

'He murdered the Emperor Carausius to become emperor himself. Towards the end of the 3rd century, it happened. Carausius was a soldier – well, actually he was a sailor – who had broken away from Rome and declared himself emperor of Britannia, and, I think, an area of northern Gallia too – that's France, of course. Allectus then had to confront the rightful emperor of Rome, who did not want any part of his empire to be controlled by one who was an usurper. So he invaded Britain and beat Allectus in a big battle, and took Britannia back under Rome's rule.'

'Where did that battle take place?' asked Lady Laura, who had been listening too with her mother.

'Ah, that's the thing,' Lord Selborne said. He stopped walking and turned his body like a windmill, with his arms spread wide. 'I've long had the feeling – ever since our earlier discoveries – that the battle was fought around here, close to the Roman road that passes across the edge of our estate on its way north to the Roman town of Silchester, which may have been occupied by Allectus as a stronghold. Many coins have been found in our area, some in the last century, as has been recorded – thousands of them. Perhaps they – and those we have just found – were part of the pay chests for Allectus' army. Some leading antiquarians share my view, William Curtis, for instance, at the museum in Alton: he favours my theory. The Reverend Mr. Joyce from Silchester, who has done much work on the Roman town there, is less sure, I believe. However, I feel it is quite possible the battle could have taken place somewhere near here, perhaps towards Oakhanger or Woolmer.'

At the house, the cart with the urns aboard, still embraced tightly by George, had arrived in the courtyard. Mrs. Broughton, hearing shouts and rattling hooves on the cobbled paving, came out to see what was going on, followed by the house steward and one or two other servants.

'Lordie me!' she exclaimed, 'none of that is coming into my kitchen.'

She was immediately appeased on learning that the workshed was to be the destination, and followed the bearers of the urns, including George, into its interior, where the urns were placed most carefully on the bench that ran against one wall.

'Is there no end to them Romans?' was her one comment, and then curtsied towards Lord Selborne, on seeing him come through the workshed door himself.

His lordship only had eyes for the urns and went over to examine them. 'No more coins have come loose, have they?' he asked.

'No, my Lord,' George answered.

'Good'.

Now was the time for George to confess to the coin he had placed in his pocket, but for some reason he did not.

'I shall work here later today,' Lord Selborne said. 'The coins will need to be loosened where they have stuck together, taken out and separated, some perhaps cleaned a little, and then taken to my study. Maple, I would like you to help me with this.'

'Of course, my Lord. I would be most keen to do that, sir.'

'Good, Good. I will inform Mr. Whiteley.'

'Right, we'll all leave now,' Lord Selborne said, looking around the workshed, and seeing a face at the window which immediately dropped out of sight. 'I'm sure you all have other work to do. Let me have the key,' he said to the head gardener.

'It's in the door still, m'lud.'

'Ah, yes.' Once they were all outside, Lord Selborne turned the lock and extracted the key. 'I'll keep this for the time being. I don't wish anyone or anything in this shed until I have finished working here myself. Any gardening needs will have to wait.'

'Of course, m'lud.'

'Well, that's quite a to-do,' said Mrs. Broughton, on re-entering her kitchen. 'A new plaything for Lord Selborne, as if he doesn't have enough to do. And you've got yourself a smart new job too working alongside his lordship,' she said, turning to George, who had come into the kitchen behind her. 'How some move up in the world.'

George, seeing the eyes of the maids on him, felt himself blushing. That was absurd. He had not sought this new work. It wasn't he who had found the bloody coins, was it?

8

The next morning, George worked in the library as normal. Mr. Whiteley's periodic grimness had returned, and he was quite sharp with him at times. Clearly he had been told about George's new work in company with Lord Selborne, for he kept making comments such as, 'Get this finished this morning before you disappear' or 'No time for a break, I fear. I want those cards done now'.

As Lord Selborne had not given any intimation to George, himself, about when exactly he would need him – whether today or on a later day, or for how long – he felt somewhat put out. All he wanted to do – and to do well – was whatever job was put before him. If that upset one person or the other, it was hardly his fault.

His lordship appeared suddenly in the library just after noon. 'Take your lunch now, Maple,' he said. 'And come to the workshed at one o'clock. We'll start work on the coins then.'

It was not the use of his surname that perplexed George. He had noticed that Lord Selborne only used his Christian name when they were alone together. In front of other staff, it was always surname alone. But he was surprised by the curtness, which contrasted with the amiability that had been earlier shown by his lordship. And he would have liked to have known more about what was expected from him and how long it was to last, and how indeed it was to fit in with the library work at which he was growing increasingly confident, and indeed enjoyed doing. In other words, he supposed, he wanted to be treated with more consideration, and not just as some sort of menial or chattel to be ordered to 'come here' and 'go there'. But perhaps he was developing ideas well above his station.

After a rushed lunch, with a harassed and irritable Mrs. Broughton looming over him, once he was in the workshed with his lordship – who had clearly already been there some time – he found matters were very much more to his satisfaction.

'Ah, George,' was his lordship's greeting, a glimpse of a smile playing briefly over his face, with its domed, balding top and fringes of sparse, greying hair. 'Let me explain to you the system we are to use.'

He then explained how the coins from each urn were to be taken out, singly or in clumps (to be separated later), then each coin to be examined by him provisionally to see if an immediate identification could be made, by metal type, emperor's name and mint mark, if possible, and then placed in a numbered envelope labelled with these summary details. A register was also to be kept. The work, his lordship emphasised, must be done as slowly and carefully as necessary, with no requirement for haste. 'They have been here for some 1500 hundred years already,' he said, the smile returned to his lips. 'They will bear a year or two further of our care.'

Years! George thought. Am I to do this work that long?

'Your task,' Lord Selborne continued, 'will be to write the register and envelopes to my dictation, as I process each coin. Yet, I would hope you will be able to develop your own knowledge as we proceed. From my first examination, many of the coins seem to be identical, that is they were minted from the same die, likely at the same time. I have already seen many coins of Carausius and Allectus that I recognise from the earlier finds made here at Blackmoor.'

'We will work here in this shed to begin with,' he continued. 'But, as we become more skilled, I think we may be able to remove coins in quantity and take them into the house for the detailed identification work to be carried out. It will be much more comfortable there and the gardeners will be able to have their workshed back. We will keep the urns, of course. Once they are thoroughly washed, they can be taken into the house as well.'

And so they began their work.

'It is lucky I retained some coin envelopes from the earlier discoveries,' Lord Selborne commented, as they got under way. 'I have now made a large order for more to be delivered from the stationers in Alton. A very large order.'

The last he said with a chuckle. 'And lucky as well,' he went on, as if to himself, 'that I have the time away from London at present.'

His head was bent over the first of the urns, from which he was extracting a single, loose green-coloured coin, and looked up at George with a broad smile on his face, as if he had suddenly thought of a joke which he wished to share, even with this most junior underling.

'Mr. Gladstone and his troubles will have to wait,' he added with a bark of laughter.

'Indeed, my Lord,' was all that George could think to say.

And that, for some reason, brought another brief rumble of amusement from his lordship, until with an obvious effort he squared his shoulders and regained his poise, as befitted master and servant, lord and commoner.

This initial work of clearing the coins from the urns and recording them lasted for two weeks, working for several hours in the morning usually, but once or twice in the afternoon as well. George learnt to write the details, as requested, in his neat hand on envelopes and register, and to tuck each coin away into its paper cell. By the last day of the second week, the supply of the envelopes had run out and the work was of necessity held up. Yet, the level of the coins in the first urn seemed scarcely to have dropped.

'I am expecting the envelopes on Monday,' Lord Selborne informed George. 'But we must break for a while, in any event, as I am needed in London for an uncertain period. Mr. Whiteley, I know, will be pleased to have you back with him full time.'

He placed the key to the shed on the workbench in front of him. 'I will entrust this to you, George. It is the only key for the present. There is probably another in the house somewhere that I will seek out. I would like you to check in here each day and ensure all is well. I want no one else to enter here. Is that understood?'

'Yes, my Lord. 'Of course.'

George thought his lordship was over-cautious. What did he expect his staff were going to do? Break in and steal his Roman treasures? No one would dare go near them, even if they were left totally unguarded. It seemed Lord Selborne trusted few, perhaps a trait – George had the temerity to ponder – he carried to his colleagues in government. But it was not a matter to be mentioned to any other staff member, not even to Harold when they would chat in their small room, while waiting for sleep to take them from their labours for just a few untroubled hours.

While Lord Selborne was away, and with the agreement of Mr. Whiteley, George was allowed a half-day's holiday. This was in addition to the regular half day allotted to all the staff, in rotation, on Sundays, when attendance in the morning at Blackmoor Church was required.

George mainly used his free time in walking the lanes and field paths around Blackmoor. One place he visited was Woolmer Pond – an extensive area of water surrounded by reed-beds. Here was where the Reverend Gilbert White, whose book on nearby Selborne he had now catalogued and partly read, had written of Roman coin discoveries a century ago. The pond had been largely dried up then, but now its waters stretched away full and clear. If it hid any further coins, it would be impossible to find them. Just as well, George thought, I have quite enough for the present. He had found the work interesting at first, but very repetitive and, he had to admit, becoming somewhat boring. And yet, given the quantities of coins still in the urns, it was clear the task would take many months yet to complete.

Returning from Woolmer Pond, he walked by the lanes to the small village of Oakhanger, where he drank beer in the Red Lion. Lord Selborne had told him of the great Roman road running close to Blackmoor, and he had said its course could be seen at Oakhanger. He could see no obvious sign of it, however, but then he did not really know what he was looking for. Part of the lane ran very straight, however, so perhaps that marked the road: he had learnt by now of the straightness of Roman roads. He pictured the Roman soldiers marching along in their polished breastplates and plumed helmets, banners flying above them – as he had seen once in a picture at the Mechanics' Institute in Alton – but he found it hard to think of them here, crossing these green fields under these broad skies, with dark clouds on the horizon blowing in from the west. He turned on his heel and hastened back down the lanes to Blackmoor House, arriving back just as a storm broke with rumbling thunder like the sound of the Roman gods in anger.

Work began again on the coins when Lord Selborne returned some ten days later. His lordship had brought with him in his carriage, arriving for dinner – much to Mrs. Broughton's distraction at this impromptu event – two gentlemen, 'of a middling look, though one a churchman', as the summoned house steward was to describe them.

George had received an instruction through Mr. Whiteley to open up the workshed at nine the next morning and be ready to recommence his tasks there. So he was surprised to find that when Lord Selborne arrived shortly afterwards he was accompanied by the two strangers. All three men were wearing long coats, for the weather had grown very cold of late. The workshed, indeed, was like an icehouse, and George was grateful to have borrowed from Harold a grey, thick knit sweater, which he wore in place of his own increasingly worn jacket.

The introductions, which his lordship had the courtesy to make, told George these gentlemen were the Reverend Mr. Joyce, rector of Stratfield Saye, currently excavating at the Roman town of Silchester – or *Calleva*, to give it its Roman name – and Dr. William Curtis from Alton, who had founded the Mechanics' Institute there with its art gallery, library, and museum displays. By chance, Lord Selborne had met the two at a function given by the Royal Society of Antiquaries at Somerset House and invited them back to Blackmoor House to see his new discoveries. They were to be taken on to their homes later that day in his lordship's own carriage.

George was introduced to them as 'George Maple, new to my staff and assisting in my library: he is developing a considerable interest in antiquities' – this last gaining a murmur of approval and even a 'Good for you, my boy.'

There was now much animated conversation as the two visitors viewed the urns, peering inside, and fingering the upper deposits of coins. Then they inspected some of the already catalogued and packaged coins, peering learnedly at the details George had recorded in his careful hand.

'All, bar one or two, appear late 3rd century,' the Reverend said in a high, clear voice. He was clean-shaven, short and rather plumpish, with a broad, friendly face and keen black eyes, and he had the habit of enunciating each syllable very carefully, which made his delivery somewhat slow. George, standing with eyes lowered, to indicate his modest presence in this august company of gentlemen experts, found himself wondering at the length of his sermons.

'Yes, Carausius and Allectus are very evident, and none later,' the Reverend added, after further study of the identified coins. 'Unless, of course, such are still to emerge from the urns. The indications of a late 3rd century hoard are definitely present, however, but it is too early yet to do more than surmise until the urns are further emptied.'

Dr. Curtis, who wore spectacles, and whose impressive jutting jaw bore a flourishing white beard, added rather more cautiously, 'This deposit might well – as you have suggested, sir – indicate a hiding away of personal, or indeed possibly state wealth, at a time of considerable disturbance of the province. I can think of no more likely period than the disorganisation at the time of the breakaway from Rome, and the re-invasion of Constantius.'

'So there you are, Roundell,' continued Curtis, his familiarity with the Lord Chancellor indicated by the use of his Christian name, the first time George had heard it spoken by other than his wife. 'You may well have built your house upon some station set up by Allectus. Or just possibly the camping ground of his army was here before the battle that saw the second of the usurpers disposed of, as the panegyric tells us. The coinage in these urns, together with that found earlier at Woolmer – and elsewhere nearby too, I believe – was part of the treasury of Allectus.'

'I think that unlikely, sir,' the Reverend said immediately. 'The coins revealed so far are all low denomination. They would not have paid many men. My feeling is that these monies were hidden away by some great land owner, who may have had his *villa* close to the road nearby. Allectus' stronghold, in my view, and possibly the battle site, is much more likely to have been behind the strong walls of *Calleva*.'

Dr. Curtis – George thought – looked irritated by this quick challenging of his theory. Lord Selborne intervened. 'We shall undoubtedly learn more when I have examined all the coins – although that will take some considerable time.'

He smiled, to George's surprise placing a hand on his shoulder. 'This young man, I think, would rather be in my library in the warmth, cataloguing books.'

'Oh, no, my Lord. Not at all.' George felt the blood rushing to his face as the eyes were turned to him. 'I enjoy this work. I would wish to learn more of these Romans. I find they interest me greatly.'

'Good, good, my boy!' the Reverend exclaimed. 'That is a spirit I like to hear. If only the labourers I employ had more desire to learn of the period, and of the method of the digging and of what is found, and how the record must be made, then I am sure they would find their labours more congenial.'

He turned to Lord Selborne. 'If you would care to release him to me in the summer, my Lord, I could teach him. I could do with another man on site during our season's work.'

He looked at George. 'It is the Roman town of *Calleva* I am excavating, you see, my boy. By permission of the Duke of Wellington – the 2nd Duke, that is, of course – whose land it is. He has a strong interest in the work. Piece by piece, trench by trench, we advance each summer. For some nine years now.'

His lordship looked somewhat surprised by the sudden request. 'Well, I don't know. There is much to do here....'

'I would pay him whatever you pay,' the Reverend persisted. 'There are funds enough for that as we stand.'

Lord Selborne looked at George. 'Would you like to do that?' he asked. 'I could perhaps let you go for a few weeks: it could not be for longer.'

'Er..I'm not sure. I mean....' George was indeed genuinely bewildered, but then realised that this truly was something he would welcome: new experiences, new companions, new knowledge. Surely it was the way forward for him.

'I think I would,' he said. 'But where would I stay?' He was so overwhelmed by the prospect that he forgot to use his master's title.

'There is a farmhouse near *Calleva* that would take you. One of my labourers lives there also. A bed, a breakfast and an evening meal. There should be no further expense. It will mean hard physical work, though.'

The Reverend Mr. Joyce added the last, scrutinising George more closely now, thinking perhaps he should have stated this fact first.

'I am not frightened of that, sir.'

'My labourers have been used to pick and shovel all their lives, but I feel you will have youth on your side.'

'Well, let us see,' said Lord Selborne, more firmly now. It was clear to George that he would make no decision at this moment.

Little more work was done on the coins after that. Lord Selborne had returned to London in company with Lady Selborne. Only two of the daughters were present at the house – Lady Sophia and Lady Sarah. George found it strange to refer to them by their titles, which made them seem old and very grand. They were scarce older than his own eighteen years.

George had returned to his library work, now on his own, for Mr. Whiteley would be absent for two weeks also, partly to be with Lord Selborne at his London house in Portland Place, and partly to take his own holiday.

'I go to Kent', he had told George, opening up to him for once and seeming very much friendlier, to the extent that George debated whether he might address him by his Christian name, Alfred. He decided, however, it was a step too far for the present.

'My family have a house at Hythe,' Mr. Whiteley continued, removing his pince-nez and wiping their lenses. 'It is very peaceful there, at the edge of the Romney marshes that have been until lately the haunt of smugglers. There are a few scattered remnants of a Roman castle too close-by. As you are interested in that civilisation, as I hear from his lordship, you should make a visit.'

Yes, I would if I could, thought George. But how does he expect me to do that? Is he offering me accommodation with his family? Does he think I might make a visit with him? The thought did not appeal. Alfred seemed to him the permanent bachelor and he felt ill at ease in his company.

By now George had got to know several of the house maids, whom he had to admit to finding attractive. He would try to take his meals with them, and, feeling somewhat more confident now, exchange some banter with them, hoping to make them laugh. He would also seek to pass them at their work in the corridors, whenever the opportunity arose, if only perhaps to gain a smile of recognition. Otherwise the day, staring at books and cards, inkwell and blotting paper, could seem deadly dull to a young man coming into adulthood.

Any more positive approach to the maids, however, during work times, other than for some passing quip or pleasantry, would seem to be impossible, and very likely frowned upon, even directly forbidden, although that was not stated in the printed list of staff rules he had been given. Those rules were also set out sternly on a notice board positioned on the wall above the kitchen table. Perhaps some rules were considered so obvious they did not need to be written down.

The maids, for their own part, did not seem to show too much interest in him, whether of their own volition or in response to his small overtures. He was a little put out by that, although he tried not to be. His self-confidence in such matters was only wafer-thin and he would find himself wondering, often in the midst of his cataloguing, what it was that they found off-putting about him. He thought himself a well enough set up young man, growing in his maturity, who might be expected to set a heart a two a-flutter. But clearly he was mistaken.

The particularly pretty maid he had first spoken with – her name was Marie, he had learnt – with a glorious crown of yellow hair spilling out from the frilled cap she wore at her work, attracted him the most. Yet he had never gained the chance to say more than a passing word or two to her, and then mainly about the weather. The maids kept very much to themselves under the house keeper's supervision, a frosty, beanstick-thin matron of advanced years, who rarely made an appearance in the servant's hall, taking her own meals in her basement room.

Harold, the footman, however, seemed to have few inhibitions about making his approaches. He boasted of a conquest of the beautiful Marie, with whom, he had said, he had walked out one Sunday into the Great Wood, and there enjoyed her to the full. George, however, innocent as he was in such matters, did not believe him. Harold's story was told from his bed in their narrow room, and George suspected it came rather from that unspeakable sin about which the Alton curate at Sunday School had once spoken in guarded language, and which, judging by the other sounds he could not help hearing, Harold might be indulging in at that moment. He rolled over and tried to sleep, but his visions of the glorious, innocent Marie were spoilt – although he doubted by any actual fault of hers.

While Mr. Whiteley was away, George found the library, where he now worked for the most part alone, was visited rather more often than had been the case earlier, by the two family daughters, Sophia and Sarah. He could not imagine this was for any reason other than the purest chance.

The young ladies appeared particularly interested in the works of Jane Austen, of which the library held several first editions. George had found a particular problem in cataloguing them, for the author was given as 'By a Lady', and he had had to learn from Mr. Whiteley the correct form of adding 'Jane Austen' to his descriptions, and making sure the books were indexed under both appellations. He had to admit that a mere six months earlier he had never heard of this lady, who had once lived so close to Alton and frequented the town often. These facts he had learnt from a book, recently published, entitled 'A Memoir of Jane Austen', which had arrived in a parcel from the publisher some time ago, and had remained on a shelf, with others, unwrapped.

When the two Selborne daughters were together in the library, they ignored George, who sat working at his desk in the room, other than to ask him occasionally to fetch a book from a higher shelf, or to return others they had finished with. When Sophia was by herself, however, she would speak with him, which flattered George that she should interest herself in him as anything other than a mere member of staff. Yet he found her asking increasingly personal questions about his background, and she would sigh and purse her lips as he told her of his troubled childhood, of the aunt who had brought him up but betrayed him, and of the bank where he had worked, as well as his very good fortune that her father had used that same bank and given him this chance.

She looked astonished by his story, as if the world beyond her father's house was something she had never contemplated before; that it could be such a strange, unsettled, fearful place, so greatly different from the sure horizons of her own life. What George had told her, at first hesitantly, then gradually growing in confidence at speaking to such a lady, albeit one of much the same age as himself, clearly made an impression on her.

'I wish to be a writer,' she confided in him, looking into his face as if suspicious that he would show some hint of amusement at such a proposition.

Instead, he answered, 'You will have much to write of – this house and all that lies about you, the fine ladies, the noble gentlemen, the banquets, the carriages.'

'No,' she said snappily. 'Can you not understand? None of that interests me. I would rather write of more ordinary lives – yours, for instance.'

'Mine!' He could not hide his astonishment.

'I express myself poorly. Not you personally, of course. But someone of my own creation who has suffered tribulations, as you clearly have, and yet still found a worthy path in life.'

She is not as pretty as her sisters, he thought. Her face is too broad and her mouth small and pursed when her mood is ill. But then what do I know of women, in particular those high-born? She has a passion, though, that I can understand. Her dark, curling hair was unpinned, falling loose halfway to her shoulders, and she wore a grey, linen dress, lined with thin black stripes, ballooning out from the waist. The high neck was lined with white ruffles.

She then immersed herself in the book he had fetched for her, and did not speak again. When she left the library, she gave him the merest glance.

9

The day of the grand celebration and ball at Blackmoor House for the two engagements of the Selborne daughters had come. Guests arrived from mid-afternoon, well before the winter daylight faded into night. They arrived in their carriages up the gravelled drive to the turning circle in front of the main door, one after the other in a procession that brought out the villagers – all tenants of Lord Selborne – from their homes to watch.

Having been emptied of their expensive occupants – in black, velvet evening suits and starched white fronts, or scarlet uniforms laden with medals and gold braid, the ladies in fine, glistening gowns, much bejewelled, all hidden for the moment beneath coats, furs and mantles for the weather had recently grown cold – the coachmen then drove the carriages away, a few to the courtyard stables, but most by a second driveway to a piece of land set aside for the purpose, where the horses could be watered and fed. Flares and lanterns were set about the house and its grounds, and when it grew dark, they were lit, so that the house, with its windows uncurtained, looked like a great ocean liner washed up from the Solent and stranded here in the darkened Hampshire countryside.

George's task, wearing his borrowed footman's uniform, was to help the commissionaire, an ex-army man hired for the occasion, who wore a plumed fore and aft bicorn hat and a crimson sash across his massive chest, and was fully briefed with the names and titles of the guests. George was very busy leading individuals, couples, and even entire parties indoors, and taking their coats and other outer garments, as required, to the cloakroom. Each set of guests was accorded a number, which matched the appropriate peg or locker where their garments were placed.

As George had feared, full control of this system was soon lost. In his eagerness to announce the guests in the reception hall, where they would be met by Lord and Lady Selborne before proceeding onwards to the great hall, the commissionaire would often give George an incorrect number from his list, or neglect to give any number at all. So George, burdened by his loads of assorted coats and mantles, furs and wraps, would have to choose the next available locker at random. He soon lost hope that the storage position of any of the later guests' property bore any resemblance at all to the numbered order set out so carefully on the commissionaire's guest list.

Once all the guests had arrived, and there was no sign of any further late-comers, George went to the kitchens, where he was shooed away by a Mrs. Broughton driven frantic by the multitude of tasks she must see done with her kitchen maids. The scene there that met George's eyes was one of absolute pandemonium. A master chef – a Frenchman, also brought in for the occasion – was working with Mrs. Broughton, and did not seem to be getting on too well with her. All about the kitchens were lines of footmen, some preparing to take food to the gathering, others collecting drinks on silver salvers from the butler, who appeared already to have had more than, what might be termed, a casual tasting to check the quality of his wines.

Lady Selborne, her hair piled high and fixed in place with glittering jewelled feathers, arrived to inspect the proceedings just as George was about to leave. He came face to face with her in the passage outside, the two performing a quick side step of a dance to avoid the other. She tut-tutted crossly, her face flushed.

'Is all going well? 'Is all going well?' she kept saying to no one in particular, clearly on edge with worry. Then she turned to hasten back along the service passage, just in time to meet her two engaged daughters who, hand in hand, were at that moment coming down the hall stairway in all their glamorous finery. They were greeted with a fanfare played by musicians brought from London for the evening. Lord and Lady Selborne, re-united, then stepped forward to greet their daughters, before passing each formally on to their respective fiancés, to the accompaniment of more music and much applause from the assembled guests.

George, hearing the distant clapping and music, and seeing the continuing turmoil in the kitchens, decided there was no role for him in the proceedings for the time being. His tasks would only recommence when the guests began to leave. Then would come the inevitable confusion in finding their coats, for which it was likely he would be blamed. Yet that would be several long hours yet.

So he took the servants' staircase to the uppermost floor and shut himself in his room. He had been given no other instructions beyond some general portering and helping the commissionaire, but he could imagine that, if he went downstairs again, he might well be dragged into some role or other for which he had received no training. It was, therefore, best to stay where he was for at least an hour or so until he could judge if, or when, the party was moving towards its conclusion. That would surely be a long time yet, for a ball was planned to follow dinner. Thus, feeling rather selfish to his fellow servants, and inwardly cowardly, he stayed where he was.

When he did eventually emerge from his room, it was to hear music playing below in the bowels of the house, swelling above a general backdrop of animated voices that seemed to rise and fall as if in harmony with the music. Was dinner finished then already and the ball underway? His lack of knowledge about a formal occasion such as this was almost complete. No one, not even Harold, had sought to enlighten him.

As George descended the lower flight of the back stair, by chance he came upon Harold now, just about to ascend. Beside him, almost leaning against him – had they in fact been holding hands, now snatched apart? – was Marie, the pretty maid whose attentions George had long hoped for.

Harold sounded out of breath, his face flushed. Marie's face also, George thought, did not show its usual calm: it was reddened, and looked – how could he put it? – guilty. What had he interrupted? Good old Harold, having his way, was he? But surely not here in the house. They would be taking a fearful risk.

'They're at the dancing now,' Harold said quickly, clearly eager to turn George's attention onto other matters. 'They'll be at that for a long time yet. And then, I'm sure, will come more speeches. It could go on much of the night. We may all be up until dawn'

Hell, I hope not, George thought.

'What I should do, if I were you,' Harold said, his arm on his shoulder, something George always shrank from, 'is to go back to old Cummings – the commissionaire, that is: I've had some good chats with him in the past, a ladies man, if there ever was one. My God, what he hasn't done!'

His gaze met Marie's, who smiled and dropped her eyes. Those two are certainly up to something, George deduced. He thought sulkily, what has Harold got, I haven't? Just the confidence and the chat, I suppose. I've never been good at that.

'Cummings has the run of the porter's rooms,' Harold went on. 'Scratchy Catchpole's away, you see. He's the chief porter at the north lodge, if you don't know him. He could never work with Cummings, anyhow, which is probably why they gave you the job of helping him. Didn't Cummings say anything to you, George? But he'll have a fire in his room and a bed probably; at least a comfortable chair to have a snooze in. You'll be on hand then for whenever you're needed again, when we can get the last drunk on his way. Hopefully, most of us will be given the following day off.'

'Right, that seems a fair idea', George said. 'When are you next on duty, and Marie here?'

Harold placed a finger alongside his nose and tapped it. 'That's for us to know and you not to bother about.' Marie giggled.

George was irritated now. He turned away abruptly, thinking, I've had enough of Harold. I wonder if I could get a room somewhere else. And Marie's clearly a trollop, if she's doing what I think she is. Not on my bed, though. Please, not that. Turning, his head, however as he walked away, he saw that Marie was still standing at the foot of the stairs. Only Harold had gone up. So had he misjudged them? He didn't know. He didn't care.

But he was to care later, very much so.

Dawn was breaking when the last of the guests was helped into his carriage, assisted by George – who by some sort of miracle had been able to sort out the muddle in the cloakroom with very few delays – and disappeared up the drive, leaving the house to slumber on quietly for a while – but not for long. Maids were already at their duties of clearing, cleaning, wiping brushing; handymen were dismantling screens and tables, Mrs. Broughton, bleary-eyed, was surveying the stark disorder of her kitchen, only a little of which it had been possible so far to set to rights. It was not – as Harold had hoped – to be a day off for anybody, other than for the ladies of the house, including the two now formally betrothed, their heads filled with dreamy romance, who slumbered the morning away.

Lord Selborne had not come to bed at all. Also absent from his bed was Harold Wilkins. When George awoke from the two or three hours of sleep, which was all he was able to have that night, it was to find Harold's bed empty. It had clearly not been slept in. The reason for George's awakening was a sharp knocking on the door.

When George pulled open the door, greatly wondering, for nothing like this had ever happened before, it was to find another of the footmen there.

'You are to come down to see Mr. Whiteley in the library now,' the footman said impassively, his face devoid of expression.

'Why?' The one astonished word burst from George's lips. The footman said nothing more, but turned on his heel. 'At once!' he called over his shoulder.

George splashed his face with water from the ewer in the room and dressed as quickly as he could. He found his hands were trembling in anticipation of something being really wrong. What it could be, however, he had no idea. He pulled on his usual clothing, leaving Harold's borrowed uniform on its hanger where he had slung it crookedly in his exhaustion on coming to bed. Like this, he blundered down the silent stairs, passed through equally deserted passageways and came to the library. There was no one there. Mr. Whiteley must be in his office, George thought. He knocked on the door.

'Come in'. He heard Mr. Whiteley's precise tones. He had not seen him since his return from holiday. He must remember to ask him if he had enjoyed his break.

He pushed open the door, and almost recoiled at the sight of Lord Selborne, sitting grimly behind the desk, with Mr. Whiteley to one side of him.

'Before you sit, Mr. Maple,' said his lordship in a hard, clipped voice, 'will you show me the key to the workshed which I entrusted to you.'

'Of course, my lord.'

His heart thumping, George felt in his right jacket pocket, where he always kept the key, but it was empty. He searched the other pockets. He had lost the key! Surely not. How had that happened? He was always most careful to check the key every day, whether he needed to use it or not. Was this what all this was about? He had dropped the key somewhere and it had been found. He was in trouble for that.

'I think this is what you are looking for,' said Lord Selborne, holding up a large, black-metal key. He raised a second key. 'And I subsequently found this one too. Last night I had occasion to use it when I wished to show one of our guests the Roman coin urns – a most distinguished man, he: Mr. Tennyson, our Poet Laureate, no less, who, with his wife, had honoured us with his presence. Fortunately, as it turned out, it was only he who accompanied me to the workshed.'

George stood frozen to the floor, wondering what was to follow.

'So, Mr. Maple, where do you think your key has gone to? You know, don't you, that you gave it to the footman you share a room with – one Mr......?'

'Wilkins, my Lord,' Mr. Whiteley interjected.

'Ah, yes. Mr. Wilkins. Who has now left our employ. He informed us you had lent him the key.'

'That's a lie!' exclaimed a shocked George. 'I would never do that.'

Lord Selborne looked steadily at George for what seemed a very long half minute.

'You know, I do believe you – which is as well for you, or even now you would be joining your room companion in the porter's lodge, from where, once his few possessions have been bundled up, he will make his journey to Liss railway station.'

'He must have taken the key from my pocket after I put on the footman's uniform,' George said, gabbling a little in his shock. 'I thought of transferring it, but there was no suitable pocket, my Lord. I would not have believed he would do that.'

'Still, you have been careless and I had trusted you,' said Lord Selborne, rising to his feet. 'You will be docked a week's wages.'

'Yes, my Lord.' George hung his head as he knew was expected of him. Mr. Whiteley's eyes had been boring into him all the while.

Daringly, for he knew a suitable abject retreat was expected of him now, he asked, 'Why did Harold – er, Mr. Wilkins – want the key, my Lord? I have never known him show any interest in the workshed, and little enough about what I did there.'

'Why did he want the key? An astute question, Mr. Maple. Have you heard of the expression *'in flagrante'*?'

'No, my Lord'.

'It means 'caught when in full pursuit of something improper'. Now, do you understand?' George looked blank.

Lord Selborne sighed. There was a gleam in his eye, a touch of humour about his mouth, another astonishment to George, who was already reeling in his tiredness and confusion at what had happened.

'He was not alone,' Lord Selborne said. 'One of the housemaids was with him.'

Immediately to George's mind leapt the name Marie. Of course, that's why the bastard had taken the key. A secret rendezvous, but far from secret after all. He felt no sorrow for Harold, but he did for Marie.

'Imagine Mr. Tennyson's surprise,' said Lord Selborne in level tones. 'By the light of the lantern – an innovative use of a workbench, perhaps, luckily well away from the urns. The poet told me he might compose an ode about it, something along the lines of: 'man oft spurs on the panting race of life.''

And now he did chortle, and continue to chortle, head bent forward, gasping, while Mr. Whiteley joined in diplomatically. George, glimpsing an understanding now, felt he should slip quietly away, which he did, closing the door soundlessly behind him.

Later that day, seeking some fresh air, for he had no duties to attend to, he saw two womanly figures, well-wrapped in cloaks, walking away from the house along the south drive. The elder had her arm around the other, who was bent forward, holding a small bag in one hand. He could not see her face, but he knew it was Marie, and such was his sorrow and embarrassment, that he turned and walked the other way.

10

One advantage to George of Harold Wilkins' departure was that he had the room they had shared now to himself, although that situation might only last a short time until a new footman was appointed. However, as the days went by and no new faces appeared, it seemed that neither the errant Harold or lovely, disgraced Marie were to be replaced – at least not for the present.

George's work with the coins alongside his lordship continued, until at last one of the urns had been emptied entirely, although a substantial block of coins taken from the very bottom remained to be separated. This work, Lord Selborne said, could now be carried out in his study, where the surroundings would be much more comfortable. The second urn was also to be taken into the house. The wet mud which had caked it had long since dried, and George had spent some time scraping these deposits away with a blunt-edged knife. A few of the coins already catalogued, coming from the top of this urn, had proved earlier than those of the usurping emperors, Carausius and Allectus, so perhaps the coins of the second urn would prove of more varying dates than those in the first.

Occasionally, when George was alone in his room, he would bring out from his waist pocket the coin he had taken, and gaze at it intently. An oared galley sailed across one face, and on the other was the bearded portrait of the emperor Allectus, wearing a type of spiky crown. The coin still had an overall greenish patina, but the most prominent points of the face and of the galley had by now been rubbed to the original bright bronze colour. He debated again whether he should declare it to his lordship. He could easily explain he had picked it up from the ground when the urns were found and had placed it on his person innocently, and had forgotten about it until now – but something about its now part-polished condition would seem to belie such an explanation. He decided to keep it. He thought it will make little difference to his lordship's overall project or the report on the coins that he tells me he will eventually write. Other coins were almost certainly lost at the time the discovery was made.

Christmas arrived. This proved both a merry and a very busy occasion for the staff at Blackmoor House. Many of the Selborne family's extended relations came to stay, some to see in the new year. There were meals to be cooked and rooms to be serviced, titled ladies to dress, and gentlemen to humour and serve drinks to in their smoking and game rooms. There was also to be a shoot across the park on the 27th December.

Mrs. Broughton had triumphed with a magnificent Christmas Day lunch, which was then served the next day to the servants by Lord and Lady Selborne in person – at least nominally so, but the gesture was much appreciated by housemaids, washermaids, footmen, grooms, coachmen, gardeners, porters and sundry all, who crowded onto a long table in the barn on the far side of the kitchen yard. Cider and ale flowed here, a concession from the usually abstemious Lord Selborne. He made a small speech to his servants, thanking them for their loyal service and wishing them a merry time and a happy, healthy new year to come.

Dancing followed – country reels and jigs, played by two fiddlers from the Red Lion at Oakhanger, of which George knew no steps at all. But, emboldened by the strong cider, he managed to cavort amongst the dancers without bumping into too many or treading on any toes, and found he had the delight of an arm around several young maids' waists, who now looked brightly into his face and seemed even to welcome his attentions.

He retired with one to a side table made from a barrel and asked her name. She had dark, merry eyes, and brown hair, pinned up under a head scarf, being still in her maid's clothing, as she had to return to service very soon. Her name was Barbara, she told him, known to most as Babs. He asked her if she would walk out with him one evening when the days grew longer, and she said she would.

For the first time since being at Blackmoor, and indeed for all the long years before that, George felt a real glow of happiness within him. But he knew he must leave this merriment soon as well, since Mr. Whiteley expected his presence in the library, in case any of the family or their guests wished to use it, so he offered to accompany Babs back across the yard to the house. She said she would stay a little while longer. When George looked back from the barn door, he saw that another man – one he did not recognise – was already seating himself with her, and they were laughing together. This immediately chilled the pleasure he had been feeling. Yet, he had the sense not to return. She had promised to walk with him, and that was what they would do, other suitor or no. Or so he thought. He had no idea – how could he? – of what was so suddenly to come about.

George had seldom drunk alcohol until now. As he walked across the yard, he felt the first real effect of the strong country cider he had quaffed. It made the cobbled surface of the yard seem to heave beneath his feet, momentarily unsteadying him, but not to any great degree. He felt he could easily throw it off.

He knew he had not been slurring to the lovely Babs, as he had heard others doing in the barn. They must then have been much deeper into their cups than he. The trouble was that the uneasy feelings within him now seemed to be increasing, rather than lessening. They were not sensations he liked at all.

He thought he would go to the WC, so he could free himself a little of the cider, and then wait until his head had cleared somewhat. This he did, but, after urinating and waiting a few minutes, someone pulled at the door to come in, so he had to leave. Ignoring whoever it was outside, he headed for the kitchen, and walked through quickly, not trusting himself to indulge in any banter. He felt better when he was by himself in the corridors of the house – there was the sound of a piano playing in the distance and voices singing – and, taking a deep breath, he turned the door to the library and went in. No one was there. He looked through the open door to Mr. Whiteley's office, and thankfully found that empty too.

He sat down at his table and pulled a box of catalogue cards towards him. He was feeling somewhat better now, just irritated with himself for allowing his pot to be topped up from the cider jug in the way it had been, when he knew he needed to work afterwards. He found it hard to concentrate, however. His eyes kept drifting from the small black characters on the cards, and it was difficult now to match the precise quality of his usual handwriting. He knocked over a pile of the cards by an injudicious sweep of his arm, and some cascaded from the desk onto the floor. He was bending down to retrieve them when he heard the outer door to the library opening and the swish of a lady's gown.

'George,' said an imperious voice – that of Lady Sophia. 'Do we have copies of 'The Fortnightly Review? I'm looking for an article by Mr. Huxley.'

'Just a moment.' George was on his knees, an arm outstretched, trying to retrieve two cards trapped between the desk and the wall.

'I haven't got any moments. We're presently discussing Mr. Huxley and Mr Darwin, and I need the article now!'

'Can't you see, I'm trying to get these bloody cards together!' The words slipped out before he could stop them. Greatly alarmed, he now scrambled to his feet, only to see Lady Sophia carrying the ladder that was used to reach the upper library shelves.

'Let me have that, my lady,' he said desperately. 'I can get what you want now.'

'No, no. You are far too busy.' She had positioned the ladder at the bay where she knew the journals were kept, and had begun climbing to reach up to the top shelf.

'Allow me, please, miss.' He was fearful now. He had failed in his job. He sensed worse would happen.

A pair of neat ankles encased in white silk was before his gaze, and, above, a lacy fringe of petticoats. She was reaching higher, and was pulling out a cardboard box with both hands. A foot slipped. With a scream she fell backwards into his arms, and he onto his back on the floor, all this happening in a trice, his arms about her bodice, his fingers against her round plump breasts, the whale bones of her corset pressing hard against his thighs.

'How dare you! How dare you!' She struggled from him onto her feet.

'It was an accident...'

Yes, your fault, not mine!' She was at the door, strands of hair plastered to her forehead, her face bright red.

'Please, miss. I'm so sorry.'

'And so you will be.' With that, she was through the door, which she thumped to behind her.

George was distraught. He stood in the centre of the room, not knowing what to do, his hands held out at his sides. They were shaking.

The door opened. Mr. Whiteley came in. He said sharply, 'I hear there's been some sort of incident. Go into my study and stay there. Lord Selborne is being told.'

George sat in the study, his head in his hands. 'What have I done? What have I done?' he moaned to himself. 'Oh, that bloody cider. Why did I drink so much?'

After some minutes, he felt a little calmer. It was *not* my fault, he told himself. If she had not been so impetuous, I would have helped her. It was only a matter of seconds. She's always been so headstrong. I saw that in her a long time ago. Perhaps I was beyond my station in getting a little too close to her. But I saved her, after all. And I've hurt my back in doing so. He had, indeed. The base of his back against the rear panel of the chair felt very sore. He wriggled against the chair to try to ease it.

Lord Selborne came in, accompanied by Mr. Whiteley. His lordship looked furious.

'Stand up!'

George complied.

'My daughter is very upset. She says you would not help her and swore at her.'

'No, no, my lord, it was just....'

'Just, nothing. Your job is to give help as required immediately, there is no just in it.'

'But, but...'

'And worse, I understand you have been manhandling her.....feeling, feeling....I can hardly bring myself to say this....feeling her body.'

'No, my Lord.' Through his fear, George was growing angry himself. 'I was helping her and saved her when she slipped. I was hurt, my lord....'

'Oh so, she is wrong, is she? And you the hero too.' George would not have associated the sneer with the calm, debonair Lord Selborne, who was normally so mild in his manner.

'I was only trying to tell you what happened my lord. I admit I was tardy in responding to Lady S-S-Sophia's request.' In his distress he could not at first remember her name. 'But I was....'

'No excuses. I want you out! Straightaway. What is owed you can be sent on.'

'But I have nowhere to go, my lord.'

'You should have thought of that before you offended so. And after the incident in the workshed as well. I was lenient to you then, but not now.'

George's blood was chilled, standing wretchedly like an animal about to be slaughtered, his head lowered, the eyes of the two men fastened on him.

Then the warm blood began to flow in him again, and his sense of worth, and the wrong he believed done to him, returned, so he raised his head defiantly, looking from one man to the other, pleased to see Mr. Whiteley unable to meet his eyes.

'Very well, my lord. May I say I have enjoyed my service here...until now, that is. I am very sorry, which is all I can say.' He turned to leave.

'Wait a moment.' Lord Selborne's voice was still harsh but perhaps a little more ameliorating. 'As it's the holy season, you can stay at the main porter's lodge until you have found out what you will do. Take your things there. I will send a message to Mr. Cathchpole, so that he knows. You can remain there for a few days, if you wish. His wife will feed you. But I want you gone entirely very soon – from this House, from my estate. Do you understand? If I find you still around, I will report you to the constabulary and they will deal with you. That's all I have to say to you.'

And with that he turned and left, and Mr. Whiteley too, leaving George all alone, his heart pumping, lost between desperation and fury. For a moment he thought I will wreck that catalogue I have put so much time into, and scatter those stupid cards everywhere, piss in all the corners too, set fire to the house – but he did none of those things. He went to his room, ignored the stares of the staff he had worked with, and went out from the yard and onto the drive with the same bag he had carried when he arrived. He gave no forwarding address, for he had none to give. And he ignored the porter's lodge, but walked out along the lane in the chilled evening air, not knowing at all where he would go and what he would do. It was yet Boxing Day.

11

George Maple never seems to have told anyone what he did to survive that first cold winter night – the night which followed a day when families traditionally exchanged presents in great jollity around decorated spruce trees, a custom greatly encouraged by the Queen's late, much-lamented Consort, Prince Albert. Perhaps indeed it was a spruce he tried to sleep beneath, huddled up in his inadequate clothes, a thin, icy rain falling. More likely he simply kept walking the black lanes to keep warm, all he owned in the small, hempen bag he carried, now sodden with rain. In time he may have been able to find an isolated barn where at least it was dry. The weather that winter was notoriously wet, with a mixture of sleet and rain falling day after day until the early spring. He would have had some money, so he likely obtained a meal or two at an inn or perhaps a farm. Possibly some Christian soul, realising he was not of the usual brand of tramps, took compassion on him and allowed him to stay for a few nights. He never spoke about those days.

    He did, however, tell an army friend that he worked for a while as a porter in Basingstoke Market, then washed up pots in the evening at the local coaching inn. In the spring of 1874, he seems to have worked his way north, helping out on farms probably for no more than a roof over his head and a meal. His intention now, he admitted, was to reach the Roman town of *Calleva*, where he might meet up with the kindly-sounding Reverend Mr. Joyce, to whom his late master had introduced him at Blackmoor House. Perhaps he could take part in his digging and become a help to the reverend gentleman. After all, this idea had already been proposed by the Reverend when in company with Lord Selborne. But, of course, that was before his downfall. Such thoughts were likely bubbling in the young man's head.

Certainly, the Roman civilisation had made a strong impression on him, and he might have hoped to develop this interest – then study perhaps with the Reverend's guidance – to take him on to who knows what? The subject of the past, and of how the material remains of our forbears are often to be found beneath the soil, clearly attracted him. His great fear, of course, was that the stain upon him that he had acquired at Blackmoor would make any such hope fruitless. And yet, was not the Christian message – as he remembered it being taught to him – one of compassion and second chances? If anyone would help him now, it was surely the Reverend Mr. Joyce.

It was an early May day of sunlight and showers when George reached Silchester, the village that stood closest to *Calleva*. He was directed by a passer-by to the site of the Roman town, and came by a muddy track to a low bank with a great, grey-stone wall running upon it, tumbled down in places and much festooned with trees and bushes that were just coming into leaf. Finding a break in the wall, he saw, beyond a broad area of green fields grazed by sheep, further lengths of the same wall that curved away to make a great enclosure, clearly marked by the trailing creepers and bushes growing from their sides and tops .

He scrambled up onto the wall, dislodging some loose stones and fragments of red brick. Now he could make out more clearly the circumference of the town, the wall continuing on all sides to form what seemed an irregular oval. Opposite him, and filling a wide opening in the wall, he could see the red-roofed buildings of a farm, and close to those, where the land rose a little higher, the low, pointed tower of a church.

Lowering his gaze to the central area of the Roman town, he noted a number of long mounds set upon the rich grass, at points where the earth had clearly been opened up, forming large, brown patches amongst the green: the mounds must be formed of the excavated soil, George reasoned. Even at this distance he could see the straight lines of stones running across these grassless areas, which were presumably the walls of buildings

The sides of some of the open cuts in the earth were draped with what looked like sacking, and similar coverings were laid over other areas too, being weighed down by large stones and, it seemed, wooden crates. One area in particular to his right adjacent to the wall had been treated in this way. A large wooden hut, painted a dark red, stood there close by.

These coverings, he thought, must be the places where the Reverend Mr. Joyce was currently carrying out his diggings. It seemed they had yet to be removed for any new work to be carried out this year. He was filled with sudden excitement, but did not know exactly why. All he really knew was that coins and other metal objects could be found; old pots too, he imagined, and possibly bones. Presumably walls and floors might be dug out as well and traced to see how far they went. If the Romans had lived in houses here all those years ago, anything they had used and left behind might still be here to be discovered.

George stood spell-bound. Had this space before him really once been filled with buildings and streets, where people came and went – traders, soldiers, slaves, perfumed ladies borne in litters, horses and carts, chariots too?

He wanted to climb down into the field and walk across to the excavations – which was the correct term for these diggings, he remembered, having heard the Reverend use it. He realised, though, that without permission this would probably be regarded as trespassing. The land, he had learnt, was owned by the Duke of Wellington. Anyone watching from the farm might see and report him snooping about. He did not want to get into any further trouble after that previous unfortunate misunderstanding. Every time he thought back on what had happened to him that terrible day, he grew angry at how unjust it had been. He did not wish to tempt fate again.

There was a path, stamped out through thick vegetation, that allowed him instead to follow the wall to his right. He came to a lane and walked along it, seeing the tower of the church ahead of him. Two farm workers in corduroy trousers and sleeveless jackets came towards him. They looked at him curiously, and grunted a greeting. One carried a long-handled scythe.

George nodded back. He did not wish to speak. He felt he was close to something that could end well for him – very well, almost as if predestined – but in what form that would be he could not have answered. All his troubled life to this moment seemed set towards what he would find along this lane and his anticipated meeting with the Reverend Mr. Joyce.

He came to the church. It stood close to the large, red-brick farmhouse he had seen from afar, with its barns and sheds around a muddied yard. Was this the church of the Reverend Mr. Joyce? He tried the door handle. A musty smell assailed him. In the grey light he could make out rows of high box pews. He called out, 'Hello', but there was no answer. He left, banging the door to, and walked into the graveyard. There, bent over, tending a grave, was a woman in a long, black coat, wearing a bonnet with a spray of white blossom pinned to it.

'Can you help me?' George asked. He hoped he had not frightened the lady, as his appearance might seem a little wild these days; his clothes were stained and ragged and he had grown a thin beard that just seemed further to dirty his face.

But the lady straightened herself and smiled. 'How may I help?'

'The Reverend or, Mr. Joyce. Is his rectory nearby?'

A furrow came to her brow. 'He is not the rector of this church, if that's what you think. That is the Reverend Mr. Fiennes. His rectory is just beyond the farm here, if you would rather see him, perhaps. But Mr. Joyce's parish is the one next to ours – at Stratfield Saye. You'll find his church close to the big house – Stratfield Saye House, that is, where the Duke of Wellington lives. It's not a church like ours, but one built of brick with a dome at its centre.'

'Thank you, ma'am,' said George, inclining his head as he had been taught as a servant. 'I shall be on my way.'

'It is quite a walk. I would say five miles, or so. The lanes twist much, but there are signposts.'

'Thank you again, ma'am'.

'I hope you find him,' she called after him. 'I know he goes much to London. His wife will help you, though.'

The lady was right about the network of narrow lanes and footpaths he came to. When a horse and cart approached, he had to squeeze right into the hedge to get out of its way. Some riders coming up behind, tall in black riding suits and top hats, also sent him scurrying into a field opening. He crossed a railway line by a bridge just at the moment that a tall-funnelled locomotive billowing smoke, and pulling four brown-painted coaches, passed underneath. Now he found himself on a narrow, straight track, bordered on both sides by thick trees that were already light green with early leaf. Because of its straightness, he thought this must be a Roman road that is heading towards *Calleva*, or, he considered gravely, coming from it, like me. Again, there was an echo of something in his mind – a passing sense of an idea largely intangible – that the road was taking him forward in the steps of the Romans to where he was predestined to go. They were strange, these feelings that he was having now. He shook his head. It was his imagination, no more.

No one else troubled him on the track, and he seemed to be walking on it forever, so that he was beginning to think it had no end. I am doomed to spend the rest of my days here, he thought, getting nowhere, as if on some giant treadmill, of which I cannot even yet make out the curve. He was growing both tired and thirsty.

Pausing at a gap in the trees and bushes on his left, he looked out upon a large green field where a shepherd was tending his flock. Even as he watched, the man was helping pull a new-born lamb from a ewe, and he could see the damp, struggling shape quivering on the ground, then raised by the shepherd into his arms, wiping at its face, and setting the lamb down once more upon the grass It wobbled now on shaking legs, seeking out its mother's udder. All around were other ewes with their young, and their bleating followed the shepherd as he moved amongst the flock.

The track made a sudden bend to the left and he came to a paved lane that still ran wet with mud from recent rains. Before long he reached a crossroads, where there was a wooden sign pointing ahead that spelt out 'Stratfield Saye House' in black lettering. Another sign, however, stated 'Church', and pointed to the left, so he went that way. Passing along the lane, he could see the park of the great house opening out to his left and in the distance many rooftops, surrounded by dark groves of trees. Further along the lane, he came to a lodge by a driveway, where stood a further sign with a pointing finger and the word 'Church' again.

Passing the open gate, and receiving no challenge from the lodge, which seemed to stand empty, its windows boarded up, he followed the narrow driveway, which curved to the right. Before him, amongst trees, he had a first glimpse of red-brick walls, with a central, green-coloured dome rising above. It was like no church he had ever viewed before. The walls in places bore creeping tentacles of foliage, studded with white blossoms.

Before the main drive reached the church, however, a second ran off to the right, and this he now followed. Here he found the rectory – not the small building he had expected, perhaps embellished by high turrets and pointed gables of the type the Victorian clergy favoured – but a large house, with white columns running along its ochre-coloured walls and well-tended gardens set about it. He trod the gravelled circle before the massive front door uncertainly, but then spotted a path that led him to a side door with a hanging bell-pull, which he tugged at. After a wait of what seemed several minutes, but was probably much less, just as he was giving up hope of anyone being at home – yet surely there must be servants? – the door was opened suddenly and a lady's head peered out.

'Yes, can I help you?' She had a pleasant face, the mouth curled into a smile, her brown hair parted in the middle and bunched in waves at each side.

'Is the Reverend at home? George asked. He knew this was no servant, but probably the lady of the house herself, the Reverend's wife, very likely.

'He is, but he is working in his study at present. What is your business?'

'I would like to ask him about his excavations,' said George as determinedly as he could. He was feeling suddenly weak after his long walk that day and his lack of food, and he felt his head begin to swim.

The lady must have noticed. She had keen, enquiring eyes. 'You'd better come in and sit down,' she said. 'You look all in'.

The lady took him to the kitchen, where there was a maid to be found in white apron and frilled cuffs, who gave him tea and a plate of small, round cakes full of currants. He eat hungrily. It was the first food he had had that day.

The lady returned as he was biting into his third cake. 'My husband asks for your name, then he will see you shortly.'

'George Maple, ma'am. I once met the Reverend at Blackmoor House, where I was then in service.'

So I have let my secret out, George thought. Will the Reverend already know of my shame? He is a man of God. Surely he will not simply dismiss me out of sight.

'Goodness. I will tell him. George Maple, you say?'

'Yes, ma'am.'

It seemed a long wait. He chatted with the maid, a youthful, fair-haired woman who told him her name was Lizzie. She told him she had once worked at Stratfield Saye House, but much preferred it here, where things were not so formal.

'They are lovely people, the Reverend and his wife', she confided to George.

'Where do you live?' he asked. 'Do you know the farms around? I may have to seek work here, if there is any available.' His heart sank a little as he spoke. That would mean he had failed in his quest here with the Reverend.

'Oh, I live in,' she answered. 'But I come from Mortimer. That's over the border into Berkshire,' she added with a flourish, as if to show her worldliness.

'Is Mortimer a big place?'

'Well, depends what you mean.' She was busy banging oven doors, checking inside, pulling out some iron pots. 'It's a straggling place, you see, some at the Hill, some the Common. There's a railway station, though.'

That's interesting, George thought. Stations, he knew, helped bring business and travellers. There might be work to be found in this Mortimer. Perhaps he'd head there next if the Reverend did not want him. Yet, what a very nice billet it would be here! Some hope, though. He mustn't get too carried away with day-dreaming. But something had to happen. He couldn't go on as he was, from job to job, sleeping rough, with only a few coins in his pocket. The more dilapidated he looked, the more difficult, he knew, it would be to get any sort of permanent, or even temporary, position.

Another lady came into the kitchen. She was tall and unsmiling, dressed all in black, her dark hair swept back and tied behind her head. He was surprised to see Lizzie stop what she was doing and make a semblance of a curtsy towards her, something she had certainly not done for the Reverend's own wife.

'George Maple? I'm the Reverend Mr. Joyce's housekeeper. I'll take you to him now.'

The Reverend's study was clearly on an upper floor of the house, for they climbed a narrow flight of stairs before reaching a broad landing and stopping before a panelled door, upon which the housekeeper knocked discretely before opening it.

'Mr. Maple, sir,' she said.

George, his nerves now very much on edge, was pleased she did not come with him into the room, but disappeared back along the landing like a shadow.

And there was the remembered broad, smiling face of the Reverend Mr. Joyce, rising from his desk at the window to greet him. He proffered his hand and George shook it. So far, so good. Perhaps the man knew nothing of his disgrace.

'I scarce recognise you with that beard, young man. Times have changed for you now, I understand.' George recalled the precise manner in which he spoke, the way syllables were emphasised.

'Yes, sir. I mean your reverence.' So he did seem to know. George's hopes began to fall again.

'Just sir, or Mr. Joyce, will do.'

There was an awkward pause. The Reverend waved George to a chair while he resumed his seat at the desk, swinging himself round to face him. 'I see from your appearance you have fallen on bad times. Lord Selborne did mention the matter to me.'

George felt a further wave of disappointment, but he was determined not to admit fault abjectly but to defend himself. 'I believe I did little wrong, sir.'

'Quite.'

George did not understand what that word meant. He said, 'I was unlucky, I believe. The circumstances, sir, were against me.'

He felt the blood in his face. If all his hopes were to be dashed, he would not rant or rave, or for that matter grovel, but just state the truth plainly, as he knew it. After all, he had been given no chance to defend himself, but been packed off from the house he had served to the best of his ability like a common criminal, which he most certainly was not.

The Reverend did not reply for a while. He was evidently thinking.

'I should probably not tell you this,' he said at last, 'but in the interests of truth in a matter that is clearly vital to you, I think I should. Lord Selborne did make a comment to me – in a private conversation, you understand, for he is a man of the law who must always seek complete truthfulness and fairness – that he acted too precipitately. The matter clearly weighed upon him or he would not have talked to me of it. I believe he had a further conversation with whichever of his daughters was involved. I do not know the details. He was particularly dismayed when he found out you had left the estate entirely. On further consideration, I believe he felt that a reprimand, and your apology, was all that was required'

'No man of spirit would have stayed on for one minute, having been so dismissed,' said George angrily, feeling the ground now more solid beneath his feet. Perhaps all was not lost after all.

'Quite, quite. But, as no one knew where you were, there was nothing to be done. His lordship is a very busy man, and has to spend many months in London on affairs of state.'

George bit his lip to prevent himself saying anything bitter. So he did not speak.

The Reverend looked long into his face. 'What then can I do for you?' he said at last. 'Why have you come to me?'

Positives are what are needed now, George knew. No more complaint, no more anger, indeed no more talk on that matter at all.

'For help,' he answered. 'I go from job to job, but none can last for long. To see if you know of anyone who might offer me work, sir. And also,' he added quickly, seeing the Reverend's gaze was still steady upon him, 'because you inspired me, sir, with your talk of the Romans and their deeds, and because I know of your digging at *Calleva*, which place I have already looked at on my way to you, and, sir, I would like to take part as well, if I could. I believe I can labour as well as any other man, and I do want to learn more. If you recall sir, Lord Selborne was going to send me to you for the summer season, so that I might help too. I would love to do so. I can't say more.' To his alarm, George felt tears springing to his eyes.

'My boy,' said the Reverend, rising from his chair and placing a hand on his arm, 'do not distress yourself any further. You have clearly suffered greatly, more than enough to atone for anything wrongful or foolish you may have done. You *did* right in coming to me.'

He added the last emphatically, beginning to pace the study, which was a large room, lined with bookcases. 'I have an idea,' he said. I have a possibility in mind, but I will need to talk to some people first. Where do you stay at present?'

George had never felt the utter hopelessness of his position any greater. 'I have nowhere, sir. The last was at a place called, I think, Sherfield, where I worked on a farm for three days, helping demolish an old barn, but I had to leave when the job was done. There was no further work for me. I got paid a shilling and was given some food in the evening. Last night I slept out under trees. It was an old place with great mounds about it, made by the ancients, I should think. A keeper ordered me out when he found me there this morning. He gave me directions to *Calleva*, where I thought I'd find you, sir. You were my last hope.'

He finished his tale on this plaintive note, not exaggerating it for effect, as he might have done once. He was speaking from the heart.

'Well, we'll get you sorted out', the Reverend said vigorously. 'You will stay here for the time being.' He went to the door and opened it. 'Miss Webb,' he called out in a strong voice. 'Are you there? Could you come to me, please.'

12

The Reverend Mr. Joyce was a powerful man of decision, George Maple came to think, looking back on that time when he had walked into his house with his leaking boots covered in mud, his stomach aching with hunger, and been given not only a paid job of great personal interest which should last long into the future, but one which came as well with accommodation and meals.

He was to help in the Reverend's excavations at *Calleva*, joining a gang of five labourers from Silchester village who volunteered for this work each year. They were paid by the Duke of Wellington, who funded all the expenses of the excavations. It was the Duke, indeed – a keen antiquarian, himself – who had first proposed such excavation on his own land at *Calleva*. Wishing to know more of what lay there under the ground, and aware that this must be carried out with care and system, on learning of his new rector's knowledge and skills in the subject of Roman antiquities, he had persuaded the Reverend Mr. Joyce to take up the mantle, meeting all the necessary costs. How the Reverend tackled the task would be up to him, although his Grace, of course, would naturally take a keen interest in the progress made.

The Duke had been at home at Stratfield Saye House most fortuitously that day of George Maple's arrival, indeed was expecting a visit from the Reverend to discuss this year's excavations, and had agreed at once to pay for an extra labourer for the coming season of excavation, and, depending on how George worked, perhaps into future seasons as well.

The digging generally went on, weather and the Reverend's parochial duties allowing, from the end of the Easter celebrations until mid-October. After that, would come the business of writing up the season's discoveries, together with all the scrutiny and cataloguing of the various finds, which was a task George could assist with as well, one that the Reverend found a growing burden for himself each year. For this, George's experience at Blackmoor House in library cataloguing would be of value, The Duke had also agreed that during the winter and next spring George could be employed at Stratfield Saye House itself, in whatever capacity the house steward thought best, but very likely in the library there.

All this sounded like a dream coming true to George when the proposal was put to him by the Reverend later that first day as he stood before him once more in his study. But he was still worried about the legacy that haunted him from Blackmoor.

'Don't worry,' about that, the Reverend had said, flapping his hands airily. 'I will send a letter to Lord Selborne to inform him of the situation. From what he has said to me – as I have already indicated to you – I am sure he will be nothing but pleased.'

George knew that great men did not normally get involved in such matters concerning their servants. Yet, for him, that is exactly what had happened. Perversely, however much his relief and gratitude, he could not help feeling he was now subject to their whim, to be raised up or set down at their will, like some sort of amusing plaything. Yet, was that not what life was like, anyhow, for the great majority of workers? He had been at his very last gasp, and now there was a future. Perhaps somewhere there was a moral for him. He had never lost hope, even in his darkest moments.

'You have come at a very good time,' the Reverend had told him, rubbing his palms together, which George was to come to recognise as a habit of his when particularly pleased. 'I am due to re-open *Calleva* on Monday – weather permitting, and it seems to be set fair now – and today is Friday. So, if all is to your liking, you will have time to gather yourself and prepare yourself – yes, prepare yourself for your new life if that does not sound too melodramatic.'

'No, indeed, sir', replied George, not sure what melodramatic meant.

'I will teach you, George,' the Reverend had said earnestly. 'The archaeology, as it may be termed – the actual digging – is only part of the process. There needs to be time as well for the cleaning of the finds and labelling them, for drawing plans of the work that has been completed, for writing up a full and detailed record of all that we have done and found, our objectives, our conclusions, and so on. And I must also, of course, reserve time for my true vocation. However zealous I am for the archaeology, it lies but a poor second to my zeal for Christ.'

When he shows emotion, George had thought, he loses his usual slow, pedantic way of speaking, and seems much nicer, more normal. A normal life was what he wished so very much. He no longer wanted to follow around titled lords and ladies, picking up the crumbs that they let fall. He wished now to be more of his own person, so to speak, mixing with ordinary people, doing things that he knew to be of great interest, or even extraordinary, pushing out the bounds of knowledge – and finding things.

Yet there was far more than that. He was coming to understand there had been past worlds now long vanished, where people had lived and had their dreams and their troubles, just as he was experiencing today. Then, they had lived and worked by different fashions and by different practices than those familiar to him now. It was to understand such lives out of those dead worlds that he most sought.

He had never thought about the past before. The present had been enough to occupy his mind, but he was now realising that in its essence, if not exact detail, everything that happened today had happened before. Down the long centuries people had been born, been abandoned or been loved, had risen like meteors or crashed down like stones, had loved and hated, been disappointed, had fought and won, but, more often, very likely, lost. In the end, indeed, everyone lost, as the ending must be the grave and oblivion, but the object surely – the path to real fulfilment – was to leave something good and worthwhile behind.

He knew that to understand all this better than the few thoughts he was trying to piece together would involve reading what others had written down on these subjects, thereby learning far more, and talking with others with much greater knowledge than he – but none of that deterred him. He enjoyed reading, whenever he had had the chance to do so. He wanted to learn everything he could about the Romans, their peoples, their beliefs, their civilisation – what they looked like, what they ate, what their empire had achieved, what buildings they had erected, what lands they had conquered, what battles they had fought. The Reverend Mr. Joyce would be his teacher, and one day it would be he – George Maple – who was setting out trenches across other sites, and employing workers to dig the holes and sift the earth. Wonderful things he would find, wonderful knowledge he would gain! And his name would stand out with the other learned men: 'George Maple – have you read of his latest discoveries? They say he knows the Romans better than any man.'

George was to sleep in an attic room of the rectory, hastily cleared of lumber stored there, on a truckle bed that was wheeled into the house by an elderly man, whom Lizzie later told him was one of the gardeners. 'It's kept in a shed over the way,' she said vaguely. 'You're not the first who's arrived suddenly and been put up here.' George hastened to help the gardener take the bed upstairs to the room.

Afterwards, he had a meal with Lizzie in the kitchen – a good meal of beef stew with carrots – the best food he had eaten for a very long time. They were just finishing when the housekeeper, Miss Webb, came in, looking displeased. 'My, what a trouble you have caused me,' she was muttering. 'Bed clothing to sort out, old clothing of the master for you too. Whatever next. I tell him, this is not a mission station.'

'I'm sorry,' said George, putting on his most abject expression.

'Oh, it's not your fault. His reverence has his mind on his archaeology now.'

'I know. I'm going to work with him.'

'Oh, you are, are you? What digging those trenches? You won't be able to keep up with the others: they're all hard men, used to digging all their lives.'

'I'll do my best.'

'Oh, I'm sure you will. What, are you learning the subject then?'

'Yes, I hope to.'

'How old are you?'

'Eighteen. How old are *you*?'

'Now don't be cheeky. A lady never tells. How old do you *think* I am?'

'Er – about forty.' George was wishing he had not got into this conversation.

'What! I'll clip your ear, you crazed boy.'

She made to swipe at him, but George ducked away. He knew she was only pretending to be angry. But she seemed a little more human now than when he had first met her. He noted that Lizzie only laughed when they all did. It seemed she was in some sort of awe of Miss Webb, but he could not understand why.

The Reverend's wife took him under her wing in the late afternoon. He was amazed by the generosity of spirit she was showing him. She reappeared in the kitchen, with a grey, woollen cape thrown over her shoulders, for the day, although sunny, had a chill in the air.

'I am going to the church,' she told him. 'Would you like to come with me?'

'Why, ma'am, yes, of course.' He scrambled to his feet to indicate his enthusiasm, although within him he felt an unease that he would know what to do or say in her company. He had never been a great one for church attendance. He had only visited Alton's church to see the lead musket ball splashes on its pillars from a battle fought there in the Civil War. The verger – a thin, wheedling man – had shown them to him, and then offered him communion wine in the vestry from a flask left after a service. He had shrunk away and never been back, despite the exhortations of the rector who sometimes visited the bank.

Mrs. Joyce and he walked side by side. The church lay just a short distance by a gravelled path through verdant grass, studded with the bright yellow crowns of dandelions. The red brick walls of the church, softened in places by creepers, rose before him. An octagonal tower at the church's centre was roofed in copper.

'Some people say they dislike the look of this church,' said Mrs. Joyce, with a wry smile. 'They think the design is ugly. But I love it. It was built at the end of the last century. The old church had been nearer to the main house – too near for the gentleman who lived there then, they say, so he had it pulled down and this one built in its place.'

'I think it's very nice,' said George – dishonestly because he could not admire its brickwork, which reminded him of the houses that had been built in recent years on the outskirts of Alton.

Mrs. Joyce smiled towards him, but made no further comment. She does not believe me, he thought. I must make my voice sound more sincere. He knew by now all about the need at times for pretence.

They passed into the church through a portico pierced by three open doorways, each matched by a round window above. Over all, was a high brick pediment with the domed tower rising behind. The inner wooden door was stiff to push open.

'It needs some oil on the hinges,' Mrs. Joyce said. 'I must tell the verger.'

Within the church, George was confronted by a view of tall-sided pews, overhung by balconies on three sides, that were painted in – to him – a ghastly blue-green, when seen against the rendered, cream-coloured walls. Various stone-sculptured heads stared down, the deeds of these worthies set out in Latin on ornamental plaques beneath.

'So peaceful,' breathed Mrs. Joyce. 'I always think of green leaves and white clouds when I first come in.'

From one of the transepts where she had been arranging flowers came a lady in a light grey dress, trimmed with fur, and patterned all over with silvery fronds. She is like some hot-house plant in motion was George's first ignoble thought. Mrs. Joyce introduced him to her, and he made a bow with his head as he briefly touched her hand.

'Mrs. Deverill, this is George, who is staying with us for a while. He is to help James at his diggings this year.'

'Oh really. That is most interesting.' She gave a sudden shrill of laughter, quite unaccountably. 'I must try to visit this year. Lots of old things to be found, I am sure.'

'Yes, we hope so, ma'am', George said, his head respectfully bent. He was surprised by his ambitious use of 'we'.

'And you have dug before?'

Mrs. Joyce now intervened to George's relief. 'George has a connection with Lord Selborne, my dear. He assisted with a Roman coin hoard found at Blackmoor House, through which he came to my husband's attention.'

'Oh that is very good,' Mrs. Deverill trilled. 'It is so wonderful to hear of young people getting on.'

George was grateful for the comment. He knew he had lost much of his recently acquired confidence. His own past was now sullied. He had much to do to recover himself. He wandered around the church while the two ladies talked. He stood before the altar, looking at the cross standing there, wondering if there was a God. He would like to believe there was. He would like to believe that a meaning and a purpose lay behind everything. And then he thought: has not God brought me out of my trial into this haven? He has shown me a task that will be mine to do to my very best. And in that moment he did believe.

Back at the rectory, he was given a meal in the kitchen by Lizzie, this time with Miss Webb present too. It was growing dark outside. Lizzie lit the lamps.

'You will need to take a lamp when you go to your room,' Miss Webb told George. 'Do your ablutions first. There is a wash room you can use: through that door there.' She pointed to a white boarded door set in the far corner of the kitchen. 'Down the passage, then the first door on the left. The gardener uses it too. It'll be your responsibility to keep it clean'.

'Don't take the second door,' said Lizzie with a giggle. 'Or you may get a surprise.'

Miss Webb frowned disapprovingly, but said nothing.

George went there now, and was pleased to find a water closet by the single sink and a blurry mirror hanging from a cord above. He relieved himself and washed his face and hands as best he could, using a hard cake of green-coloured soap that proved impossible to work into any sort of lather.

'I'll show you to your room,' said Miss Web when he returned 'I shouldn't think you could find it again by yourself. We go up by the back stairs, of course.'

And that was true. George's tired mind was growing muddled. He had never known such attention, so suddenly and unexpectedly. All sort of thoughts and impressions were popping into and out of his mind, without any overall view of his situation being allowed to settle. He must sleep – how he craved sleep! – and then all would seem much better in the morning. The great news was that, almost miraculously, he had found a situation for himself, where he could live into a future that he wanted. There would be no more sleeping out and moving on, without plan, not knowing where he was going. He had *arrived* now, and all looked promising, very promising indeed. It was like being in a golden dream after a long, dark nightmare, almost too good to be true. His mind hung over those last words. Was everything in fact just too good to be true?

He stumbled after Miss Webb up the steep and narrow, wooden stairs, trying to note this time the landings and doors he passed. On the very upper level right under the roof, she opened a narrow door, and along the passage with its low, sloping ceiling was the door to his room. In the shifting light of the lamps they carried, he saw the narrow bed that was his. A sleeping gown was laid across it. The bed occupied almost the whole room. There was no window. Against the far wall was a wooden chest with a ewer and dish set upon it. A ceramic plaque on the wall, bordered in purple, spelt out in black letters. 'Prepare to Meet Thy God.' Not yet, thought George. I want to live, not die.

'Sleep well,' Miss Webb, said closing the door. She opened it again. 'Your chamber pot's under the bed, by the way. You empty it yourself when you come downstairs. There's a cloth to put over it.'

There was no lock, he noted briefly. He dumped on the floor the bag he had carried all this way, containing everything that remained of his old life. Only a few sad relics they were. Then he laid himself down on the bed, fully clothed. The air was chilly here. He did not undress and pull on the nightgown. He fell asleep in seconds.

It was long after dawn when he awakened. Daylight was filtering greyly under the door, but he slept on. He came to with a start, wondering where he was. There was a rattling at the door. 'Are you awake, George?'

'Yes', he tried to call out, finding his voice choked. He scrambled from the bed. 'Yes,' he called again in a firmer voice. The door opened. Miss Webb stood there. She wore a different dress from yesterday, one of a light blue, with ruffles on the skirt and at the bodice. Her hair was no longer bound up. Her long black tresses tumbled to her shoulders, catching the light from the landing window behind her. He was surprised by her sudden beauty, feeling almost naked in his small space before her, the sleep still in his eyes.

'Are you coming down? Breakfast is long over, but Lizzie is still in the kitchen. She'll feed you, and then you are to see the Reverend later.'

'Thank you.' He didn't know what else to say.

'Poor boy,' she said mysteriously, looking at him inquisitively, her head on one side. He felt a sudden desire for her, but knew the slightest move towards her would be madness.

'I'm off to the house today, so I probably won't see you again. You'll likely be gone when I return. So good luck.'

'Thank you,' he said once more.

She lingered, staring at him, which he found unsettling. 'You didn't undress, I see. Naughty boy.' Then in a much more clipped voice. 'There're some clean things for you in the chest. Don't be long now.' And she was gone.

George was left in a whirl. He looked in the chest. There was some underclothing there – a woollen vest with sleeves and some drawers with legs almost to his knees. He undressed and pulled them on. Such luxury he had not known for some weeks.

He made the journey to the kitchen. Lizzie was there, raking out the stove. 'Here, take these to the bins outside', she said, handing him a scoop of still-glowing coals, scarcely turning her head. He did as he was told.

When he returned, Lizzie was laying some cutlery on the table. 'Well, sit down and I'll cook you some bacon. There's a loaf here you can cut and butter.'

Lizzie is nice and normal, George thought, watching her slight, bustling form in a striped dress, her hair covered by a white kerchief. That other one. She seems half-crazed to me.

'Miss Webb,' he said between bites of bread. 'She said she was going to the house. What did she mean?'

'Diana Webb? She often works for the Duke at Stratfield Saye House. And other things too...' She had crossed the kitchen and was busy fetching jars down from a wall cupboard. Then, turning to him, her sleeves pulled up to her elbows, her hands on her hips, 'When did she tell you that?'

'Just now. She came to my room to wake me.'

'Did she now? You watch her, young man, you don't want to become entangled with her.'

George felt himself blushing. 'That's ridiculous.'

'Perhaps. Perhaps...' Lizzie was busy at the oven.

'What do you mean, other things?'

Lizzie laughed, turning back. 'Now that would be you asking, and me telling.' Then suddenly sharp, 'More than my job's worth. I leave you to guess. I pays her great respect though, I tell you, young man, as if she was of the family herself. Now do you see?'

George didn't, but he said no more. He would ponder upon the matter later. In the meantime he was hungry, very hungry.

13

George had shaved off his beard. It had hung wispily from his chin most unsatisfactorily, so he knew he must now remove it. He felt it was expected of him, to rid himself of every trace of his legacy as a vagrant and to become a well set up young Englishman once again.

A razor had been left for him in the washroom: who by? – he had no idea. Perhaps indeed it was the gardener's whom he had been told shared the basin and closet, but he had yet to meet him. George opened the cut-throat blade and applied himself to the task of shaving, which was a difficult and painful operation without a soapy lather. But after some minutes he had removed the longest straggling hairs at his chin, and concentrated next on scraping away the patches of stubble. He only nicked himself a couple of times, but was able to staunch the thin trails of blood oozing from his skin with scraps of wetted cloth. He examined himself in the tarnished mirror and thought the result was satisfactory. Then, with a piece of cloth, he rubbed at his teeth to remove their furry feeling on his tongue. He hoped his breath did not smell. Harold, the disgraced footman at Blackmoor, he recalled had had particularly bad breath, making his female conquests seem even more implausible.

Once back in the kitchen, subject to Lizzie's close examination – 'you've cut yourself', then rubbing the place with her own handkerchief, pulled from her apron pocket: 'that's better' – he did not know what was expected of him.

He tried to help Lizzie put dishes and plates in the cupboards, but she shooed him away – 'Best leave it to me, but I thank you for trying. The Reverend will send for you soon. He's busy at this time on his Sunday sermon.'

An half hour or so later, the Reverend Mr. Joyce appeared at the kitchen door, looking into its interior with a smile on his lips, surveying with apparent satisfaction the neat ranges of burnished copper pots, the blackness of the grate, the scrubbed table tops.

'Ah, there you are, George,' he said. 'Did you sleep well?'

'Yes, sir. Thank you. Like a top.'

'That is good,' the Reverend said. 'If you come with me now, I will tell you more of the excavations I am making at *Calleva*, and explain something of our working methods and what you will be expected to undertake. And also, of course, I have not yet told you where you will be staying during that time.'

Stay? thought George. I had thought I would be at this house. And then he remembered that the attic room was to be his only temporarily. He had been too tired last night to think further. Silchester, as he now knew, was some distance from Stratfield Saye: it would be too far for him to make the walk there and back each day.

He followed the Reverend through the house, passing Mrs. Joyce in the hallway. She smiled benevolently at him, but did not speak. A maid he had not seen before, in black dress, white apron and cap, was on her knees before the fireplace in the large drawing room they now entered. She froze in her work as they passed, unable to rise to make the expected bob of the head or curtsy.

'All well, Ivy?' the Reverend called out.

'Oh yes, sir, Thank you, sir.'

She is only a girl, George thought. Stick legs and thin chest like a board, her skirt about her on the floor like a pool of black water. This is likely her first job. To work for the Reverend at the rectory was perhaps a step up from the other girls of the village.

Leaving the lounge by an opposite door, they came into the front hallway where George had first arrived, and climbed the stairs once more to the Reverend's study. George recalled from yesterday the broad room with its windows on two sides at the corner of the house, through which yellow sunlight was now striking warmly. But, in the distressed condition of his arrival yesterday, he had not paid attention to the high bookshelves that he saw now filling the remaining walls, with the Reverend's great desk – like a beast commanding its area of rich carpet – set at the centre of the room.

The Reverend did not go to sit at the desk this time, but relaxed his body into a well-cushioned chair with high arms, while waving George to another opposite. George sunk deeply into his chair, feeling somewhat imprisoned by its high sides, as if he was being borne, a captive, in some ancient chieftain's chariot.

The Reverend, clearly a man who believed in giving clear instruction, wasted no further time in pleasantries, or other matters irrelevant.

'George, on Monday morning – we will make an early start – you will ride with me in my pony trap to Silchester – to *Calleva*, indeed. My labourers – those who dig for me – five in number, they are, all live at Silchester, or close by on the farms. My foreman is Will Hankley: he works at Manor Farm, which is by *Calleva's* east gate. He will have seen the site is ready that morning, the covers removed from the diggings, and all in order to make a start. Knowing him as I do – he's an ex-army man who served in the Crimea – he'll be standing ready with the others when we arrive. Then I'll introduce you and say what your role is to be. But, before we do that, I'll take you to where you'll be staying – and that will be at the rectory close by of my neighbour, the Reverend Mr. Fiennes. I count him a very good friend, as well as a neighbour and a brother in Christ. His wife, I'm happy to say, is also very friendly with my own dear wife, who often plays the harmonium at their church, which is hard by the east gate too.'

'I called there on the way to you,' George interjected. 'I thought it was *your* church.'

The Reverend frowned and muttered, 'Did you now?' then seemed for a moment to have lost his way. 'Ah, yes,' he said, recovering himself. 'It just remains to tell you, I'll also be sleeping at Mr. Fiennes' house some nights, but at other times I will need to return here, as, of course, I have my parochial duties to attend to also, and my responsibilities to this house. My wife will occasionally come and stay with me at Fiennes' rectory too.'

George remembered that when the Reverend had spoken with Lord Selborne at Blackmoor about his working at *Calleva* he had said he could stay on a Silchester farm. But now he was to be alongside the Reverend himself at this other rectory, a presumably much more comfortable billet. That was surely a great advancement, was it not? Again, he could scarcely believe his luck and the trust shown in him.

Joyce went on, 'I have already written to Mr. Fiennes, and, although there has been no time for an answer, he will be prepared for us, I am certain, even at this short notice. I am sure he will make you comfortable in one of the servants' attics, and his people will feed you, and give you whatever you will need to carry to the site for the day to keep body and soul together. The men usually make tea with water from a spring. I think that is all I can tell you for the present.'

But he added after a short pause, 'I am likely out some evenings – there are a number of local landowners who are interested in our work, and they can be most hospitable. However, there is much evening work to be done by lamplight, and with that I will wish you to help me, George, as I know you have the skills of penmanship I require. All will become much clearer as we proceed. By the way, George, can you draw?'

He was surprised by the question, and queried, 'Draw what, sir?'

'Could you make a drawing of a pot, for instance? Show its shape accurately, sketch in any breaks or blemishes. Perhaps make a plan of a trench, showing where the walls are that we find, or to indicate a pit?'

'I was good at drawing at school in Alton, sir. I achieved a star once for drawing a vase of violets and colouring it in.'

'Excellent! Excellent!' The Reverend was rubbing his hands enthusiastically in his habitual manner. 'I am sure you will prove of much value to me. Let us see how we go on first with the basic digging. That is sure to tire you at first. The others are used to the labour. They can dig a trench to perfection, but they could not write or draw to save their souls.'

The Reverend rose to his feet. 'I will show you two of the very best finds we have made at *Calleva*. They should whet your appetite for the work.'

He bent down to a cupboard beneath one of the bookcases. 'Although I must emphasise – as I do to all who dig with me – that it is the knowledge of the site we seek most of all, its structures, their dating, and so on, rather than individual artefacts, however glorious they may be.'

He brought out two large, hinged wooden boxes and placed them on the maroon-coloured leather top of his desk. 'Come and see, George. I keep these close to me, as they are of particular value. Many other finds are kept in our hut on the site, which we know as the 'red hut' from the colour of its painting. It makes an office for us and we use it too as a small museum for when we have visitors, which is often.'

'Yes, sir. I saw the hut when I stood at the Silchester wall.'

George rose and stood beside the Reverend at the desk. With his white, slender fingers, the Reverend pushed up the hooks that held the boxes closed. Both contained objects wrapped in white cloth. Taking up the smaller one, he unwrapped it carefully, and pulled out a metal object, tarnished overall but in places gleaming brightly. George could see it made the shape of a horse in profile – its head, its back, its tail, and its legs set as if at a gallop.

'Is it gold?' George asked, awe-struck. He noticed how the horse was engraved with a series of circular shapes along the back to indicate its flesh and hair.

The Reverend handed the object to him. 'Hold it in your two open hands over the desk. Note, it's not gold but made of bronze. We have cleaned it somewhat, for it was dark green in colour when it was found. That must be three seasons back now, when we were working on the basilica.'

'What was it used for?'

'Good question again, my boy.' The Reverend was nodding approvingly. 'Probably it was once part of some larger object that has not survived. The style of the work is of the period before the Romans – that which we call the Iron Age. The art of that time seems to have lived on even after the Roman conquest. You see, although everything and everyone was now part of the Roman Empire, many of the people still retained their old traditions – for a while, at least.'

The Reverend took the horse back, wrapped it up again, and returned it to its box. He now took up the second, somewhat larger bundle. As it was unwrapped, George made out a greenish-brown shape that eventually was revealed as a bird, its feathers most clearly cast, its head with a cruel, curving beak.

'An eagle,' he breathed.

'An eagle, indeed. In bronze too. It retains its green patina, although it has been cleaned also to some degree.'

'Was it one of the eagles carried by the Roman army?'

The Reverend looked at him, surprised. 'You know about that? You have read on the subject?'

'Only a small amount, sir, in Lord Selborne's library. I would wish to know more.'

'I will teach you, my boy.' He held the eagle up high, so it was caught in a ray of sunlight streaming through the window. 'It is good, very good indeed, to have found someone so young who has such interest.'

'May I hold it, sir?'

'You may.' He handed the eagle to George who took it in his cupped hands.

'It has lost its wings, of course. If you look carefully, you can see where they were once attached, probably spread out widely. It is an image such as we see on coins that show a legion's standards. This may be the only survival in the entire Roman empire of such an *aquila*. Each legion carried one. The bearer was greatly honoured. He was known as the *aquilifer*.'

'So how was it lost then?' George mused aloud, lost in the object he was holding, forgetting for the moment the humbleness of his position here and speaking, as it were, man to man with one of the great learned, whose sanctum he had so fortuitously stumbled into.

'Ah, that is the question. That is archaeology. It throws up much we can never answer, although some may have the imagination to try.'

The Reverend walked over to one of the bookcases, opened its glazed front, and took out a large volume bound in leather. He stood beside George leafing through the book. George saw many handsome pages filled with the coloured drawings of objects, and about them dates and descriptions, all in the neatest, flowing handwriting.

'I record all that I do in this journal,' the Reverend said. 'Set down place and purpose, what is unearthed with measurements, theory and conclusion. And I draw the artefacts and paint them in their true colours. See, the horse I have just shown you.'

He read, 'Found on 7th October 1870.'

'And in an earlier volume of the journal I have drawn the eagle too, and given its measurements. That was found on 9th October, 1866, if my memory serves me correctly. You see, my boy, I have only to turn the pages and I have the full memory of everything we have done at *Calleva*, and that record can be passed on to those who come next when my own time here is finished. You too might keep your own diary, young George. I can give you an exercise book for the purpose, such as used in our schoolroom, and pen and ink too.'

'I should like that, sir. I can add my own drawings as well.'

'Excellent, excellent.' The Reverend rubbed his hands once more. 'Well, my boy, that is enough for now. My wife has most kindly sought out some suitable work clothes for you, and indeed some boots, which you must try on' He looked George up and down. 'I fear your present clothing will not be suitable, nor would it suffice for long, as I do believe – if I may make such fun – it is coming to its last legs.'

He let out a mighty guffaw at this, which he tried to stifle with a handkerchief brought hurriedly from his pocket. 'I'm sorry, my boy, please do not think I laugh at you, but punning always has amused me.' He pressed the handkerchief to his mouth again, his chest heaving.

'You are all most kind, sir,' George said, not minding his laughter at all. Indeed, he would have joined in but for the very real emotion he was feeling now, desperately trying to gulp it back, to prevent his eyes moistening like a girl. And he remembered and gave tongue to a phrase he had heard repeated at Blackmoor House. 'I shall endeavour to serve you as your most loyal servant.'

'Quite, quite,' said the Reverend, looking a bit embarrassed, stuffing the handkerchief back into his pocket. 'I am sure you will prove your value, and return what you have been given three fold. Now is there anything else you wish to ask me?'

'Will I receive any money for my labours, so that I can buy those things I will surely require in time?' George asked. He was still mystified as to how exactly he was going to live.

'You will have some money in hand,' replied the Reverend, perhaps a little impatiently now. 'I have to talk to the Duke further about what can be afforded and what additions he might make to our grant. He wants costs to be as low as possible, as you can imagine. The digging is just an addition to the work of the estate, a luxury perhaps, carried out purely for the edification, and indeed education, of society, as befits the age of learning we live in under our gracious Queen. But, of course, it cannot be done by free labour. Most of the monies to pay you will be used for your food and accommodation. When you work directly to the Duke's steward, however, it will be different. That has not been discussed as yet: there has been no time. Are you happy with this situation for the present? I appreciate it must cause you some uncertainty.'

'I am pleased for this great opportunity, sir,' George said with an enthusiasm that was clearly genuine. 'But where I will stay during my winter work?'

'Why, with the other servants of the Duke at his great house, of course. From there next season, you can be released to my care once more – if all works out as I would hope.'

'It will, sir. It will,' said George determinedly.

The Reverend patted him on the arm. 'Good, good, my boy.'

You will attend my church tomorrow,' he said of a sudden. 'Then, you can thank God, who rules in all we do.'

It was clearly a command, not a request.

'Of course, sir.'

'Excellent.' The Reverend was beaming again. 'All will work out very well, you will see. And, with God's help too, we shall make many new discoveries.' He went to the door and rang a hand bell.

It was not a maid who appeared, but Mrs. Joyce. 'Yes, dear?' she said with the calm patience George had already noticed.

'Oh, Ellen, my love, I am sorry to have disturbed you. Is there no servant? No, of course, I forget; it is Saturday. Could you take George here back to the kitchen, and perhaps introduce him to the clothes you have that he should wear for Silchester.'

She smiled, and led George away back through the house to the kitchen, where Lizzie was still at work. Lizzie knew all about the clothes and Mrs. Joyce left her to get them for him. She took him to a store at the end of the washroom passage and pointed to a large pile of clothing, with no less than two pairs of boots placed upon it, tied together by their laces.

'You are the lucky one, young man,' she said. 'Some of these are from the Reverend's own wardrobe, others were to go to the poor of this parish, if you had not come along when you did. I should try the boots on down here, then take the clothes to your room to put on. Here, there's a basket you can use to carry them in.'

George did as he was asked. He sat outside the kitchen back door to pull on the first pair of the boots. Although a little large, they fitted him well enough. They were of good stiff leather, only a little scuffed. They were hobnailed too and seemed little used. He wondered what dead man's boots they had been; some recent death of a parish labouring man, he would guess. The second pair were thinner-soled and of a patent leather, more of a gentleman's walking-out shoes, in fact. The sides were tight across his ankles and the length on the short side, but he thought they might stretch in time. He was pleased to have them too.

In his small room, he found there were several pairs of trousers, a coat, obviously of quality with a glossy-red lining, and several shirts and a black waist coat with white buttons. He selected a pair of trousers made of a thick woollen material and with a leather belt attached – they looked newly washed – which fitted his slight shape well, if the leg bottoms were turned up. He would wear these and a fresh shirt to set out on his adventure tomorrow. There was also more flannel underwear, and two other pairs of trousers and some shirts, one nattily striped, and good long socks also. He was reborn as a king!

He packed away everything he would not immediately wear, including his old clothes, in the basket and his own bag that he had carried here. With a sudden start, he remembered the coin he had taken from the Blackmoor urn, and hurriedly retrieved it from the front pocket of his trousers already in the basket. The head of Allectus – his nose and chin and the spiky crown on his head – shone up at him from his hand. He found a secure place for it in a narrow side pocket of his new trousers. Then, freshly apparelled in trousers, striped shirt, waistcoat and socks, he padded shoeless back down to the kitchen. Lizzie was present with the young maid, Ivy, he had seen earlier making up the fire.

'My, look at you, fancy man!' Lizzie exclaimed, while Ivy smiled shyly. George paraded before them. All he needed, he thought, was a coloured scarf, and he would be the picture of a proper labouring man. Lizzie must have thought exactly that, for she went to a cupboard and pulled out a red-patterned bandana, which she placed about his neck, knotting it at the front.

'There you are,' she said, stepping back appreciatively. 'I found it by chance yesterday hung up on a bush by the lane. Perhaps it was meant for you.' And she gave him a peck on the cheek, while Ivy giggled.

'Now take yourself outside and make yourself useful with old Tom,' Lizzie said. 'You'll find him in the small garden cutting wood, or trying to. Give him a hand before he chops off his own.'

And George thought he had not felt so happy for a very long time.

The next day – Sunday – George accompanied the other servants to church, seated with them in a green-sided pew to the rear of the nave beyond its central crossing. Many staff from Stratfield Saye House were present too, although not the Duke of Wellington, whom George overheard someone say was indisposed.

The church was full. The Reverend Mr. Joyce was clearly a popular preacher. George had dressed in his old suit, dragged from his bag and given a press by Lizzie, and brushed his hair, which Lizzie had also trimmed for him, a towel, thrown over his shoulders, for it had grown bushy and overlong. 'You need to get it cut properly,' she told him. 'There's a barber's in Mortimer.'

'As soon as I can,' he said. 'Perhaps if we're rained off one day.' Secretly, though, he was quite pleased with the rather wild, unkempt look he was gaining, appropriate, he thought, to have the look of a navvy for the digging work to come.

The Reverend took the service from the pulpit, also green-painted. His wife played the harmonium, an instrument in a Gothic-styled casing of dark wood, positioned on one of the balconies. The singing of 'Ride on, Ride on in Majesty' was sung with great enthusiasm, and after a reading and prayers, was followed by 'Abide with Me', a hymn that George always found moving. To his shame, he felt his eyes watering once more as he mouthed the words, rather than singing. For some reason it made him think of his mother, of whose memory he knew only as a breathing of scented air.

Then the Reverend gave his sermon, which was on the theme of discovering God and seeing Him all about us in His magnificent works of nature – in a baby's smile, in the blessing of a warm, spring breeze, and in the gentle rains that would bring forth the fruits of the earth; all such things being the glorious works of God.

Excellent, thought George, particularly the bit about the fruits of the earth, for which they would soon be digging. He did not know for sure, but he suspected that interpretation might border on the blasphemous.

When the majority of the congregation rose, including the maids and other servants about him, to go forward to the altar to receive Holy Communion, George remained seated. This was something new to him which he had never partaken in before. He felt he was not entitled. Afterwards when he was leaving the church, the Reverend pressed his hand and said, 'Are you looking forward to tomorrow, George?'

'Yes, sir. Very much so.'

'May God bless you then, and all of us in our endeavours.' The Reverend did not ask him why he had not taken Communion. George was grateful for that. He wondered if he were even baptised.

With others of the staff, he walked back to the rectory. As there were no chores set for him that day, he occupied his time in reading a history of the early inhabitants of Britain, brought for him by Mrs. Joyce from her husband's shelves, as the Reverend was locked up now for the rest of the day in his study and 'not to be disturbed.'

The book was titled, 'The Celt, The Roman, and the Saxon', and had been published some twelve years earlier. He took it into the kitchen and pored over it, propped up against a sugar bowl on the scrubbed table top. Lizzie and Ivy came and went occasionally, but he was too engrossed in the book to do more than acknowledge their passing presence. Lizzie was dressed for walking out. It was her afternoon off, to do as she wished. Ivy, finding him engrossed in the book, soon left to sit outside in the late spring sunlight – a warm day giving prospect of the summer to come.

There was a map in the book headed 'Britain under the Romans', and George pored over it, seeing the many place names across the map, given in Latin, and he wondered what towns of today they corresponded with. He could see Londinium (of course, that was London) but to the left (or west) of that, joined by a thin line that must represent a Roman road, was Bibracte (he had no idea where that was) and then Calleva (which he knew now was Silchester). Coming south from Calleva, a line ran to Venta Belgarum (was that Winchester, he wondered? – the museum display in Alton told of Roman remains there). Beyond Venta Belgarum, the road ended on the coast at Clausentum, which he thought must be Southampton, or a place very close to it. From there, a road ran parallel with the coast past Regnum (he had no idea where that was) to Anderida (a mystery to him as well). How he would like to go to those places and find out what remained there of the Romans, walking their roads, following in their footsteps. Had anyone ever done that and written about it? He must ask the Reverend when he could get his attention.

Looking further at the map, he could see from the Latin names that the Romans conquered as far as the south of Scotland, as well as west into Wales, and even deep into Cornwall, all parts of Britain he had never visited and had very little idea about. Yet, less than two thousand years ago, the Romans had roads that could easily carry you west and south, east and north.

He turned to the index to the book and looked for 'Allectus', the usurping Emperor whose coin he still had in his pocket. Lord Selborne had said in the conversation he had overheard with the Reverend and Dr. Curtis that he thought that the battle which had been fought to overthrow and kill Allectus had been fought near Blackmoor. But the author of this book merely gave the battle's location as 'possibly in the area of London'.

There was so much more to read in the book: the chapter on the British warrior queen, Boadicea, for instance, enthralled him. He was still deeply buried in it when it began to grow dark, and Ivy returned to cough diffidently into his silence.

'Sir,' she said. 'Mr. Maple. I am to prepare you some food, the mistress says. For Lizzie is out this evening. Shall I light the lantern, sir, for the light is going and it must be hard to make out the words you read?'

George looked up abruptly as if stung. Seeing Ivy in front of him, small and shy, wearing a full length white apron that looked too big for her, with hands clasped before her and concern clear on her face beneath her frilled white cap, he smiled. 'How old are you, Ivy?'

'Sixteen, sir.'

'You don't need to call me sir, Ivy. Please know me as George. I am a servant here too, much mindful of my debt to the Reverend Mr. Joyce and his wife, who have allowed me to stay at their house. I go away with the Reverend tomorrow to dig for him at Silchester.'

'I had heard, sir. And will you return?'

'Why, would that concern you?'

She blushed. 'I but asked, sir.'

'Of course. The answer is I am not certain myself. In the winter, when the work with the Reverend is done for the year, I am told I will be given work at the big house. I shall presumably stay there at that time.'

She had turned away now and had taken the globe from the lamp to light it with a tool that struck a spark. The flame flared upward suddenly. She trimmed it down, and replaced the globe.

'Well done, Ivy. You are very skilled at doing that. What is the food you have?'

'Just some cold meat. Cold lamb, it is. But I can boil some potatoes, and there are some early lettuces from the garden. And bread and jam too.'

'That sounds wonderful. Have you eaten today, Ivy?'

'Yes, sir.'

'When then? I know your master and mistress are invited out to a neighbour's house this evening, and so there was only cheese and biscuits at midday. I have not felt hungry until now, but you must be.'

'I will have something after you.'

'Oh, no, you won't. You will prepare for both of us and sit here with me to eat, and we shall talk. You will tell me all about yourself and how you came to work here, and I shall tell you about myself.'

'There is little enough to tell, sir. Sorry, I mean George.'

He laughed. George makes a heavy sound, does it not? Rather pompous perhaps. I would prefer something short and sharp, let's see – Will or Dick or Matt. I do quite like Matt.'

'Oh no, George suits you.' She laughed. How her face lights up when she smiles, he thought. She will become a real beauty when she grows older and fills out. And likely she will make someone a very good wife.

When he went up to his room later that evening, he took the borrowed book with him, and sat reading by candlelight for a while. Then he got into bed under the covers, for he wished to sleep well, and he suspected tomorrow would be a memorable day with much he must learn and remember.

He heard the Reverend's pony and trap outside, and the sound of voices, and the pony, unharnessed, being led to the stables. Lizzie must have returned as well, for he heard her voice too, a door closing with a thump, and feet on the stairs, somewhere in the house, but not close to him at all. And then there was silence, long and deep, and he closed his eyes to sleep. A full moon had risen and its light was penetrating the thin curtains of his attic window.

George fetched his new coat with the red lining from where he had rolled it up in the basket and managed to fix it over the window. Then he slept long and deeply, with dreams of Romans colouring his inner consciousness – soldiers in golden helmets, sailors on oared galleys, seagulls crying, traders with weighing scales, the hubbub of a market, men and ladies in long robes, and slaves with fair hair, tied together by their feet. There he was too, standing with Ivy watching these scenes, and he knew he wanted to be with her, but she was falling away from him, and he thought he had lost her – somewhere, somehow, he didn't know why. Then he awoke with a start. Sunlight was bathing the room through the thin curtains. His coat had fallen to the floor.

14

It was before nine that Monday morning when the house had breakfasted and the stableman had brought the Reverend Mr. Joyce's pony and trap from the stables to the front door of the rectory. The dark-brown pony was small but sturdy, and the cart it pulled painted a bright yellow, its shafts and the spokes of its two wheels picked out in red, so the result was perhaps gayer than might have been expected for a reverend gentleman to make use of.

George climbed aboard with his two bags, and the stableman handed up further bags and a large, stiff-leather case with metal catches that belonged to the Reverend. George seated himself on the driving bench where the Reverend, in an attire of fustian and corduroy, with a round priest's hat jammed on his head, joined him and took up the reins.

Mrs. Joyce had come out onto the gravelled drive to wave goodbye, with Lizzie and Ivy beside her, and the stableman and one of the gardeners looking on too.

Mrs. Joyce stood by the trap, and her husband, bending low, kissed her upturned lips. 'Look after yourself, James. Don't catch cold. Remember your chest. Wear that flannel I gave you, however warm the weather may seem.'

'Of course, my dear. Do not worry about me. I'll see you on Saturday, if not before.'

'Enjoy yourself, young George,' Mrs. Joyce called out, waving her arm, as her husband, making a clicking sound with his mouth, urged the pony into motion. Turning his head, he saw many hands waving at him, Ivy's and Lizzie's too, and he felt a sob of happiness that he had been so suddenly welcomed here, almost as one of the family. How he would strive in every way to maintain such good opinion of him, and to grow better and better in everything he would do. After a long black nightmare, the colours had surely returned to brighten his world again – this exciting new world of meaning and moment he was now part of.

By high, hedged banks they went, the pony's hooves rattling on the stony surface of the lanes, the freshness of spring leaf all about them, ploughed fields seen in sudden glimpses through the hedgerows already showing a brush of green, as if smeared by some master painter. The sunlight struck in dappled pools of yellow through the early leaf above them. Horses grazing in cottage paddocks raised their heads to watch as the trap passed by, the willing Molly pulling at a steady trot.

They passed between the cottages of Stratfield Saye village itself. Some labourers, on their way to work in the fields, touched their hats to them as they rattled past, with the Reverend raising his own hat in acknowledgement.

They swung to the right at a junction by a farm, the lane partly blocked here by cows being led into an adjacent pasture – much calling out and dogs yapping, dirty-faced children out in the lane too, a girl trying to bowl a hoop – then moving on with the Reverend raising his hat again to the confusion they were leaving.

They passed onto a broad, well-metalled track running straight as an arrow's flight, and George recognised the Roman road out of *Calleva* he had followed those few days back, when he had first found the Roman town. Thick woodland now lay to the left, with clumps of dark firs standing amongst tall beeches, their bare branches rising like great skeletal fans, starkly outlined against the pale blue sky. A cloud of black rooks circled about them, with raucous cries that could be heard clearly above the clatter and rattle of the trap's motion. An inn passed next on the left: George did not recall having seen it when he had walked here; perhaps he had not spotted it over the high, thick hedges, or noted its sign at the mouth of the drive leading to it from the Roman road.

'That's 'The Silchester Arms',' said the Reverend, speaking in his ear. He had given the pony its head now and it was trotting fast, the rushing of the breeze and the jangling of the harness making conversation difficult. 'It's very popular with visitors who pass by from Mortimer station to see the *Calleva* excavations. Or return afterwards, for that matter The inn's better known as 'The Jackdaw,' although I know not why.'

'Do you get many visitors?' George asked, raising his voice, then finding he was shouting as the Reverend reined back the pony.

'That's enough, Molly. You've had your run, now let us return to the dignity of our passage as befits one of the cloth with his acolyte.' He chuckled. 'This stretch of the old road is known as the Devil's Highway. Molly always wants to gallop here as if she knows the devil comes this way.'

So he thinks of me as an acolyte, George thought. What is an acolyte? It is something good, I think. Yet, he scarcely knows me. I still have to prove myself. He is a true Christian, though. He has given me this chance, whereas most, hearing my story, would have told me to be on my way.

'Oh, visitors,' the Reverend said, as they slowed to a steadier rate. 'Yes, we have many during a season. Various individuals and societies pay us visits. I generally give them a guided tour, show them what we have revealed, and give them a talk about it, depending on what I judge to be their level of interest. Some learned – very learned – societies want to see everything and hear everything in the greatest detail, which I endeavour to fulfil. We even give them refreshments at times. Later in the summer, there is a tent we put up, so the ladies may rest out of the sun. And we have our 'red hut', of course, where some of the best finds are on display, and many others kept in boxes. The most important items, however, such as the horse and the eagle that I have shown you, I take away in case some thief should break in. There is money to be made, you see, from the plunder of coins and other objects. It is wise not to trust anyone, even the local village people, who are otherwise most supportive to us. It only takes one bad apple, you see, and irreparable harm might be done.'

'I understand,' said George. 'It all sounds most interesting – most exciting.'

He found that everything the Reverend told him – the bad, as well as the good – only added to his fascination with the whole subject. And yet he knew nothing yet of the reality of taking part in an excavation, in particular an important excavation like this one. Listening was one thing, doing quite another. Reality was fast approaching, though. It was very close now!

They came by an ever-narrowing lane to a steep-sided mound on the right, covered by dense evergreen bushes that included great banks of prickly holly, impenetrable to all but the most undaunted. The Reverend halted the trap here at the opening to a side-track, the pony's head going immediately to a clump of rich grass at the margins of the lane, which it began chomping at with relish.

'This is the place of *Calleva's* amphitheatre,' he said. The mound you see is where the seating rose. On its far side is the arena floor where the gladiators once fought. You've read about gladiators, have you, George?'

'A little bit, sir. Indeed, I was reading of them yesterday in one of your books that Mrs. Joyce fetched for me. They were a Roman sport, it seems.'

'Yes, I suppose that is one way of putting it. A very brutal sport, to be sure. The Romans may have used an arena to train their soldiers too. And they held fights with wild beasts – men and dogs fighting wild bears, or boars, perhaps. Sometimes too exotic animals were brought from overseas, but that would have been very expensive. The subject is not the highest point of Roman culture, I must admit – but the people liked it. I would very much wish one day to make some diggings here too, to see what walls and rooms survive, and to lay clear the entrances.'

'Were there many amphitheatres in Britain?' George asked.

'Oh, yes. We know the sites of several, but little excavation work on them has been done as yet. I believe, though, some digging on one at Richborough – that's the great Roman fort on the eastern shore of Kent – was undertaken some years ago, although I have yet to see the report.'

The Reverend was struggling to get the pony to move again. She still had her head deep in the lush green grass. He pulled hard at the reins. 'Hey up, Molly. Hey up. Off you go, girl.'

Reluctantly the pony moved back onto the lane. The progress was slow now, passing some children, the girls in white pinafores, the boys in short trousers and long socks, who waved at them, and the Reverend called out, 'Get to your lessons, children. God be with you.'

'They have a way to reach the school,' he told George. 'It lies on the far side of *Calleva*, north of Silchester village at the edge of the Common. There are many temptations to delay a child reaching there by the time the bell is rung.'

Yes, George thought wryly. He know well of temptation. He had gone out into the hop fields at Alton rather than sit in class to be hit over the fingers by Miss Turner's boxwood ruler. He understood now the value of all lessons, however unappealing they might seem. At least, he did learn his letters and numbers, however ill his attendance had been at times.

'We go to Mr. Fiennes' rectory first,' the Reverend said, 'to drop off our bags there and make our greetings, then to the site to make a start.' He took a watch from out his waistcoat pocket. 'It is a quarter to ten. I said I would be on site at the hour. I know my men will be there already, and all will be prepared. Will Hankley is a most reliable man. I feel sure you will like him, George.'

'Oh yes, sir, I hope so.'

George knew that at all costs he must get on with everyone, and, as he would be very new, and they all, he assumed, experienced, he must learn the correct procedures quickly or he would be an encumbrance, rather than a help. Whatever came, he must not complain.

'George, I will have you digging first with the rest,' the Reverend said, 'before I move on to teaching you other matters, like the correct way to record and measure and write up what we have done. You see, what we dig away, we dig away forever: there is no putting it back. So we must keep as good a record as we can – of how the ground was when we came to it; what exactly we have done, and what we have found, with all the appropriate measurements of heights and lengths and depths taken.'

Ahead, George saw a jumble of red roofs surrounded by the stark branches of tall trees, spread against the sky like skeletal hands.

'That's Manor Farm,' the Reverend said, 'where're we'll be going after we've called on Mr. Fiennes. But here is the rectory now. It's a tall, brick house, fairly recently built.' He chuckled. 'My colleague says he likes the old to look at, but the new to live in.'

Turning into a driveway, they came in sight of a large house, its lower walls covered with roses, already in early bloom. As they scrunched over the gravel at its front, a lady appeared from the front door, accompanied by a male servant.

The Reverend took off his hat in greeting. 'Alice, how lovely to see you again.'

'And you too, James. I fear Wingfield has had to leave early to attend the needs of a parishioner. I expect him back by lunch time. But I imagine you just wish to leave your bags for present. And this is your protégé?'

George was introduced, stepping down from the trap to take the lady's hand. So I am a protégé now, he thought. Just now I was an acolyte. I wonder if they are the same thing. I shall have to look up the words in a dictionary.

After some further pleasantries, the bags being handed to the attendant servant to take indoors, George resumed his seat in the trap, and with a flourish of his hat, the Reverend urged Molly away for the final few yards of the journey.

'We go now to the farm where the men will be waiting,' the Reverend said. 'We would normally walk it, but I have a case with me I will need at the 'red hut'.'

It was indeed the shortest of journeys. They entered the farmyard, which George realised now was the one he had viewed from the church when he had come here those days back. Five men, leaning back against the wall of a barn, each with a spade and pick beside him, pulled themselves upright as they rattled into view. One of them, an older man, tall with a moustache, seized hold of the pony's bridle, as the trap came to a halt. George and the Reverend stepped down.

'I'll take her to the stable, sir. Give her some water.'

'Thank you, Will. Take my case out first, there's a good fellow. Molly can be put to the paddock later where the grass is freshest. George, this is my foreman, Will Hankley.'

'Pleased to meet you, lad.' Will was tall and broad-chested, with the look of a man proud of his own strength, who would dig, if necessary all day, and expect no rest. His hand in George's was like hardened leather.

'Tom, Bart, Abe, and Will the Second,' the foreman said, going along the line. 'The last is my own, coming up to sixteen now, aren't you, lad?'

The young man spoken to shuffled his feet and looked down shyly. He was dressed like the others in moleskin, belted trousers, white shirt, and black waistcoat. They all wore hats – one a black bowler, but otherwise flat caps. Their boots were stout and studded, made clearly for heavy manual work amongst earth, stones and gravels. As each man moved, his studs clashed on the cobbles of the yard.

'Abe here has dug with me from the beginning – 1864, it were, ain't that true, Reverend?' said Will.

The Reverend nodded. He was supervising the removal of his case from the trap. Abe was perhaps the oldest of them all, with a full beard, turning white, from ear to ear about his jaw.

Molly was unhitched from the trap and led away by the younger Will. The trap itself was then pulled against the barn wall.

'Is Farmer Barton here?' the Reverend asked.

'He's away at market,' Will replied. 'His missus is indoors, though.'

'I'll see her later to give her my compliments. We must make a start: first, to the 'red hut'.'

They were all gathered together now, tools over their shoulders or placed in the two timber-sided, iron-wheeled barrows that were to be pushed by Abe and the younger Will.

George was given the Reverend's large, flat case to carry, an awkward burden that he had to hold out before him. He was trying to remember all the names, wanting to appear ready and willing, to become one with this gang and not a problem to those he would be working beside.

And so they walked out into the green fields beyond, once the home of the many citizens of *Calleva* with their houses, their temples, their shops, their bath houses. and their grand halls, George felt again that sense of revelation, as if this was a place he had long known and where it had been foreordained he would one day come. He trod the soft earth with care, as if his step represented an intrusion into the lives of those who had once lived here and might resent his coming. The others, though, clearly had no such ponderous thought, but were much more carefree, their work tools raised upon their shoulders, blades honed and shining, much chatter and banter, the barrow wheels squealing as they bounced over the hummocks of turf.

The Reverend led the way, down the slope from the farm and past a row of elm trees, his short, broad figure in its rude clothes of greens and browns merging into the landscape, only his black hat with its rounded dome striking an incongruous note.

He turned. 'I see you've removed all the boards and covers,' he said to Will. 'That's well done. And at the basilica too?'

'Aye, sir. For I know you wish all to be clear to show visitors. I've shovelled away any rubble that's fallen in over the winter. And at the round temple too.'

'Good. Good.'

They were heading for the 'red hut', close to the south gateway, which could be made out as a gap in the thickly overgrown stone wall before them. Coming nearer to the wall, George could appreciate how high it was – some fifteen feet, he would guess, trying to measure his own height against it. It was hard to determine the top because of the tangle of roots and branches growing from it. Should not all that growth be cleared away? he wondered, then realised what a task that would be, just in this one section, let alone around the whole perimeter of the town. Perhaps the growth protected the stone, anyhow, preventing it being robbed any further. To steal stone however, would be to steal from the Duke of Wellington who presumably owned all that stood here.

They came up to the hut. It proved larger than it had looked to George at a distance, perhaps some thirty-two feet long by fifteen feet wide. The Reverend opened the door with a large black key taken from his pocket. The inside, George saw, held work benches and wooden shelving. Some folding chairs, were stacked at the far end The full length of one side was covered by the shelving, on which items discovered in the diggings were set out, some within small, glass-topped cases. These had cloth coverings placed over them.

George could see an amazing assembly of urns and jars, some whole, others in broken pieces, most of a grey or blackish colour, but some too highly decorated and a glossy red, a few glass vessels too, together with chunks of tile, flat and curved, some scored or otherwise decorated. One flat triangular-shaped piece had a face moulded on it, and other pieces were impressed with animal footprints. Another small fragment had some letters stamped into it.

There were metal objects too – many nails, some enormously long and thick, what seemed to be large iron keys with their flanges set at right-angles to their shafts, a curved blade, two great bolts as if taken from a door, a bronze handle showing a spiral pattern, broken from whatever utensil it had once been attached to, a pan pierced with tiny holes, what was perhaps a horseshoe – although a peculiar shape if for that purpose – some thin brass rods with hooks on them, a dozen bronze brooches in a case (he slid back the covering of this to view its contents).....

The quantity of objects passed in a blur before George's eyes. Many of the objects had cardboard cards attached that were lettered and numbered in black ink. The tile and stone, George noted, was also sometimes marked with designations that had been inked upon them, as were many pieces of broken pottery – the rims of basins, the heads of vases, and the bases of what had clearly been huge vessels. On the lower shelves, or placed on the floor beneath, were blocks of shaped stone, some square, some circular, the latter perhaps pieces of columns.

The other side of the hut contained the work benches with the one window above, from which Tom was even now pulling out the wooden shutters that had been slotted in place against the glass, a protection against anyone with ill intent trying to break in: such things were possible, even on the Duke of Wellington's land.

'All's well, I think,' said the Reverend, looking around as more light flooded the hut.

'I keeps an eye on it, sir,' said Will, sounding almost huffy.

The Reverend made no comment. He had gone outside to help the others bring in the items that had been carried to the hut. The tools were lined up neatly by the door. There were already some other tools present, George noted – long and short-handled brushes, buckets, and several wooden and iron trays of differing sizes.

The Reverend's large leather case was now carried in and laid flat on a work bench. He flicked up its catches and opened it. He took out several flat sheets of card, upon which George could see some drawings of pots and other objects, as well as what looked like the plans of buildings. One plan appeared to show the entire area of the town, its angled walls and gateways delineated in black ink, as were various buildings marked by red letters in their interiors. The drawings and plans were laid flat on the table top, and beside them the Reverend placed pots of inks and several pens.

The last item to appear from the case was a cardboard box-folder containing what seemed to be blank sheets of a fine paper. George thought that this was likely to be the Reverend's current journal, of which he had shown him one bound volume from a previous year. On these sheets he would record each day's activity, and describe and draw the finds.

Fresh digging was about to start! George felt a thrill of excitement, tempered only by his knowledge that he was a complete novice. He had little idea of how the digging was to be carried out. It must be a precise art, he reasoned – not just a crude digging away like navvies carving out a canal – or else much would be missed and lost, probably forever. Since the Roman relics here had survived for so long undisturbed, it would surely be a tragedy if they were now just hacked away with much being lost. He knew enough already to realise that this was not a treasure hunt – although finding treasure might well come into it!

But now came the Reverend's voice calling for all their attentions. Some of the folding chairs had been brought outside and opened up, positioned in a semi-circle about the hut door. The six members of the digging gang perched themselves on these, each, other than for George, already with a spade or shovel in his hand. The Reverend stood before them.

'You've all met our new colleague, George Maple,' he begun. 'I now want to introduce him more formally. He came to me only very recently wishing to help with our excavations here at Roman *Calleva*, and I have decided to take him on.

He has recently helped out with a discovery made elsewhere in the county when a large quantity of Roman coins was found, and he proved very apt at that, as the landowner in question has stated. I'll leave him to give you more details of that find, should he choose to do so. It has been published in the newspapers.'

The Reverend coughed and pulled at his collar, for once bereft of the clerical ring that was usually in place. 'George also has skills in writing and drawing, so I wish particularly to train him in how to use these in recording our discoveries. He should be able to help me considerably, as the necessary paper work is often more time-consuming than the digging!' (some chuckles at that from amongst the chairs) 'However, he must learn to dig first, so that is why I hand him over to you – particularly you, Will – to show him the correct methods of doing so. As indeed, Will, you have been teaching your own boy, young Will here.'

This last brought a few more chuckles and a call from Will of 'Aye, Sir'.

'Right, down to business. This year of 1874, we will concentrate on finishing off our clearing of the south gateway, and we'll have a further look at the round temple. Also, I would like to do more work in Block II, where, as most of you will know, some years back we found a very fine house with mosaics. We have yet to achieve the full extent of that building, and it seems there is a well in what seems to be the courtyard, which we might seek to empty. Its finds may prove invaluable for dating evidence.'

'Now, regarding visitors, we can daily expect the appearance of the curious, so we must find time – obviously, that will be myself when I can, but you, Will, might help out as well, as you have done in the past, when I am off site or too busy measuring, and the like – to answer questions and escort around. The Newbury Field Club is already booked to come to us at a date in July: there will be twenty or so of them. And of course, we can always anticipate some distinguished visitors, as our work becomes increasingly known. The Duke, himself, has intimated to me he would like to visit again this year. Our 'red hut' here will be open, of course, with its museum displays. And later in the year, the ladies – including my good wife very likely – can open their refreshments in the tent. We have the tent stored away, Will?'

'Aye, sir. It is in the barn at the farm. I can carry it over with the pony when I bring the water butts. Today, if you wish.'

'No, I think first thing tomorrow, so that we can make a start now. There should not be much material to wash until then.' The Reverend turned to George. 'We need water, you see, to wash over some of what we find – the pottery fragments, the pieces of tile, and so on, to make clear their fabric or to find any particular marks. There's a spring that bubbles up yonder in wet weather....' – he flung out an arm towards a distant point – ... 'but it's only suitable for making tea, not filling a bucket.'

George nodded to show he was paying attention, although really his head was in a whirl and he was thinking, all this sounds more complicated than I had imagined – and I had thought I would just be digging holes and pulling Roman objects out of the ground.

'So, let's see.' The Reverend swung around to look at the south gate, a short distance from the 'red hut'. 'Let's all go over to the gate and remind ourselves of last year's work. Some trenches we backfilled, I recall – or at least I gave instructions for that to be done after I had recorded and drawn the trenches – as the gate is still used to drive in sheep.'

'We did, sir,' a couple of the men assured him, as they all got to their feet.

'Indeed, I can see that now.' The Reverend paused beside a straight line of stone walling on his left, above which the main curtain wall rose, entangled at this point by a veritable jungle of roots and trailing bushes.

He beckoned George over to him. 'Last year we revealed this walling. It was totally overgrown and buried under soil from the bank. It forms one of the side-portals of the gateway. We found that the gate itself is set back from the main wall, which, most unusually, curves in on either side to meet it. Roman soldiers on the walls would thus have been able to rain missiles down on any enemy trying to break through the gate. The trenches we dug to show this are where we are standing; you see how quickly the grass grows back!'

'We also dug a trench to find the paving stones of the carriageway as it passed through the gate, where it then becomes a central street of the town, leading directly to the basilica. There were no ruts in the paving, though, which may indicate that the gate was rebuilt later in the history of the town. We also found the inner pier of the gate. It had no guard chamber: it's possible, though, there is one in the pier opposite.'

He crossed to the other side of the wall opening and kicked at a high tangle of weeds. 'That pier must have stood about here. The great wooden, iron-studded gate – it was a single portal – would have closed just where we stand. It makes you think, doesn't it? A great road entered here – the one that comes from *Venta Belgarum*, no less: that's Winchester, of course, as we know the town today. The other Roman road – the one that passes close to ....' – he realised that, with others listening, he was about to break his own secrecy about George's previous employer – '....your previous house, well that would have joined with the Winchester road to enter *Calleva* by this same gate.'

The Reverend snapped abruptly from this reverie. He became much crisper in his speech. 'Right, I want all of you to work here for the present. The ambition is to reveal a matching set of walls to those we exposed last year. At least, I imagine the layout will be much the same, unless we find a guard room too. You never know what the spade will turn up. The area is even worse overgrown than it was last year, so you will need saws and axes at first. I'll leave everything to you, Will, to get the men organised. Don't do any digging, though, until I've first seen what you've cleared.'

'No, sir. Of course not.'

'Come with me, George,' the Reverend said. 'I want to inspect the areas that we have dug and left open for visitors to see, so as to check on their condition. It will be a good time to tell you more about what we have found in previous years.'

'Yes, sir', said George tamely, although really he would have liked to make a start with the others. 'That will be most interesting.'

Walking into the buried town from the south gate, they came first to an area where the ground had been dug away in a large square, at the centre of which George could see the low stubs of stone walls, some of which curved.

'Here is the circular temple we discovered.' The Reverend stepped down into the excavated area, George following him. The surface was covered in clumps of weeds, which grew also against the walls, most of which were no more than two stones high. In places, the yellow crowns of dandelions shone out brightly amongst the greens and browns of the earth. The Reverend stood astride the outer stone wall, which George thought at first formed a circle, but then realised, in fact, it was made up of straight lengths of wall set at slight angles to each other.

'Yes, the outer wall is polygonal,' the Reverend confirmed, seeing George staring down at it. 'Sixteen sides, there are. It must have formed an ambulatory, or walkway, around the circular temple itself. The diameter is 66 feet, as we measured it.'

He stepped over the next line of stone, with George following him.

'Now we're at the most sacred part of the temple, the inner sanctum where the priests would have carried out their rituals. Unfortunately, we didn't find anything that might indicate which god they worshipped here. There are several likely candidates – Serapis is one. He has an Egyptian origin. But it could equally have been a British god incorporated into the Roman pantheon, whose name we have no idea of. We found no inscriptions, I fear.'

George stood at the centre of the shrine, looking upwards. A pale blue sky, fleeced with puffs of white sky, spiralled above him. He seemed to feel the world turning on this fulcrum, and for a moment felt unsteady on his feet.

Sensing his unease, the Reverend said, 'Yes, I often feel dizzy looking upwards here. Perhaps there is a void created that we are being sucked into – back into time.' He chuckled. 'Or more likely, leaning back, the blood rushes into our heads. Come, George. I will show you the forum next.'

Some further yards over the green turf rose the long, broad mound that George had noted earlier, a distinctive feature at what seemed the very centre of *Calleva*. As they approached it, George could make out an increasing amount of debris amongst the grass – pieces of broken pot, many oyster shells, and scattered fragments of Roman brick, some with flanges, others scored with wavy lines, even one he saw with a long, rusted nail protruding from it. He stooped and picked up a thick, red chunk of brick. At its centre was the print of an animal's paw – a dog, he thought: he could make out the shape of the pads and even the sharp points of the nails.

'Can I keep this?' he asked, as the Reverend came up beside him.

'Yes, of course, my boy. We have found scores like it – imprints of dogs and cats in the main, pigs also, but occasionally a human foot too. The last we keep. You'll see some examples in the museum. They are usually pieces from tiles. The Romans clearly laid them out to harden before firing, and, it seems, their animals had a habit of walking over them. Many places – from military sites at the great northern wall to the villas in the south – show the same thing. If you are very fortunate, you might also find writing inscribed on a tile, which, of course, is important. I tell the workers to look at every piece they dig up before it is discarded.'

They now stood beside the mound, which George could see was formed largely of earth and clay, with many stones and gravels amongst it, and very many more chunks of red tile, some of which had been stacked up like small chimneys.

'You get the best view from the top,' the Reverend said, scrambling for a foothold amongst the scree of loose stones and earth, and eventually mounting the steep slope to the mound's flattened top. George followed him. Before him, he could see a large square area of reddish-brown earth that had been cut out from the surrounding grass. As with the temple site, the earth was thick with weeds, which grew thickly as well against the grey, stone walls that he could now see. These walls ran in straight lines across the cleared area, ending at right-angled corners to make a series of what – even to George's untutored eyes – were clearly rooms. In some places, he could discern a few curving lengths of wall as well. It was a most confusing sight, which he could not even begin to understand.

The Reverend was beside him, however, to explain, with his right arm thrust out, finger pointing, as he indicated the various features and gave them names; just like a rather portly

Caesar was George's fleeting thought, based on another of those pictures he had seen at the Alton Institute .

'To the right, George, you see the gap in that long straight wall? It is the entrance way into the forum – the market place, where the citizens of the town came together. The forum itself is the open, rectangular area beyond.'

His finger waved up and down, as if to score out in the air what George should be looking at. 'The rooms either side of the entrance were shops. You should understand that wherever people gathered together like this, there were others selling goods to them. So there would have been many traders here, some in the shops, others perhaps at stalls set up in the actual forum – just like a market place in an English town today. You likely paid a lot of money to have a shop here, or perhaps knew someone on the *curia*. The *curia* was the town council, which was responsible for regulating everything that went on in *Calleva*. Its members had to be elected, but, if you had wealth and position, you stood a much better chance of getting in than the ordinary citizen – it ever was, and ever will be, I suppose.'

'What did the shopkeepers sell?' George asked.

'A good question. Let's walk down there now and I'll tell you, for I was able to gather some evidence.' They slithered down the mound, George's boots uncovering the pinkish-coloured earthenware head of what might have been a flagon, still with a piece of its handle attached.

The Reverend bent to pick it up. 'Perhaps we should have kept that piece. Sometimes the handles are stamped with the maker's name. Ideally, all such items should be recorded, as should the details of the place where they were found, and a catalogue kept: that is the sort of work I will want you to do, George. If the workmen throw pieces like this away and don't put them in the trays, then much is lost. Most of my gang are skilled by now, but one or two are impatient. Pieces of old pottery seem of little value to them. They want to find coins and other items made of metal. My foreman knows the score, but he can't be everywhere.'

They walked over to the small square rooms that the Reverend had said were shops. Standing in one, Joyce said it had likely been a fishmonger's, because large quantities of oyster and other mollusc shells had been found there. And in another shop adjacent, he speculated it had been a butcher's, because much animal bone, as well as pieces of a steel-yard, had been unearthed, this perhaps for weighing the meat. A third shop could have been a jeweller's, for a small bar of solid silver had been found as well as a number of finger rings. *Styli*, for recording sales on wax tablets, as well as door hinges, keys and locks had also been recovered from a pit.

They came out into the open area of the forum. 'George, you have to imagine here a tall building with a red-tiled roof towering over you – that is, the main basilica, what we might term today the town hall. It was some 230 feet long by 40 feet broad. Facing us would have been a great row of Corinthian columns, of which we have found several of the capitals. Inside, the *curia* met. It was where all the sacred symbols of the Roman state were kept – statues of the emperors, busts of local great men, possibly even the standards of legions and other military units, in much the same way as today we lay up the banners of our regiments in our cathedrals.'

The Reverend led him inside the excavated walls outlining the basilica. 'Here, we are in the nave of the basilica, again just like a cathedral. Indeed, the builders of our first great churches copied the basilica form. This curving wall you see is the apsidal northern end.'

Turning to his left, the Reverend stepped over further low walls. 'These are the rooms where the official business in the basilica was conducted. It was here we discovered the eagle that I have shown you, George.' He pointed down. 'It lay at this spot beneath some charred deposits that may have come from the roof when it burnt down and collapsed.'

'Why should it have been in the roof, sir?' George asked, puzzled.

The Reverend rubbed his palms together. 'That is a question which goes to the heart of what archaeology is all about, or at least *should be* about. You see, even if we will never be able to say for absolute certain, we can, nonetheless, *deduce* from the evidence we gain, if we use great care in our excavation and don't just pull out artefacts without considering the deposits they lie within. Only through a careful examination of those deposits can we hope to make a deduction about how and why an object, such as our eagle, came to be placed there. It takes patience, and knowledge, of course, to do this. So many who dig, just hack and hack and look for exciting things, and destroy most of the evidence at the same time. So we have to teach those who take up the archaeological spade that they must employ it carefully and by set methods. And, above all, they must make a detailed record of all they do. Do you understand?' He laughed, surprising George. 'I confess it is a hobby horse of mine.'

'I understand you well,' George said – and it was true, he did.

'Good, good.' The Reverend had removed his hat and was mopping his brow. 'The sun is growing warmer. The first warm day, I believe, we have had this year.' He replaced his hat. 'Now, to answer your particular question: the eagle could have been hidden in the roof timbers, perhaps at a time of unrest, and it was forgotten, only to fall when the basilica was burnt down in a period of great unrest, very likely when the town was the headquarters of the rebel emperor, Allectus.'

George noted that name Allectus, again, whose coins had been in such abundance at Blackmoor House, and about whom he had already heard much speculation. He seemed to be followed by this man, above all the many emperors who had ruled Britain under Rome.

The Reverend continued, 'Or, indeed, the eagle could have been hidden beneath the floor – in some hideaway chamber or other – only to be covered by burning timbers when the basilica was in flames. Whatever the case, we are very fortunate to have found it. It is one of the wonders of our Roman Britain, even if now shorn of the spreading wings that it would once have had. When it was hidden, those may have been dismantled and hidden separately. It would be wonderful to find them yet. I have dug to a certain level, but much more work could be done here.'

The Reverend moved on, stepping over another low wall. 'This room, I believe, was the main debating chamber of the *curia*. You see, there is a raised floor here and we found several fragments of an expensive marble, which surely indicates its status.'

He pulled out a watch from his jacket front. '*Tempus fugit.* Let us press on, and then we shall return to the south gate, and you, George, can then make a start digging with the men. First, though, I would take you to the patrician's house we have opened up and show you his bath house.'

Further north, beyond the outer basilica walls, there was another block of earth opened up, with a second great mound of debris ranged alongside it. More walls, most standing higher than those of the basilica, made a criss-cross of shapes here.

'Someone wealthy must have lived here,' the Reverend said, picking his way between the walls, with George behind him. 'It is right by the place of power at the centre of the town, so perhaps it was the home of one of the *duumviri* – that is, the magistrates of the *curia*. We found two floor mosaics, one of which was patterned: the Duke has had it raised to re-lay in his own hallway. The other floor you see here is plain, being of red *tesserae*, as we know the small squares pieces they used, cut from tiles. You will soon learn these terms, George, and they will become as natural to you as English words, so don't let them worry you for the moment. There were many pieces of painted plaster found as well that would have decorated the walls, and even perhaps the ceilings.'

The Reverend came to a wooden cover, with iron handles set into it. 'The Duke had this installed, and there is another also. We keep them in place and only open them when we have an important group of visitors. I won't lift them now, but you'll certainly see them raised at some time. They cover the heating system – the hypocaust, it is called – that the Romans used to heat their houses, and their bath houses too, for such a building lies beneath the second cover over yonder.'

He extended an arm, and George could just make out a further, even larger cover set in the ground close to the edge of the excavated area. 'That one is over a steam bath, and is clearly but one part of the bath house, which I hope to be able to reveal more of at some future time.'

They walked back to the south gate to find the gang hard at work. They had already cleared away the tangled undergrowth and cut out some roots and earth beneath to reveal the top of stone walling that seemed to match the appearance of the coursed stone on the other side of the entrance way. Will was now directing others to clear an area a few feet into the town's interior from the great outer wall. They began clawing away the tangled mass of bushes and briars here to reveal the ground surface beneath. The cleared wood, leaf and twisted, prickly briars were lifted into a wheelbarrow, which was then trundled back out through the gateway to be dumped at the edge of the field beyond.

'We'll burn that later, sir,' said Will, wiping his brow with the back of his hand. The sun was higher in the sky and the air growing ever warmer. The sky had cleared of earlier haze and shone now a peerless blue.

'I'll set out our trench,' said the Reverend. He had brought some wooden pegs, a mallet, and a card of thick string from the 'red hut', and began to hammer the pegs into the newly-cleared ground and running string from them to delineate a large box-like shape. 'If we find the same arrangement as on the other side, this trench should be large enough for present purposes. If there is a guard chamber, we shall have to extend. The east gate had two: it may have been considered the more dangerous approach to the town – although that doesn't make too much sense, really.'

'Place the spoil close by for now, Will,' the Reverend said. 'We must backfill as soon as we've dug and made a record. We don't want any sheep falling into deep holes. The Duke would not be pleased by that.'

Will chuckled. 'He might pay for a cover then, as he did at the bath.'

'More likely we'll just need some simple fencing. Farmer Barton will probably be able to help. But I feel it may not be needed. We should get this task completed in a couple of days, unless something unexpected turns up.'

'Always a possibility,' he murmured to himself, walking away. 'Always a possibility.' He swung round. 'Of course, whatever we find, it will all have to be measured and drawn.' He looked at George. 'That's something you could help me with, George. It would be a straightforward exercise where you could learn the practice.'

George felt the curious eyes of the others on him. He felt uncomfortable being signalled out like this, even embarrassed.

Would they be sympathetic to his purpose with the Reverend? Or would they be resentful of what they might think his 'special role'? Why should they be? He would show them he could dig as hard and well as they.

And now here was his opportunity, for the trench was to be dug. The stringed off area was large enough for two teams to work – Will, Abe, and George at one end, Tom, Bart and young Will at the other.

Will thrust a spade into George's hands. 'You cut first, George, Abe will shovel for you. He'll pitch up the spoil to where I stand and I will sort it. You see', he said for George's benefit, 'we always look through the dug earth in case there's anything in there that might be missed, which is easily done, I'll tell you. I've found coins, brooches, and even half a horse's skull in one clod before now.'

As George tentatively wielded the spade, pushing it down at the soil with the strength of his arms, Will called out, 'No, spade it. Use your foot on the shoulder. Force the blade in that way.'

Looking across, George saw this method being used by one of the others, and immediately followed the same action. He turned out his first bite of earth to Abe, who, gathering it up, flung it to land at Will's feet.

'And another. Give him much more to shovel. Keep your eyes on the earth. This is where the Romans walked, farted and died. Anything could be there. Think on that.'

Some more guffaws came from both ends of the trench. 'You'll soon get into the hang of it, George.'

It was hard work, he found, using muscles little required before, the soil being stony, so in places he had to shuffle the spade backwards and forwards before he could get a good bite of earth to make a spadeful. He began to go a bit deeper in the area where he had already dug.

'No, not there yet. Go to the same level all over first. We don't dig holes, unless we have to. We're not digging bloody railway cuttings.'

More laughter at that sally. George decided he should join in the laughter. They were not really making fun of him. He was new – very new, an innocent amongst these men who had worked manually all their lives. Yet, he was part of this gang now, sharing a common cause, doing what he most wanted to do. He must keep that at the front of his mind all the time, because he already suspected it might prove not quite as easy, or as exciting, as he had thought.

'You'll soon learn the method, George.'

And he did.

15

Extracts from George Maple's Diary (I)

Monday 11th May 1874

What a thrill! Excavation at Calleva begins (Rev. Joyce uses the Latin name rather than Silchester). Meet the others who dig for him. All nice, polite. They have much experience. I am the new boy. But learn fast – I hope. Make my first finds. Some pottery rims and a handle from a vessel. These are kept. Later Will II (as his father – our foreman – calls him) finds a coin. Small and green. Can't make out the emperor's name. Reverend takes it away, spitting on it and wiping it with his handkerchief. We dig at the South Gate to find the inner tower (other one exposed last year but now covered again). Find walls. Dig trench about them but still going down. Aches and pains in evening and blister on right palm. Much use of spade and shovel. Knees sore too from kneeling on the ground, scraping with spatula tool. Very comfortable at Silchester Rectory. Mrs. Fiennes very kind. I have good room, v. good bed. They treat me like a guest, not servant. Eat dinner in kitchen with servants (all friendly), but given tea in drawing room later when meet the Rev. Fiennes. He seems rather severe and not so friendly. He indicates he is doing our Rev. a great favour, but, as he is being paid for it, why should he complain? I cannot believe how fortunate I am. A week ago I had nothing.

Thursday 14th May 1874

Some light rain. Delays start. Shelter in the Red Hut. The Rev. shows me finds from glass case. Many brooches, one enamelled red and blue. Many coins – sesterces and one large dupondius. Head of Caracalla, Rev. says. Small bronze bell with engraving, beads from necklace, finger rings, and a red intaglio (think I have that right) showing a galley with letters above – hard to see, but Rev. has magnifying glass back at Stratfield and has studied it. The best finds he keeps there, or they go to the Duke. Rev. tells me he brings the Eagle and Horse to the hut, when he knows he has important visitors coming to see Calleva. The farmer – Mr. Barton – came to see how we did. He watches over everything. Will says he has his own collection of finds picked up in the fields: I believe the Rev. must know of this, but they are not for showing, or so Will says. I find that strange. Barton has two fierce dogs he lets loose at night. When rain stops, we dig once more at South Gate. No guard chamber. Rev. disappointed. He measures and draws. I help him. He shows me what he does and explains his methods. I try to follow but it is difficult. I prefer to wield the spade!

Friday 15th May 1874

Measuring and drawing again with the Rev. I made a drawing of wall and gateway, and also of a large carved capital, which Bart had found in a pit he was digging out. It took three of us to get it from the trench. Drawing the capital proved too hard for me. The Rev.'s drawing I thought very good. Will declared it to be the most exciting discovery for a long time, and at the very start of the season too. The Rev. said it had once topped a column. What we have dug – two trenches – will be kept open for the present. A visit by a Society is due in June, the Rev. tells us. As it is, visitors come and go often and ask us what we've found. Our gang has moved on to another area now – Block VI it is called. I went there in the afternoon and, digging with Tom, found a large storage jar which we had trouble cutting out and lifting – unfortunately it broke, but can be stuck back together again, the Rev. says. Blisters bad. Mrs. Fiennes gives me ointment. The very nice maid – Poll – wraps a bandage on my hand. She .... *[scratched out]* .....more than friendly. The Rev. tells me my drawing is 'good' and should get better as I learn, so I am pleased.

Sunday 24th May 1874

The Queen's Birthday. A special prayer offered up for her in morning church. Army on manoeuvres camped in nearby field. Several officers at church. Red tunics and gold braid. Shining buttons and Medals. Walk out in afternoon with Poll and see camp. White tents like little pyramids. Coarse jokes at us over fence. I urge Poll away. Rev. Joyce returns in evening. Poll, very delightful. *[rest of entry, scratched out]*.

Wednesday 10th June 1874

Visit this day of the Newbury Field Society, or a name like that. About 30 gentlemen and several ladies. I learnt they came by train which made a special stop at Silchester Bridge, from which they walked up the lane. Rev. Joyce met them at the church and brought them round the various places to see what found. He gave them a long lecture about Calleva at the basilica, standing on the spoil heap to do so. They then came around our trench in Block VI where the six of us were at work on a Roman house. I was the 'star exhibit', coming from the well we found a few days back with mud on my face and half a glossy red dish in my hand (!), of what Rev. J says is Samian ware – or terra sigillata. Afterwards tea was served them by two ladies from the village in the tent the Rev has had put up next to the Red Hut. Mrs. Barton made the farmhouse available for the ladies' necessities, although I saw three gentlemen pissing on the far side of our South Gate wall. Rev J, who saw it too, was not pleased.

16

From his diary, it is clear that George had settled in well as one of the Reverend Mr. Joyce's digging team. He appears to have learnt quickly and been able to get on with the other diggers, despite the difference in his background. He records in one diary entry that the grizzled, bearded Abe had asked him during a lunchtime break what had been his work before, and he had told them 'a bank cashier', which had made them all scratch their heads. Not even foreman Will, for all his life experience, knew anything about the inside of a bank and what went on there. When asked why he was not doing that work now, he said because they did not need him anymore, which brought a chorus of sympathetic grunts. He told them he was now in service to the Duke of Wellington, but wanted to be an archaeologist like Mr. Joyce

'But you cannot do that forever,' Will said. 'Even the Reverend only does his digging when he's not giving his sermons and blessing the babes and old ladies.'

'Then I'll be a footman all my life,' George answered. 'Or a secretary or a librarian, or whatever else I'm given to do.'

'That ain't much of a life for a man,' young Will said. 'I couldn't be at no man's beck and call all the time.'

'You'd better get used to it, son,' his father commented with a chuckle. 'It's what I've been doing all my life. What about the army, George? Fancy a spell in that? You'll get to see the world, go to other places where them Romans were too. I seen what they's built even in the Crimea...' and he went into a long account of Sebastopol and how the Russian guns had shattered 'some old walls said to be Greek, which was Roman too, weren't it?' while the others scratched and fidgeted. They had heard it all many times before.

It made George think, however. Was his a useless dream? Should he not try something a bit more adventurous? All he knew of the army was what he had seen of soldiers in Alton occasionally (mainly the worst for drink) and at the recent camp outside Silchester, when they had made bawdy comments to Poll over the hedge. He had pulled her away, but she had laughed back at the soldiers. Was he not too serious? Shouldn't he rather seek out life while he was still young?

His evenings he spent watching the Reverend write up his journal, while he read out to him the measurements they had made together, and tried to copy the drawings he made. He had taken his coin of Allectus from his pocket and made a drawing of the emperor's sharp-nosed profile. The Reverend had said the drawing was excellent, but he did not ask where the coin had come from. Perhaps he had guessed.

One evening in late summer that year of 1874 – a very hot day – he accompanied Poll to the Jackdaw Inn, close to the railway on the Devil's Highway. Mrs. Fiennes had already intimated to him, in her loving, caring way – just like Mrs. Joyce as well, the mother he had never known – that she did not think he should be walking out with Poll.

'It is not seemly,' she had said.

He hated to disobey her, but he felt he should be his own master now, certainly in 'affairs of the heart', as he told himself grandly, however kind and thoughtful Mrs Fiennes was to him. He had convinced himself that this was truly the case with Poll, whom he admired greatly. He had even dared to kiss her once, on the cheek, and she had smiled but said nothing.

The inn was busy. Some of the customers, whom George recognised, were from a party that had been at *Calleva* that day. Eyes turned to gaze upon Poll as she entered the tap room by his side. With good cause, for she was looking exceptionally pretty in a tight blue bodice with a white collar and full dark blue skirt with a modest bustle, her dark brown hair parted in the middle and tumbling about her ears. Food was being served, but both Poll and he had already eaten. She accepted a glass of cloudy cider, which he ordered for himself too, a pint of it in a china tankard pulled from a hook above the bar. They carried the drinks outside to sit on a bench in the garden at the front of the inn. Some rustics were there too, who seemed to know Poll, for one spoke to her and looked at George curiously.

They drank and said little. The occasional rider passed by on a plodding horse, and a cart pulled by heavy shires, the driver halting to take a drink handed up to him on the box. Then came suddenly outriders and sleek, black horses, pulling a fine carriage with yellow sides and a coronet on the doors, passing the Jackdaw at a good pace.

'The Duke,' someone muttered, and George was amazed to see men rising and knuckling their fists to their brows, although the carriage had now passed, leaving only a cloud of dust behind.

'He's in a hurry,' said one.

'His wife must be calling him.'

'Nay, they say he would go fast from her opposite way.'

George found this talk outrageous. Didn't the Duke pay his wages and he was a servant to him? Shouldn't he rise to his defence? He made some comment to Poll, but she just smiled and said, 'Don't be silly. They mean no harm. My, this cider is strong.'

And it was too. George felt his own head swimming. He remembered what has happened to him the last time he had drunk cider. After a while, they rose and left, leaving some of the cider behind. Every step they took, Poll's beauty took on a deeper allure for George. He stopped by a gate and tried to kiss her, but she pulled her head away. He felt rebuffed, swaying there a little, hanging on to the gate with one hand. Then suddenly she was upon him, pushing him through the gate, her mouth on his, collapsing on top of him in the warm grass.

He felt a sudden fear. He didn't know what to do. But she showed him. He was always a quick learner.

After that, George's days passed in a somewhat dream-like state. He was not so attentive to his evening work, and the Reverend had to speak quite sharply to him at times, although his digging on the site remained as vigorous and conscientious as ever. When Will was away for a few days with his son, attending to the harvest, the Reverend put him in charge of a new trench across the bath house in Block II, where there was a section of the hypocaust to dig out to its lower floor. Many fine artefacts came from this trench and much burnt material from the stoke hole. There was a pair of fire-irons, hinged at the top and twisted by heat, that might have been used to stir the coals – if indeed the Romans used such a fuel – or at least to turn over burning logs. And an iron shovel as well that looked to have been very worn when discarded, or lost, here. A heap of white, calcinated bone that they came upon, the Reverend said might have come from when the building had fallen out of use, possibly roofless, and the old heating systems was being used to cook food.

When he could get away, and Poll was released from her duties, he saw her in the evenings, and she seemed now more lovely than ever to him. He thought he should ask her to marry him. After all....but his thoughts would go no further than that. She let him make love to her, but she never gave herself to him again.

One afternoon, which the Reverend had allowed him to spend away from *Calleva* for a 'well-earned rest', he came across Poll under a railway bridge when he was out walking alone. She was kissing a soldier and he watched them going off into the woods, and he knew his dream was broken.

He soon recovered, however, knowing he had been a fool. Shortly afterwards Poll gave in her notice and left. George could see the relief on Mrs. Fienne's face, which she must have imparted to Mrs. Joyce, for, when he returned to the Stratfield Saye rectory in early October, at the end of the Reverend's digging season, she said to him. 'I hear you have had an adventure, George, which is now over. You have been a silly young man, but I suppose it is only natural.' She said no more and George blushed scarlet. He did think, however, this is none of these two ladies' businesses.

The Reverend Mr. Joyce, however, did not alter his attitude to him. Perhaps he was not informed of these other matters. He told George how very well he had done, and how pleased he was with him – well, most of the time, barring his occasional evening inattention, which was understandable, for the work day after day was indeed most taxing.

But now he had to earn his keep at Stratfield Saye House – and that George was dreading – the dreariness of it, the servitude, the minding of your Ps and Qs – after a whole, bright, new coloured world had been opened up to him, and he had tasted of its fruits fully. His body had developed, his mind too. He was growing into a man at last, overcoming his timidity with people, determined not to be foolish, but to be successful.

And so we must trace him over the next three years by the Diary he kept, and also through the memories of people who were to come to know him, one of whom even set down a brief account that has survived. Much, though, is speculation out of the few facts that are known for sure.

17

Extracts from George Maple's diary (II)

Wednesday 21st October 1874

The 69th anniversary of the Trafalgar battle, according to the Duke of Wellington's secretary (or rather his junior secretary, I think, although that is my own estimation of her rank, not from her lips) Yes, this 'secretary' is indeed a lady, and one I have already met – Miss Diana Webb. I didn't like her when she was at the Rev. Joyce's house (as his housekeeper, I recall), and now I am to be beholden to her again. The Duke's principal secretary is a far grander person – a Mr. McPherson, who wears formal evening dress all day, perhaps even in bed! He did have a brief word with me. The Rev. Joyce, whom I haven't spoken with for some time, as he has been with his son – for the record, I did not know he had a son, but he is Arthur, aged 16 or so, returned from school (I know not which one: a precocious lad, I fear to say I did not like him) – anyhow, Rev. J must have briefed D of Well or perhaps McPherson about me and what I did for Lord S, for I have been put in the library again, and – very good news! – will help look after the small display the Duke keeps of finds from <u>Calleva</u>, yet I must have a uniform and be a footman too, when the need is there. Also – and this is good too – the Rev. J may take me back to the rectory, should he have a particular task re <u>Calleva</u> he would like me to do.

I have a very small room in the attic of Stratfield S House, but at least to myself. The House is large, but not enormous; yet, it is hard to learn the routes servants must use, or even find the understairs where the kitchens are. The maids are all old and ugly, so no Poll to lead me astray (unfortunate mol). The household seems very quiet and subdued. Some have even worked for the most illustrious 1st Duke, who died not long before I was born. I am to get a few extra shillings as pay, which is good, as otherwise I have very little money in coin at all. At least the uniform will keep me from the need to buy clothes. By the by, looking back to where I referred to Trafalgar, there is apparently a man on the Duke's estate who is said to have fought at that battle. The 1st Duke asked that he be looked after, and so he is still. And he in the navy and the Duke an army man! I would like to meet this old tar – such a link with the past, he makes – but doubt I will ever get the chance. Who next? – a Roman who knew Allectus still living in the woods. Now that would be a real sensation!

Thursday 26th November 1874

Being on footman duty this day, and positioned in the entrance hallway, I had moved from my place to look more closely at the Calleva mosaic that has been re-laid there. Suddenly the Duke arrived, surrounded by an entourage of his fellows, all in country tweeds, and some great dogs, so that I was all but knocked over. 'Get back to your post!' the house steward – a Mr. Blakely, whom I do not like – hissed at me. His face was so red, he nearly spat out his false teeth, which normally wobble, anyhow.

Friday 24th December – Sunday 26th December 1874

Rev. J very busy with his Christian duties. The time of Our Saviour's birth. I attended church with the whole estate – or so it seemed for the numbers were large – on Christmas Day. In fact, I have never seen a church so full, even standing between the pews. The Duke and his wife, and members of family, were present. Afterwards to Christmas lunch by invitation of the Joyces at the rectory, but not, of course, at their table. Lizzie and Ivy there. Happy, merry time. I kissed both under the mistletoe. Ivy held my hand. She is not used to the sherry that was passing round the kitchen, a gift from the Rev. Joyce. Ivy is a lovely girl, but she needs to get more flesh where it matters. That sounds nasty. I should cross it out. I don't mean it, but she is a bit clingy, like her name! She is turned 17 now, but I missed her birthday. The blessed Arthur was given a bicycle as a present, one with the new high front wheel. He fell off as soon as he got on and near-broke his wrists, as well as tearing his velvet pantaloons. I told him 'Hard cheese', but he doesn't acknowledge me, thinking me but a servant.

Wednesday 14th April 1875

Calleva is ready for digging this year. All is much as last year, although young Will is not present. His father says he does not wish to do this work anymore, and, as there is so much to do on Culham's Farm and the farmer pays better than most, he is kept there. The Rev. Joyce brought me from Stratfield, but he has returned to SS. We have opened the new trench in Block IX he showed us, but not much found yet: no walls, only a dump of tiles, one with what looks like writing on (or are they just squiggles?). Will has placed it aside for the Rev. to see when he comes tomorrow. [Interposed later: 'this was writing and has been translated as a quotation from the Roman poet, Virgil']. I have the same room as last year. No Poll now to disturb me! The Rev. Fiennes speaks to me rarely, but he did caution me as to my behaviour this year, when I came face to face with him this morning when about to leave for

Calleva. His wife is much kinder. She plays the harmonium sometimes with Mrs. Joyce at the Stratfield church, and also here at Silchester, I believe. The people love the music to break up the dusty prayers!

Wednesday 26th April 1875
In the Rev. Joyce's absence, and Will's unwillingness – he does not like public speaking and sees it not his duty – I gave a brief talk on what we are currently doing in our Block IX trench to an unannounced party of some five gentleman who suddenly arrived on ordinaries, and even, to my astonishment, two ladies accompanying, riding side-saddle on machines similar. It being very dry weather of late, they brought – some even rode – their machines up to the Red Hut, which they entered unsupervised. I hastened across and told them of the Rev.'s absence, and could I help? The ladies were very pretty, they apologising for their presumption, while the gentlemen looked typical 'hooray henrys', being entirely ignorant of the Romans, thinking they fought at Hastings! I informed them those were Normans! I escorted them up to the trench which we currently dig and they looked on astonished. Abe brought up at that moment a half of mortarium, with its maker's stamp, which one lady asked me if she could have. I could not allow that, of course, but I gave her a piece of tile with a sheep's hoof mark pressed in, which she said she would keep by her always even as she slept, making my head swoon, fool that I am! They then asked the way to Stratfield Saye House, which I told them. They gave the impression they knew the Duke, but I doubt that be true.

Monday 3rd May 1875

High excitement! The Rev., who returned to us this morning, tells us the Prince and Princess of Wales are to visit Stratfield S in June, and he is to preach to them in his church. He thinks they will come out to Calleva too, so we must be ready for the visit, with something 'major' to show them. I said, 'Such as? A golden urn?' and he said I was cheeky: it was not like me at all. I did not speak after that but thought, what is the Prince of Wales to me? The stories at the Jackdaw is that he is a licentious old *[scratched out]*.

Saturday 19th June 1875

I returned to Stratfield Rectory last evening with the Rev. Joyce. He is in a state of some agitation. He is to have Prince/Princess Wales at his church tomorrow. The church has been cleaned and polished every inch, even the altar cloth changed and wall coverings taken down and washed. Mrs. Miller from the village was on her knees scrubbing every inch of the floors, helped by Ivy with her hair piled high under a cloth. I thought Ivy looked quite charming and told her so, but she cast her eyes down and asked me to empty and re-fill her pail. So much for my compliment!

Sunday 20th June 1875

HRH Prince Edward and HRH Princess Alexandra arrived at Mortimer Station yesterday afternoon and were met by the Duke of Wellington, then proceeding in carriages to Stratfield Saye House escorted by horsemen from the Royal household and the Hampshire Yeomanry. Many villagers and gentry lined the route to welcome them. A welcoming arch had been erected near the House and beneath it a chorus of small girls in white dresses lined up to sing as they passed. However, the

Royal carriage did not slow and their voices were quite lost by the sound of the hooves and the wheels. Some of the girls were in tears, their teachers consoling them. I attended the church and stood close to the Prince, who is a fleshy man with a dark beard. The Princess, I thought, very beautiful. She walked with great grace, he beside her trudging up the nave like a fat trooper with his spurs on.

Monday 21st June 1875

I returned with Rev. J to Silchester rectory this morning, and then to Calleva. Rev. has organised a find of coins to be made in Block IX (our trench is almost complete but largely barren) when the Prince and Princess visit tomorrow. I am instructed to make the revelation, the Rev. trusting to my judgement as to when to announce it. We have reburied part of a pot for this purpose, filled with a number of denarii from Rev. J's private collection.

Tuesday 22nd June 1875

On coming into Calleva early this morning, we found a large number of villagers, and many we knew not of at all from elsewhere, some with picnic hampers, seated on the grass, with rugs spread out, all very cosy, children running and playing, the girls with red, white and blue streamers in their hair, the boys in sailor suits. Others as well were trying to enter Manor Farm, and being kept out by Mr. Barton as he was on tenterhooks too – awaiting the carriage of the Royal couple and their escort into his courtyard, from where they would walk to see the excavations. It was only with some difficulty that we were able to make our entry with Molly.

The Reverend, assuming a joviality which I know he did not feel, managed to jostle the visitors back to the South

Gate, allowing a respectful distance around the Red Hut. I set up with the others in the trench, spades newly cleaned and burnished. We waited and waited, leaving the trench only to take tea brought from the farmhouse by Mrs. Barton, who was wearing her best clothes with a full-length white apron. Then we waited some more, seated on the trench edge. Abe lit up his clay pipe and took a puff. The Rev. consulted his pocket watch. I could see many of the families who had waited so patiently, with ever discontented children needing to be fed and using the field behind as a privy, and – as I suspect – the Roman wall too, were beginning to leave.

'Right, they are not coming,' the Rev. declared at last, coming over to us. 'It is now noon. I was given a time of ten. I had been told they might change their minds. I have to say I am bitterly disappointed.' And with that we resumed our proper work. Looking up a little later, I saw most of the visitors had gone, the very last being a courting couple cuddling and kissing, until an angry Joyce chased them away.

Friday 27th August 1875

A very hot day. It has been very dry for weeks now. Across the town where the grass has yellowed you can make out lighter lines, which the Rev. says are those of streets, and even in some places other lines which he says are likely to be the walls of buildings. I tried to map out some of these with him, as he says they will provide an indication of where we might dig at a later date.

Thursday 16th September 1875

Today, looking up from the trench newly opened in Block VII (near the round temple), I was amazed to see Lord Selborne wearing a black frock coat and top hat being escorted around by the Rev. They did not come up to me, so I was spared any embarrassment, nor did his lordship look in my direction at all. I feel sure that the Rev. would have told him long ago of my presence as one of his labourers. Would he recognise me, anyhow, for I have filled out, my chest size is bigger, I have muscles in my arms where there were none at all before! I am also burnt brown by the sun and my hair is long over my shirt collar, as I do not know where to get it cut. Ivy, who cut it for me once, is away at present, as her mother, on the staff of the Duke too, has had a fall and has to be nursed at the big house until recovered: Ivy will also work there for a while. I have no time or money to go into Mortimer for the haircut to be done. One of the Duke's valets cut it one time, but he made it far too short, like an army man.

On another day some two weeks back– I forgot to record this at the time – a large man with a bushy beard visited, wearing a long, grey cloak that fell almost to the ground. I recognised him as Mr. Tennyson, who had come to Blackmoor House to see Lord S at the time of the unfortunate incident in the workshed, which was to cause me such trouble, although no fault of mine. Having been ushered around the trenches by Joyce, and paying no attention to me – and why should he? – the great poet then seemed content to walk round and round the Roman walls, stopping occasionally to write on a pad he carried. I could only assume he was composing a poem, or at least setting down ideas for one. How you write a poem, I have little idea. I thought of a line the other night:

'*What eyes are seeing? What faces faded? Eyes of ashes.*' which I thought quite good. But I don't think I can take it any further.

18

After the 1875 excavation season, George Maple's diary entries become very much briefer and much less frequent, as do the drawings with which he used to fill the margins of the pages. He seems at some time – possibly during the Christmas season of 1875/76 – to have become involved with Diana Webb, to whom he sometimes worked at Stratfield Saye House during the periods when he was not being utilised by the Reverend Mr. Joyce at *Calleva*.

Certainly, for the 27th January 1876 he makes an entry, 'To Lovejoy booksellers in Reading with Miss Webb to select books to be bought for DoW's library.' They went apparently by train from Mortimer station, to which they would have been ferried by a Stratfield Saye coachman, although the diary provides no detail. It does record 'late return', although no further detail is given. One wonders why it took two of them to order books at a bookseller's in a nearby town.

The diary entries following the above, for most of the *Calleva* excavation season of 1876, are very sparse. George seldom writes up now the excavation work he is doing, nor what is being found. The entries he does make begin to use a type of code to indicate people and events, which causes the reader to think that he is being more careful about what he actually does set down, perhaps in case the diary should be picked up and read by others.

Indeed, the diary at this time becomes much more a personal one than earlier, when its prime purpose had been as a record of his excavation work, as the Reverend Mr. Joyce had suggested he make. Whether the Reverend was in the practice of examining the diary we do not know: perhaps in the first year he did so, when George's descriptions of the site were detailed and accompanied by drawings. Yet, from the very beginning of the diary – as we have seen – George had used a narrative style to his entries; that is, he wanted to tell a story, as well as setting down a record, which it is doubtful the Reverend Mr. Joyce would have approved of. He is unlikely to have interfered in the matter, however, his main task, absorbing much of his time in the evenings, being the entering up of his own 'official' journal, a task in which he expected George to help him.

The code – perhaps too strong a word to describe this – used by George from 1876 is very elementary and can be interpreted easily enough. It is usually simply a truncated form of text, e.g 'ct tr to twn.' (i.e. 'caught the train to town') People's names are given by their initials usually in lower case and between inverted commas, e.g. 'dw' for Diana Webb and 'dow' (which he had used already at times, although then in upper case) for the Duke of Wellington. He had already made use of various forms of entry for the Reverend Mr. Joyce's name, but settles now for 'rj'. The rectory maid Ivy, whose clear devotion to him at this time he seems not to have recognised, is given as 'ib', the 'b' being for Bedser, her surname from a local Stratfield Saye family. The maid Lizzie, though, always appears simply as 'L'. One individual's abbreviation that occurs often is 'erp', whom it is impossible now to identify, as no one with those initials is referred to otherwise in the diary. However, something that happened later, as will be related in the year of 1878, creates a suspicion – or even a likelihood – of the identity, but remains unproven. However, it is clear 'erp', was a woman. Some abbreviations of personal names that

George made (for example 'ls' for Lord Selborne) was clearly for his own convenience in the labour of writing, rather than any purpose of secrecy, the names being elsewhere spelt out in full, or given in another contracted form, according to his whim.

Further coded information refers to places and is usually made in upper case, for example, 'JD', almost certainly the Jackdaw Inn, 'RD' Reading; 'CAL' *Calleva*; SS Stratfield Saye; SSH Stratfield Saye House; STR Silchester; and 'MRT' Mortimer. Other abbreviations must be to locations around Silchester and Stratfield Saye, for example 'SC', Silchester Common'; 'GC' perhaps Garden Copse; and 'CG' Chequers Green. Some, however, are impossible to interpret and can only be guessed at. Dates now are also seldom written out in full. For example, the entry for 2nd March 1876, the first sfter that of 27th January 1876, already transcribed above, is written 2-3-76. For some reason, he seems to have wished to compress information, perhaps to lessen the labour of entry, but more likely to give at least a veil of secrecy.

It is probable too at this time that George began to go over what he had written previously, scratching out from the pages, probably with a razor or other sharp blade, any over-indiscrete comments he might already have made. Even some coded entries were given similar treatment by a later inking over. The cheerful, open young man had been replaced by someone who had grown older and less innocent, with good reason to be careful. What might that reason be?

We can deduce readily enough that he was having an affair with a woman, possibly even two affairs running concurrently, while a third admirer – whose love and devotion he was eventually to accept when his world was totally overthrown – looked on sadly from the sidelines. But that is to jump well ahead in this story.

19

Extracts from George Maple's diary (III)

2-3-76

'dw' tells me 'dow' not plsd wi her. Hs wif had cause to repr her for rudnss. He thretns sak her. At JD wi her 4 nites bak. Walk wi 'dw' to HEW *[?]* and more. Sum *[sic]* worries.

9-5-76

Dig begins CAL. 'rj' not there until evning. Out wi 'erp' SC. Hav missd her grtly. 'rj' has me drawin half night. he wants big progss this yr.

7-7-76

Back at SS. Stomach bad. Sick. L brings me medicine, 'ib' tends me. Ib says I shd rest, but bak to STR nxt day. Ib in tears evening. No not y *[?]*. Mrs.J v. considerate. She tells me don't be silly.

8.7.76

'erp' at GC. Back to rectory late. Both Fiennes and 'rj' reprimand me. I say sorry. Worth it wi 'erp'. We ly long. She crd. Says *[inked out]* bts her.

19-7-76

'dow' at CAL. he to stay at rectry overngt. 'dw' with him. The house noisy and can't sleep. Who needs sleep?! Better things.... *[inked out]*

20-7-76

'dow's baillie organises removal of mosaic for SSH and many things from the mus at red hut. To be layed *[sic]* with other in SSH hall. I am to catalog items this wintr 'dw' tells me. 'erp' at site. I told her no, but says must c me.

22.7.76

With 'erp' alday (day's rest at CAL). Say -----*[inked out]*. She *[inked out]*. Upset with myself. Fool! and *[inked out]*.

9-8-76

Arth'r J comes to CAL. He trips, falls. Breaks <u>terra sig</u> bowl and snaps good bone pin with lady's head. 'rj' ill-plsd – makes him brush out hut. Men find it funny but dare not show it.

22-10-76

To worship SS church. 'rj' preaches on sin. I take communion – 1st time. Feel much better in myslf. 'The sinner who repenteth... *[ink blot]*

4/5-12-76

Cataloging with 'dw'. Objects from CAL placed new cases. 'dow' comes, says v. plsd. 1st time spoken me directly. Walk in park later with 'dw' *[inked out]* near where Cophagn buried. Must escape ..*[undecipherable]*. Spoke with old sojer at Bull. Like Will, he was in Rushenwar *[sic]*.

26-12-76

Servants dance and dinner. Waited at table Xmas day. Danced with 'dw' and L. 'ib' at rect to attend Mrs.J, who was ill. Sorry for that. *[inked out]* misseltoe *[sic]*.

Except for one made in the first week of January 1877, the coded entries, so prevalent the previous year, cease. It seems to have been an experiment George had tired of. Perhaps a new year's resolution was to become much more open once more, according to his true nature, and to take up his digging work again with the enthusiasm he had first shown. He seems by this time to have realised the futility of thinking he could make a career for himself out of archaeology, and was perhaps casting around for other occupations he might do, possibly that of being a soldier. But now he is determined to be his own master again, pursuing his original dreams, and not to be blown about by 'outside interests', when he had had to live furtively at times, scared of being 'found out'.

It is a wonder, perhaps, that he did not rip up or otherwise destroy those redacted, but still fully revealing, diary entries of 1876. A poor, confused state of mind had clearly troubled him for much of that year. Now, as he enters 1877, the entries become much fuller again, although here too the very occasional phrase has later been hidden. When then did he make the various scratching and inking outs? Very soon afterwards, seems most likely, although a few show signs, from the greater freshness of the ink, of having been done very much later, perhaps even towards the end of his life.

20

Extracts from George Maple's diary (IV)

Wednesday 14th February 1877

Diana Webb has been dismissed! The house steward – Theo Twink (or Stinky, as most call him privately) – told me this yesterday morning when I was working in the Duke's library. He said I would answer directly to him from now on, and His Grace would want a report from him as to whether I remained satisfactory. I was somewhat put out by that, as I have always done my cataloguing work most conscientiously, despite the distractions I have had to put up with. Stinky will not report badly on me, I feel sure. He knows I could say a lot about what I saw him doing in the latrines that day with something more than a bar of soap in his hand *[the last can be read although an effort has been made to hide it by scribbling over in pencil]*.

    I cannot say I am sorry Miss Webb has gone. She was friendly – most amiable, in fact! – one moment, then a complete b---h the next. Lizzie at the Rectory loathed her, as likely did Ivy too, although she is too gentle a person to speak ill of anyone. I wonder why Miss W was given the boot. I think I may know, but I am resolved from now on to keep such thoughts to myself.

Wednesday 4th April 1877

An early start at Calleva this year. I was very pleased to return to the rectory and see Lizzie and Ivy again. All there is as it was. Mrs. J particularly pleasant to me, ruffling my hair, and calling me her 'favourite boy'. The Rev. J said not to tell me that, as I would grow big-headed. He is eager to start digging. We are to open a whole new building in Block VIII, which may prove to be the biggest house found so far at Call. Last year the long period of dry weather showed in the grass; paler lines appearing where the grass dies first, there being walls beneath. The house appears to be set around a very large courtyard, like – so the Rev. tells – a big villa in the countryside. He is excited by the prospect of opening it up.

Friday 6^h April 1877

Dig with Bart, Tom and Abe. Will not present as he has hurt his back, and laid up to recover. Rev. J says he will be paid nonetheless. So I am put as temporary foreman to the others, which they seem to accept willingly enough. To be in charge now – under the Rev's watchful eye – cutting into virgin <u>Calleva</u> soil, such progress to have made! I am most fortunate. I cannot believe I thought of leaving last year, my troubles seemed so great. I might now have been at a barracks somewhere doing square-bashing – as I think they term it!

We cut straight down on a most beautiful wall, very well laid, and so far we have dug it to a depth of three feet and more. The Rev. J spent much of the afternoon drawing its every stone, with a spade alongside for scale. I am very far from matching his skill. He is indeed an artist and tells me he is to paint the scene of Christ's crucifixion, to be placed in Silchester Church after the restoration of that church, which is to begin quite shortly. I was pleased to hear about the restoration because I have often thought the church 'mouldy' – the term I once heard a lady make use of, who had gone into the church after viewing the excavations.

Monday 9th April 1877

In the trench many pieces of painted plaster have been turned up, which Rev. J says must come from the paintings that once adorned the walls. He says that Roman rooms were often highly coloured with mural paintings, some with scenes showing human figures, trees, flowers, and animals. Such have been found at villas in England, but most prolifically at the remains of the Roman town of Pompeii, where painted room after room can be visited, the walls still standing very high as they were dug out from the ashes of a volcano that destroyed the place. How I would love to dig there, or at least to go and see this Pompeii. Rev. J tells us to keep the bigger pieces of plaster as he may be able to join them together later to see what scene they once made. The rest we tip back into the trench, although I kept one small piece that shows a yellow bird's head. Later I pulled it from my waistcoat pocket and found the painting has been mostly rubbed off – a lesson not to do similar again. Now that bird can never fly again owing to my foolishness!

Saturday 23rd June 1877

At the Stratfield rectory, the Rev. Fiennes and his wife being present too, as they were staying the weekend, Rev. Joyce told us more of Allectus, the false emperor who had ruled in Britain at the end of the 3rd century of our Christian era. Rev.J looked quite fierce – not a look I have known before, with passion in his eyes, his plump cheeks reddened – as he declaimed that he was a treacherous man who had poisoned the earlier emperor – he also an usurper – a former admiral of the British fleet (classis Britannica) named Carausius – who had been accused by the real emperor of piracy, and so assumed power and split Britain from Rome. The result of this was that the true emperor, one Constantius Chlorus, invaded

Britannia to win the province back to Rome. Allectus was a coward and fled before the invading army, taking his treasure with him. Calleva was likely his capital and he may have been trying to get back within the shelter of its walls. He was caught by Constantius' army before he could do so, and he was killed and his army destroyed.

The site of this battle – as I have already heard said – may very well have been in the Blackmoor area, although Rev. J prefers a site nearer to Calleva. I still have the coin of Allectus I took from one of the great urns we found at Blackmoor. Sometimes I feel it to be almost alive in my pocket, as if the owner of the head would like to escape into our world – but what a fantasy is that, a subject perhaps for a poem! Allectus, and all those of his time, are long dead. We move now within the ashes of their eyes.

Ivy came into the room to ask about serving tea after the Rev.J's declamation had finished, and stood listening too. I saw her standing there with her dark eyes bright in her small white face, her black hair swept back under a frilled cap, her hands linked prettily together before her, and she saw me looking and gave me such a lovely smile that I began to think.....and then stopped, for my life has become complex enough as it is, and I want to be rid now of all complexity so I can live free.

Tuesday 3rd July 1877

There is scaffolding erected about the Silchester church. A wagon pulled by shires, with a heavy load of long wooden poles and boards and planks, was already there when Rev. Joyce and I walked into the yard of Manor Farm. As we watched, the first uprights were being sunk into their great base-planks, and a team of men like monkeys were swarming on the walls, lashing and tying with rope and wire. When we returned later in the day, the whole north side of the church, and the tower too, was covered like one of Her Majesty's warships in Portsmouth dock, to be re-masted and rigged – not that I have ever seen such.

The Rev. Fiennes was there watching: he seems more agreeable to me now, and even smiles at times. I suspect he is a cautious man and takes a time to feel sure of you. He told me – for Rev.J had left by now with Molly and the cart for Stratfield (he will return tomorrow when a visit by Oxford antiquarians is expected) – that the roof is to be restored, both internally – where it will be rebuilt as an open roof of English oak – and externally too, being re-tiled, and the tower's stonework strengthened. The four windows of the chancel are to have new stained glass and the high box pews replaced by seats of pine. All is to be paid for by the good Duke – some £1000, said Rev. F, gleefully, as if – I thought – he had won some prize at the county fair.

I have to state the Duke's beneficence is to be seen widely, and I have benefited from his generosity too, although I had feared my former foolishness might upend me.

Friday 14th September 1877

Rev. J has stopped our digging for the season. We work in Block VIII on the 'big house', which Rev. is calling now a <u>hospitium</u> (this not a hospital but a type of inn, Rev. J says). We have found a bath house with a large hypocaust and <u>pilae</u> stacks up to 8 tiles high. Much more wall plaster. Some pieces appear to show sea creatures. These have all gone to the Red Hut and are laid out for visitors to see. Will has returned: he has been laid up the whole summer and is angry with himself and with all else, it seems. He chased a small village boy out of the trench, threatening to whip him, then came close to throwing punches at the father – a very large bearded man whom Abe says is a thatcher – who chanced to see what he did. Once the boards and covers are laid on the site and made secure I am to return with Rev. J to help when a special visit is made in November. He would not tell me what this special visit would be about. It has been cleared with SSH, however, and Mr Twink told, otherwise I would be expected there wearing my hated uniform.

Saturday 15th September 1877

I am to return to SSH next Monday. It has rained hard all this day and the gardener says looks to do the same tomorrow. So I shall stay in, using the Rev.'s library, with his open permission. Mrs. J tells me he is busy with his painting for the Silchester church. Ivy came in as I read on British chariots and the revolt of Queen Boadicea, flicking a duster over everything, and then over me. I seized her and held her. She was like a skinny, struggling, colt in my arms. I was filled with a sudden urge for her. I released her and she went away giggling, flourishing the duster back at me in a cheeky manner.

Sunday 16th September 1877

Later in the day, after church, once the rain had ceased around 11 o'clock, I walked out with Ivy – it being her free afternoon – along the devil's highway to Silchester, a walk I had not made since I first came to Stratfield Saye, being always driven in the cart. The distance passed easily, she looking happy to be at my side, perhaps wondering at why I had asked her now, and not earlier, though the question was never made. I like Ivy. I feel at ease with her, I enjoy her company and can relax with her, and it was a companion I wished this day, but I sense there is nothing more, or can be anything more, although once..(but I write not of that now). She has grown and filled her figure – as indeed I have done too. We all age together! She must be nigh on 19 now, so I am her elder by two years or so.

We came to Calleva and I showed her the town, and the trenches where we dug, the latest boarded over. As the Red Hut was locked, I could not take her in there, so I decided to show her the amphitheatre, a feature of Calleva I have seldom visited, not liking the place for reasons I cannot really tell, but which many visitors do include in their itinerary.

We entered from the lane, passing beneath a huge bank covered with holly bushes, ferns and foxgloves, and so came into what must be the floor of the arena, once covered in sand, where gladiators had fought each other to the death. Grass, neatly clipped by sheep, now stretched over this space where blood had once flowed freely. The tree-hung banks extended around us to make a great O, yet rather, in fact, an oval than a circle. From here the spectators had watched the fights, and bayed for more blood, not just of men who fought, but of criminals too, men and women, who were to be executed. Animals also were killed here, some perhaps captured in far-off regions of the empire and carried here caged on carts – lions and elephants possibly, but more likely the native British bear, brought here from Caledonia to have dogs set upon it. All this I had read in the Rev. Joyce's books.

And so we journeyed back to Stratfield Saye, in time for a meal and evening prayers. I felt downcast at the end of an otherwise very pleasant day. Of course, I know the reason for being downcast, fool again that I am, but I will say nothing more of that here. I have written down too much already. It is time I closed this book.

There are no further diary entries after that, only a few details of some work in November of 1877, when George helped the Reverend Mr. Joyce with experiments carried out on behalf of Charles Darwin, the eminent naturalist and biologist, by his two sons, Horace and Francis, who visited *Calleva* for the purpose. These experiments were concerned with whether earthworms could penetrate soil, and even mortar, so as get between stones into the very heart of a wall. It is likely that George was very bored.

Much from now on is speculation, yet the conjecture is informed, and what follows in this reconstruction of George Maple's life is far better founded than simple imagination.

21

Let us continue by returning first to the *Calleva* amphitheatre where Ivy and George lingered that 16th day of September 1877. This is likely what happened to them there that afternoon.....

There is no doubt George felt oppressed by the arena, by the idea of fighting and dying for the fun of it before crowds baying for blood, out for a day's entertainment. It is probably why he had only visited once before in all the time he had dug at *Calleva*.

'I feel it to be haunted here,' George said to Ivy. 'I sense the past pressing in on me. All those people, who would have lined those banks above us, may still be there, looking down at us.'

Ivy laughed. It was a pretty sound. She was a little more confident with him now, still astonished by his attention to her, that he should be bothered to bring her here to share his interests with her. She struggled to try and see what he saw in these strange places that she had never visited, or thought about, before, and would never dream of going to by herself. She could understand the lure of finding things amongst all those old walls – treasures of gold and the like – but she felt no particular fascination, as he clearly did, in wishing to immerse himself in the past.

'We would have been very frightened if we were captives here,' she said, trying at least to show she understood his thoughts, although she could not really share them. It seemed such a silly thing to ponder upon, standing here in the late summer sunlight, with the breeze on her face and the scent of the flowers about her.

'Yes. That's true. But I would fight to save you.'

'You would?' She looked up at him anxiously. She never quite understood his moods. Was he about to make fun of her?

'Yes, of course I would.' He loved her worried, dark eyes. They seemed so trusting, so innocent. He felt strong. He was the fighter who would protect her from danger. With her, he felt a man, which had not always been the case with the others. He recoiled a little from those memories.

'Ivy...'

'Yes.'

He leaned forward and she let him kiss her, at first on the cheek and then on the lips, although she turned her head when he moved to do the same again, and so he kissed her chin instead.

'Come,' he said, aroused, taking her arm and pulling her towards the bushes on the bank.

'No,' she said. 'No, I don't want that.'

She tried to move away from him, but he still held her by the arm, his other hand on her bodice now, feeling at the soft mounds it covered.

'No!' she cried, sharply now.

'Come on, it'll be fun. Haven't you done it before?'

She had torn herself from him, and was walking fast towards the amphitheatre entrance, through which the processions had once come with trumpets blaring, the chariots garlanded for an emperor's presence, the black horses high-stepping, the roars of the crowd echoing out.

He realised the mistake he had made. Fool that he was. He had shattered her friendship, her trust, her dreams.

He caught her up. 'I'm sorry, Ivy. I just got carried away. You are so lovely, you know.'

She said nothing, but walked on, turning into the lane, he following her like a shamed puppy, his heart in his Roman boots. And so they returned to the Stratfield Saye rectory, to an evening meal and prayers, as George was to record so faithfully in his diary.

Lizzie looked at them curiously as they entered the kitchen, George still trailing Ivy and seeming very downcast

'What did you two get up to?' she asked. Ivy did not reply.

George tried brazening it out. 'We've had a good day, haven't we Ivy?'

Ivy said not a word, but left the kitchen to go to her room. Lizzie could see she had been crying.

22

George spent the winter of 1877-78 at Stratfield Saye House, employed there in much the same way as every winter since 1874. He still answered to the house steward, known to all – but never, of course, to his face – as Stinky. This particular close season, however, The Duke of Wellington asked for him in particular to help him with his own displays of *Calleva* finds. He had managed to recall what the Reverend Mr. Joyce had told him of the young man in his service who might do this, if not his name. Stinky had to provide it.

His Grace's displays – rather like the Reverend's own – were laid out in glass-topped cabinets in one of the inner sanctums of the house, where a small section of mosaic from the town showing a figured scene – a cherub like face with wings – had also been set most artistically into the wall above one of the cases. It was labelled as being from the 'basilica bathhouse', but George did not think that quite correct, according to the latest excavations. Yet, he decided to say nothing.

The Duke was a benign looking, elderly gentleman, who sought an easy comfortable life in his later years without any further pressures of public service. He had lived in the shadow of his illustrious father for very many years, which state had continued even after the great Iron Duke's death. His poor relations with his wife were the stuff of popular gossip. It could not be said, though, that he had a lack of interest in attractive, usually younger, women. He liked them to be around him, and there were several scandals which were talked of privately at the time and which there may be hints of in this present story. He was a tight disciplinarian, however, and liked all to be proper and circumspect around him. Any straying from that strict rule was likely to get a servant, even of his inner household, removed from his presence, and very often from his service entirely, without any ceremony or argument.

He had been paying George Maple's wages for four years on trust that this was of benefit to his own interests in *Calleva* and because of his confidence in the Reverend Mr. Joyce's judgements. He trusted him to carry out this project and was prepared to meet any expenses, within reason, so incurred. George was just one further small expense, but he decided now to look over the investment in person, to see who and what he was getting for his money.

So one morning in December, when George was preparing for the much more mundane job of polishing the brass door knobs in all the servants' quarters, by orders of one of Stinky's under-stewards, the summons to the Duke came, being passed from 'flunky post' to 'flunky post' from the distant quarters of His Grace, where he spent much of his time. George was to attend the Duke in thirty minutes in the library. This library, where George had already done some book cataloguing a previous winter, was not nearly as large as Lord Selborne's in terms of the extent of its shelving, but it was much more richly decorated, being entered from the main hall through a screen of porphyry columns. Paintings and prints adorned its walls together with the ranks of books.

There, George, freshly scrubbed and in his newly cleaned estate uniform, was duly escorted by a toffee-nosed senior footman. The Duke was bent over a table top as he entered.

'Mr. Maple, your Grace,' intoned the footman.

'Ah, yes, Mr. Maple', he said looking up from the table, upon which George saw a number of relics, presumably from

Calleva, spread out, taken from what looked like cardboard shoe boxes. He could see an iron lock and a number of large keys, a chunk of painted plaster, a bronze toilet set, a curving piece of bronze of uncertain origin with a ridge cast along its centre, a very fine fragment of painted glass, and several coins, one that looked to be of gold. Much more seemed still to be in the boxes, as more iron and bronze objects were poking out of one of them.

'How are you enjoying working at Silchester for our indefatigable Reverend Joyce?'

'Very much, your Grace.'

'He tells me you have worked well and have learnt much.'

'I'm honoured to hear it, your Grace.'

He has snow white hair and looks tired, was George's thought. Also, there's a blot of what seems to be egg on the lapel of the velvet housecoat he's wearing. Has he no valet to tell him, and no wife either? The Duchess, he knew to be away at present, in service to the Queen.

'I would like you to help me with the identification of certain of these objects.' He cast a blue-veined hand over the table top.

'Yes, your Grace, but I don't know if I can be as precise as the Reverend....'

'Don't underestimate yourself, Mr. Maple. I am sure you can. The Reverend Mr. Joyce is away at present, as you will know.'

That was true. George had learnt from Lizzie that the Reverend was spending some time with his wife at a spa in Germany, having suffered a bad cold in the autumn. Mrs. Joyce had told Lizzie that 'he neglects himself' and must gather his strength in time for his Christmas responsibilities. In the meantime, his parochial duties were being met by the Reverend Mr. Fiennes.

'It is the proper wording, sir, that I do not know. The Reverend would add Latin to his descriptions.' There was a hint of panic about George now. Was he about to be dismissed entirely?

'Plain English will do for me, young man. You can write English, can you not?' The Duke sounded disagreeable. He seemed a mild and temperate man, but George suspected that he could be easily irritated, like so many others in positions of power.

'Of course, your Grace. I shall do my very best.'

'That is good, that is good.' He even extended an arm to pat George briefly on the shoulder. 'We shall work together. You see I want these all arranged with my other collections when the Society visits in the new year.'

George wondered what Society this was. He did not like to ask. He learnt later it was the Society of Antiquaries, who were to pay a visit to the *Calleva* excavations and take tea afterwards at Stratfield Saye House.

As it was the work proved much easier than George had anticipated in his first confusion of thought. He was able to identify all that the Duke brought before him, some of which, in any event, were already clearly marked by labels affixed by the Reverend Mr. Joyce. Others, he was able to provide further details for, in particular their site locations and the names and numbers the Reverend had already given them.

Days passed most pleasantly; in fact, George was often left alone by the Duke to proceed by himself. He began to feel they were just two persons working together, and not at all the high aristocrat and his plebeian underling. It was certainly much more congenial than polishing door knobs. As had been the case with Lord Selborne, he received envious looks, coupled with some ribaldry, in the servants' hall. He had learnt by now not to pay any attention to this.

Three weeks later, the Reverend Mr. Joyce had returned, certainly looking much revitalised by his rest. George was pleased to learn from the Reverend's review of his work that he had made very few mistakes. Almost all of the labels for the artefacts, which he had written out in his best copperplate hand, passed inspection. It was only necessary to add a little Latin, as George had anticipated, but in most cases he had carefully left space for this.

The gold coin proved to be a very fine *aureus* of Allectus, the only such yet found at *Calleva*, so the Reverend said. The curving piece of bronze, which had had no provisional description given to it, George had identified as part of a *strigil* – a metal tool used to scrape away dirt from oiled skin in a bath house. The Reverend, on examining the object closely, confirmed this purpose, complimenting George in front of the Duke for his identification.

'I had but thought it a piece of bent metal,' he said, 'but you have looked at it very much closer and have done your reading. Excellent.' The praise brought a blush to George's cheeks, of pleasure rather than embarrassment.

The Reverend had no sooner returned to his church, taking up his duties again from the Reverend Mr. Fiennes, then he was overheard by George, while on a Sunday visit to the rectory, as was his custom, telling his wife that he must leave immediately for Silchester to 'give whatever help he could'. A particular tragedy had just happened in the village, which needed the consolation of the church, and Fiennes, himself was currently away on a fishing trip at some place on the River Test, not due back until the coming Saturday evening. Mrs. Fiennes had sent this message by a carrier, so it was immediate.

'It is a man called Pope,' George heard the Reverend say. 'His wife has committed suicide, by throwing herself down a well. He is distraught beyond all comforting, although the neighbours try to help and the doctor has visited. I must go, my love, but I will return as soon as I can.'

On hearing this, it must be said that George turned very pale, and, although he was due back at the House that afternoon, he stayed in the room kept on for him at the rectory as late as he could, before he had to return to his duties. As it was, he was reprimanded by an under-steward who reported him to Stinky, and had a blot – most literally – added to his service record. Two blots, it was said, and you were out. It might be said that George's behaviour now was such that he had ceased to care. However, as the days passed and nothing further was learnt from Silchester – whatever it might have been that had so clearly troubled him – he bucked up a little.

He still loved the excavation work at *Calleva*, although, if he were honest, he might have said something like, 'It drags on me a little now. I can't see where it is to take me. I am only a tied man in service. And one day the digging will finish. What then? Is this the life for a man? How could I ever make a life as an archaeologist, anyhow? Or gain a cottage for myself and have a wife, with children playing at my feet, food on the stove, flowers about the door? It is an impossible dream, as has been said to me by the others I dig with. But I wouldn't listen to them, and I won't listen to myself now. All will turn out well.'

Yet that was not to prove true.

23

The Reverend Mr. Joyce was later opening the *Calleva* site for the 1878 season of excavation than in previous years. This was partly because the Duke's farm manager wanted a grass crop brought in before the *Calleva* fields were available for further archaeological work, and partly because the Reverend himself was busy finishing his painting of Christ's crucifixion, which was to be added to the glories of the refurbished Silchester church.

On 30th April, the church was officially re-opened on a day filled with special services, the prayers being led in the morning by the Bishop of Winchester. To the accompaniment of a large choir made up of choristers from several churches, the Reverend Mr. Joyce's painting upon the chancel table was unveiled to much applause from the crowded congregation, to his obvious great pleasure. In the late afternoon, some 300 parishioners attended tea in a large marquee erected in the gardens of Mr. Fiennes' rectory.

George had come that day to Silchester with the Reverend and Mrs. Joyce. Ivy had accompanied them as well, she to help with the tea arrangements. All four were squeezed into the small, yellow trap pulled by Molly. George on the rear seat was pushed up against Ivy. He had scarce said a word to her since that awful occasion at the amphitheatre, and he was much relieved to see her now at least meet his eyes and make an uncertain smile.

'It's good to be with you again, Ivy,' he managed to whisper, not wishing to be overheard, but she looked away and did not answer. Her leg was pressed against his, and he thought he could feel her trembling, but it was probably just the movement of the cart as the Reverend flicked the reins to start Molly on the journey.

The services at Silchester Church – which did look splendid with its polished pine pews, the smell of freshly-cut wood on the air from the great timbers now branching in the roof, its new windows glowing with the bright colours of the stained glass, where all before had been but dull and stale – carried on for several days afterwards, allowing the Reverend Mr. Joyce no time for anything other than his Christian duties. Prayers were said as well for several parishioners of Silchester, and other villages around, who had lost relatives in a terrible disaster recently when the training ship *HMS Eurydice* had been upset and sunk by a sudden squall off the Isle of Wight. Many of the 300 or so crew members drowned had come from Hampshire towns and villages.

When they did make a start in early May, with the same original team (both Wills, senior and junior, had returned), it was to dig once further on the *hospitium* building in Block VIII, with an extension of the already wide trench there. A jumble of walls lay exposed from the previous year, and the Reverend was busy with a note book noting down measurements, which George helped him in taking, for eventual transference to his main excavation journal. And so they dug on that last late spring, having to stop often because the season proved unusually wet, which meant that on some days they could not dig at all.

The season turned to June, and by now the trees and bushes covering the town walls were in full leaf and the grass, cut so recently, had already grown again unusually lush and tall, so that a further cut in the areas away from the excavation was planned for a month's time, using a new-fangled, horse-drawn mower. Then the rains came again, catching them in the open as a thunder clap crashed out suddenly from dark billowing clouds, and the rain emptied down in solid sheets of silver.

They ran for the 'red hut', but most got soaked, including the Reverend, scrambling to gather up his papers and hug them to his chest, trying to cover them with his arms. In this, he was only partially successful. One careful drawing he had made in ink of a wall, which survived to three feet high, with the possible sill of a window still in position, was irrevocably spoilt, reduced to a smeared and pulpy mess.

'We can clearly do no more today,' he said. 'We will pack up just as soon as the rain has eased.'

The problem was that the rain did not relent for over an hour, and by then George and almost all the others, including the Reverend, were shivering in their wet clothes, having been able to make only a token effort to dry themselves in the hut. One small hand towel was passed around, but it soon became soaked in its turn.

'Right, we'd better get the tools in, lock up, and make a run for the farmhouse.' It was the Reverend's decision. Foreman Will had suggested this move much earlier, but the Reverend had overruled. 'The rain will pass very soon. It's just a heavy shower.'

But it wasn't.

Once in the farmyard, the Reverend shouted at George through the still teeming rain. 'We'll go straight to the rectory and get dried. There's no point in hanging about here.'

And that's what they did, running as quickly as they could, Joyce still clutching his papers, across the lane and up the rectory drive, to be met at the already opened front door by a most worried-looking Mrs. Fiennes.

'Get inside quickly. Ah, Reverend you'll catch your death of cold.'

Which was most sadly prophetic.

It had seemed the Reverend was getting over the effects of his soaking, as George had soon done, once rubbed down and allowed a hot bath, with boiled water brought to him by the Reverend Mr. Fiennes' man servant. 'Treated like a gentleman at last,' George had thought, handed a pile of dry clothing in which to wrap himself, while his own hung up in the kitchen to dry.

However, just as the Reverend was thinking he was recovered enough to return to *Calleva*, two days having passed and a warm sun now shining from cloudless skies, he began to develop a bad cough.

'Just as I feared,' muttered Mrs. Fiennes to herself.

A message was taken by a servant to Mrs. Joyce, who ordered a carriage to take her husband home. Molly and the cart were still in Fiennes' stables, and the Reverend was in too much discomfort by now to tolerate such a small, open conveyance, anyhow.

When the carriage arrived, a rather grand affair from the Duke's own stables, the Reverend was laid out as comfortably as possible across one seat, while George and another servant sat opposite for the short journey back to his home, where he was put to bed

Although there were short periods when he seemed to be recovering – with Mrs. Joyce watching over him night and day – and a pale Ivy and Lizzie, fetching and carrying water and soups to assuage his thirst and try and tempt his appetite, while George, filled with fears, badgered them as to what he might do to help (there was little) – towards the end of the second week, the Reverend grew very much worse. His lungs were so congested he could only breathe by a painful effort. His coughing brought him great pain.

The doctor had come and gone many times. 'It's a bad bronchitis,' he had declared sombrely to Mrs. Joyce. 'I have done all I can for the present. The next few days will be critical. My good lady, you must get some rest yourself.'

The Reverend Mr. James Gerald Joyce – faithful priest, antiquarian and artist, Fellow of the Society of Antiquaries and accomplished excavator of the Roman town of *Calleva*, loving husband and father – died in the early hours of Friday 28th June 1878, just as the first rays of the rising sun were lighting the paddocks and fields to the east, along the line of the great Roman road running out of *Calleva* towards *Londinium*.

The rectory stood frozen in silence. The grief was intense. Lizzie and Ivy, and all the other servants, dressed in black moved like shadows. The Reverend's body was taken away by the undertakers and returned in an oak coffin, surrounded by flowers. Mrs Joyce slept by it at night, keeping her ever-loving watch.

One day, the children of the village were led past the coffin, carrying summer flowers in small posies, which they added to the already many flowers present. The Duke of Wellington sent an enormous wreath on behalf of himself, his family, and his whole estate. He was ill. He sent his commiserations and regrets to Mrs. Joyce. He would be unable to attend the funeral in person.

The Reverend Mr. Joyce's son, Arthur, had come home, trembling with tears. George tried to tell him how sorry he was, but he did not answer. It is likely he had not heard. George was shaken too, lost in sadness: he did not know what his future would be now. As the Duke was confined to his room with his ailment, Leo Twink, the chief house steward and secretary to His Grace, sent for him.

'You are to continue to work at Silchester for now to tidy up what you are digging. Give instructions to the other labourers. You should finish the tasks you currently have, then close up the site for the present. You understand?'

'Yes,' George answered in a dull voice. He had never felt so low. All his vain hopes had been swept away. 'And what about my other work at the House?'

'You are to be paid off.' Twink (or Stinky, as he certainly showed himself now) said this without emotion. 'Your service with the estate will be over. I always thought you a waste of the Duke's time and money.'

George slunk away, head down.

The funeral was held on Tuesday 2nd July. Stratfield Saye church was filled with the high and the mighty, with church dignataries, with representatives of all the great institutions the Reverend Mr. Joyce had belonged to, with many residents of Stratfield Saye and Silchester and the other towns and villages about. It was said 500 were present. Everyone had loved the Reverend. They grieved for his widow. Many were in tears. After the service, the coffin was borne to the grave that had been opened in the churchyard, where it was laid deep in the earth.

After all the prayers had been said and the choirs had sung their last hymn, silence returned at last to the church, as the last of the mourners drifted away. George stood in the graveyard in the evening gloom, looking upon the low mound of upcast earth with the many flowers laid upon it, and could feel the presence of the Reverend about him still.

'What do I do now, sir?' he asked, but there was no reply.

He became aware of a shadow moving amongst the graves, coming towards him. It was Ivy. She held out her arms to him, her white face running with tears, and he held her, pressing her close.

'I'm sorry', he said. 'I'm so, so sorry.'

'So am I,' she whispered.

'Don't leave me,' she said. 'I love you.'

'I won't. I would never do that.'

But he did.

24

For a few days George worked on at *Calleva*, as he had been asked, clearing the trench they had opened to a common level, finding yet another piece of wall, digging out a few more bits of pottery and oyster shell, throwing most of it away. Will senior was there with him, putting the various covers on, as was done at the end of every season. On the last day, Abe and Bart and Tom were present as well, just standing around. There was nothing more to do. These three had dug with the Reverend, off and on, for more than ten years. Then they went to the 'red hut', and Will locked it for the last time, keeping the key. They made their final farewells.

George walked across those empty fields that had once been a Roman town after the others had gone. He was returning to the south gate, where his digging had begun, when he was suddenly accosted by a thick-set young man he had never seen before, who seemed to spring out of the Roman wall.

'Are you George?'

'Why? Who are you?'

'My name is Pope. Charles Pope. Were you playing around with my wife?'

The fear in George burst out like fragments of steel, slicing into his nerves. He turned and ran.

He expected a heavy hand on his shoulder, but the man had not moved.

'The doctor said she was with child!' he heard him yell out. 'Yours not mine, you bastard. I'm well rid of ye all!'

George kept running. He ran down those lanes as he did not think he could run. He collected his outstanding pay from Stratfield House, packed what he could of his possessions into one bag, and left straightaway. It was nearly seven in the evening. Only Lizzie saw him. He gave her a folded note. 'For Ivy,' he said. Then he was gone. Greatly wondering, Lizzie opened up the note.

'I'm so sorry,' she read. 'I shall return for you. Please wait for me.'

He slept out that night in a hay shed, and the next too in a hop field, in the way he had done in those days before first coming to Silchester. In the broad August light of the next day, around noon, he walked into Alton. Taking a meal and beer at the Red Lion in Normandy Street, where he also asked for a bed and was given one, but sharing, for a modest 3 shillings, he walked into the High Street, and then to the Market Square. Here, he entered the Mechanics' Institute, and climbed to the first floor, where the museum was situated. For a good hour, he stared upon the items displayed, which included now – 'on temporary loan from Lord Selborne' – as a card stated – the enamelled beaker from Selborne House.

The memories came back to him in a rush, of being shown the jug by Lord Selborne and the great excitement there had been at that time, by all, high and low, at the discovery of the urns of coins in the grounds.

He gazed upon the jug steadily, hoping it might tell him something of what to do now: where could he recover his hopes and dreams? But it said nothing to him. Even the coin that he still kept in his pocket, that had once burnt so fiercely for him, had dulled now, its features inconspicuous – just an old coin that would not buy him anything, whether clothes or food or drink, let alone a future. His idle dreams were dead, just like that man whose head was on the coin, a useless token of what once had been. He felt like taking the coin out and throwing it away. And all the time that voice kept thudding in his head – *'The doctor says she was with child'!*

He went back to the Red Lion. The landlord, looking at the well-spoken young man, unshaven, his clothes, including remnants of some sort of uniform, much muddied, asked him what he did.

'I dig,' relied George, by now heavy with drink. 'I dig up bones and all sorts of things.'

'What you mean, in a churchyard – a grave digger?'

'Sort of,' spluttered George. 'That's sort of f---ing right, I suppose.' And he burst into a peal of laughter.

'Get yerself some fresh air, son,' said the landlord. 'You's not used to the ale, I think. I'll keep the bed for yer.'

George staggered outside. It was early evening. The shops in the High Street were closing. The butcher was slotting his heavy boards into place, washing down his step. A lady and gentleman were descending the stairs from a milliner's door. George lurched into them, causing the lady to gasp.

'Watch it, you damned fool!' exclaimed the man angrily. 'Are you all right, dear? Drunkards and it's not yet six. What are we coming to?'

George splashed his face at the market pump, steadying his reeling senses. A carriage passed him, a lady looking out. He was sure he recognised the face. He followed the carriage into the yard of the Swan Hotel, where once the father he had hated had worked. The lady alighted. He had been right. He did know her. It was Diana Webb, now expensively dressed, wearing a broad-brimmed hat. Stepping down behind her was a tall, lean figure in a bottle-green uniform – an army officer, most certainly.

George, trying to sober up a little now his curiosity was satisfied, turned to go, but Miss Webb had seen him. 'George, what are you doing here?!' she exclaimed.

'The same as you probably,' George said as haughtily as he could, but the slurring effect was not successful. 'Coming in for a meal and a drink.'

'I don't think so,' said the officer. 'Serjeant Collins!' A uniformed soldier, also in a dark green tunic with white stripes on one arm, standing next to the ostler at the horse's head, came forward, 'Yes, sir!'

'Take this young gentleman to one side, would you, serjeant. You never know he might like to join us at the depot.'

'Looks a bit untidy, sir.'

'We would soon sort that out. Do what you can. I need more.'

'Of course, sir.'

To George's hazy surprise, the serjeant was now at his shoulder. 'You mustn't bother the officer, lad. If you want to join us, I am the man you need to see.'

'But I don't....'

'Come on, lad, let me get you a drink and tell you all about the benefits of joining the army of our glorious Queen Victoria....'

It seemed ridiculous later, but in that very moment George decided that joining the army was indeed exactly what he had long wanted to do, not the stupid, oh so precious, digging for ancient Romans that he had been up to, surrounded by old men and silly, motherly women, but to be part of something manly, something adventurous, something with a future – a future also where he would not have to think at all, and where his past would not suddenly emerge to trouble him.

'You had best buy me a drink then, serjeant,' he said as steadily as he could through the beer fumes in his head. 'I know a good place just up the road.'

He heard Miss Webb laugh, and, turning, he saw her now on the officer's arm. 'She's only a toffer,' he yelled out as clearly as he could. 'I should know.'

It was hardly a wise thing to say, but the next he remembered was being back at the Red Lion, leaning on his elbows on the bar, taking great gulps from a pewter tankard, with the serjeant beside him, and the other drinkers about him laughing and cheering him on, their hands clapping his shoulders as he drank.

'Go for it, boy,' one yelled out. 'Join up. You only live once.'

More laughter. 'That's the f----ing point,' declared an elderly man who wore a round, glazed hat. 'It's your one life. Them boys'll tak it from yer quicker than your ma squeezed yer out.'

'Well, George, my lad, are you to sign?' the serjeant asked, half way through his own quart pot. His black shako with its red-tipped plume sat on the bar beside him.

George tried to retain a sliver of his mind from the call of the ale fast engulfing him. 'I'll let you know tomorrow,' he managed to get out.

Bending forward he was sick onto the shako. It was not a good start.

He reported, as had been requested, at ten o'clock the next day, still very much the worst for wear, to the stables office at the Swan, once very much the domain of his father, although he did not know that. There, in company with three other recruits, he signed his enlistment form in front of the officer, who sat at a table, dark rings about his eyes also. Then he took the oath to Her Majesty, her heirs and successors, as read out by the serjeant, who stood rigidly beside the table, his immaculate appearance scarce disturbed, his shako, freshly-sponged, held beneath his arm. There was no sign of Miss Webb. Probably she was still abed. George regretted now calling her a tart, even though a high-class one.

25

And so on 16th July 1878 George Maple joined the 3rd Bn. 60th (Kings Royal Rifle Corps). He was taken to the regimental depot at the Upper Barracks in Winchester, where he was issued with his recruit's uniform and began his training. He learnt to drill, to learn the quick march step of the regiment, to understand the workings of the Martini-Henry rifle, how to load, aim and fire, and he did not let himself or any of his fellow soldiers down.

There was little doubt, though, he soon regretted his decision to join up. His fellow recruits were largely coarse men, many of whom could not read or write, and with whom he found very little in common. However, he made every effort to bridge the gap between them, knowing he would need to do so if his service was not to descend into misery and despair. He determined to do all that they did, to share their nights out in the town, to drink with them, to chase women, to join in with their crude humour.

In time, he came to understand that not all the riflemen were like that. Some were of a much quieter disposition, with a lower profile in the barracks room, but they too were determined to fit in with this accepted idea of the common soldier, in the depot or on the way to war. As time passed, and 1878 turned into 1879, his fellow soldiers emerged much more as individuals under their assumed veneers. The corporals and the serjeants, however, were normally unapproachable, and had their own society. So too the officers, who lived in a separate world entirely.

On parade, and on exercises out into the surrounding countryside, all ranks came to glue themselves together as one, aware that they represented the regiment first and foremost, and that was what they lived for now above all.

On one occasion, a week-long exercise, as part of a battle training manoeuvre commanded by some unknown general, was to the areas of Silchester and Stratfield Saye, where villagers he may once have known lined the lanes to cheer the soldiers passing by. He scanned those watching at the lane side, hoping to find Ivy amongst them, but he could not see her within the blur of faces as he marched by.

Despite the message he had left for her, he had not written to let her know where he was. Like most things of his former life – the learned Reverend and all that work at *Calleva* year by year – she had faded already to be just a memory. Reality now was cleaning boots, oiling his rifle breech, pressing jacket and trousers for parade, squaring his pack, and marching, marching, marching, moving into meadow and wood, bent low, skirmishing, skirmishing – the role of the rifleman. At least this was how he was trained. He wondered how it would prevail on a South African battlefield.

For South Africa was where their parent battalion – the 3rd – was fighting now, in this new year of 1879. The war was against the savage, spear-wielding Zulus, who had a reputation for their great ferociousness and fighting skill. They had already defeated the main British invading column, so the terrible news had come, with hundreds of dead on the field, but now the 60th was at the front in the fight back, and winning. Soon, it was believed, the two reserve companies of the $3^{rd}/60^{th}$, of which George and his fellow riflemen formed a part, would be sent out as reinforcements.

Would the war still be going on when they got there? They hoped so. There was honour yet to be won. They all thirsted for medals and glory, and the adoring caresses of grateful girls. War, thought George cynically, has probably always been like this. He had read little about war, only about the Roman army, and that now seemed a very long time ago – which, of course it was, in more sense than one.

Only a few days later, towards the end of February, they were ordered for foreign service, collected new kit and canvas-white tropical helmets, soon to be stained brown with tea, from the quartermaster, and made ready for the great adventure. Lamps were lit late at the depot as the officers gathered about maps and planning briefs, so that everything was known and completed to the finest detail.

On 27th February, 219 officers and men of 3rd/60th, with all their equipment, left for Southampton Docks, to which they travelled by railway in covered wagons, marching past cheering crowds at Winchester Station, who had gathered to see them off. At the docks, they boarded the steamship *Danube*, sailing the same evening. On board too was the Prince Imperial, the son of the deposed Napoleon III of France, who was to serve as an officer with the British Army. The *Danube* reached Durban in Natal on 31st March, and the soldiers remained on board until the Prince Imperial had disembarked, being greeted by a cheering local population. When, the next day, the 3rd/60th came ashore, they found their own welcome somewhat less vociferous. They marched through the small town to the barracks at Fort Napier.

The heat of Durban wrapped itself about Rfn. George Maple like the densest and heaviest of cloaks, so that under the serge of his uniform he was soon running with sweat. The sun was fiercer than anything he had ever known before, the air pungent with the scent of plants entirely new to him, and the hum and chirp of strange insects and great coloured birds made him think he was in a huge glass house, rather like that at the Crystal Palace he had visited with his aunt as a small boy.

It was cooler in the barracks out of the glare of the sun. The huts were built of slatted wood and iron, some with verandas along their fronts with wood-paved walkways, framed by pillars and rails of wrought iron. Panels of corrugated iron fronting some huts had twisted in the burning heat, leaving gaps through which small creatures scuttled. One rifleman found a long green snake curled about the leg of a bed frame. It struck at him, and he later died – their first casualty. They were much more cautious after that.

Two days later, news went round the Rifles companies that a battle had been won by the British at a place the riflemen came to call 'Gin-Gin-I love-you', where, it was reported, the $3^{rd}/60^{th}$ had distinguished itself. Their officers were seen relaxing on the veranda of their mess with raised tumblers of gin to celebrate. The riflemen were allowed only small beer that came in black bottles, and tasted – so it was said by the veterans at the fort – like Zulu piss. George could not disagree.

Later in April, the two companies of $3^{rd}/60^{th}$ were ordered to march to a small place, once a mission station, called Eshowe, which had been besieged by the Zulus. The battle of 'Gin-Gin-I love-you' had been fought nearby to relieve it. There, they would join up with the battle-hardened companies of the regiment.

The riflemen travelled at first out of Durban in canvas-sided wagons together with their equipment, the officers on purchased horses. A wide landscape of open grassland and scrub stretched out before them, within which great ranges of flat-topped hills like towering battleships were set down on a pale green, grassy sea.

At a certain distance, the riflemen in their dark-green uniforms and high black boots were ordered to march both ahead and behind the wagons, as they were now entering Zulu territory. Sluggish rivers, swirling high with brown waters, beside which trees and other lush vegetation grew thickly, were crossed by ponts, but smaller streams, set in deep ravines (or dongas as they were known) had to be splashed across, the water sometimes up to their knees. The earth about the rivers changed from the usual dusty-grey to a dark red, the colour of dried blood. At night, the wagons were set into a circle and entrenched, in accordance with field regulations, with sentries posted behind the defences. The riflemen slept in the wagons, the officers in bell tents.

It took them two days to reach Eshowe, where they entered the fortifications, known now as Fort Pearson, after the officer commanding who had so recently defended the place. Here they joined up at last with the main part of the regiment.

George Maple was not the only rifleman straight from England to feel inferior and inadequate, compared with the sun-baked, experienced veterans of battle he saw now. Here they stayed while the war was fought on to its conclusion somewhere to the north, beyond the distant plateau of mountains that George could see on the skyline. He wondered why the army was fighting for this bare land, with its small scattered kraals, its few cattle, its statuesque, bare-breasted women with bundles balanced on their heads, its small, chubby, smiling children, their hands cupped for rewards. The huge, sun-seared skies seemed as alien to him as the land itself.

He thought of the green meadows and woods of Hampshire, and longed to be back there amongst the rich fields, chopping back the bushes, exposing the ancient stonework, happy in his purpose then with things he understood. He didn't think he'd ever make the sort of soldier the army clearly demanded: practical indeed, and skilled in what he had to do, but acting largely without a need for intellect or anticipatory thought. Only the officers had that: or did even they? He saw and heard them each night, ha-haaing over their whiskies and gins, with luxury campaign kits about them, bought at the Army and Navy Stores. Yet, that they were hardy and brave too, there was no doubt.

It was certainly all a great adventure, something to tell of one day..... He realised he had no one to regale with his experiences, only perhaps Ivy, and she would have long since gone, probably married to some plodding farmer, keeping his kitchen bright for him, cooking him meals, popping out his children one after another. And what did *he* have? Nothing really. Likely some lonely death delivered by an enemy of the Queen. Or even by a snake, as he had witnessed at Durban. He had seen great black snakes more than once, coiling themselves from rock to rock at remarkable speeds, luckily always away from him. They were said to be able to move faster than any horse, and their strike meant death.

The wait in camp at Fort Pearson was long and tedious. The war was being fought elsewhere and the $3^{rd}/60^{th}$ had no role now. There was some indiscipline. The worst defaulters were stripped of their uniforms and bound to a cross bar, standing for hours out in the sun. Fortunately for them, the sun was far less fierce now, as the season descended into the South African winter.

Two major pieces of news reached them. The first, terrible and unbelievable, was that the Prince Imperial had been killed while out on patrol with British officers. No one could imagine how that had been allowed to happen, but the Prince was known to be full of courage and daring, in the tradition of his ancestors.

And then at last, some four weeks later, they heard what they had been eagerly awaiting, that a great battle had been fought at the Zulu royal kraal of Ulundi, and the Zulu army soundly beaten. A small detachment from the 3rd/60th was then ordered to march to Ulundi to help escort the captured Zulu king, Cetshwayo, into captivity. He was to be brought to England to be paraded before Queen Victoria. The war was over.

The 3rd/60th, however, was to stay on in South Africa, unlike most of the troops assembled for the war, who either left for other troubled parts of the Empire, or returned to Britain. The task of the 3rd/60th now was to keep an eye on the Zulus, to make sure they were indeed 'pacified', and to maintain a watch as well on the Boers – the name they used for themselves – the original Dutch farmer settlers of the Cape, who had trekked to the north to find new lands away from the invading British. The Boers had been watching the outcome of the Zulu War with the greatest interest, but not taking part, despite an open invitation by the British to do so. They feared the British would turn on them next, and with very good reason.

The politics of this did not interest George. He had met some Boers, and found them grim, silent men, who feared God far more than anything brought against them by man. They were skilled marksman. Set a challenge, he had seen one, firing from the shoulder, at 200 paces shoot a stoneware bottle out of a baobab tree. A rifleman from his own company, firing from the ground, only hit the thick trunk beneath.

The next year, after long, profitless months by the 3rd/60th patrolling the borders of Natal to the exhaustion and disgruntlement of all, came the news that had been half-expected: trouble had indeed broken out with the Boers. They were claiming back control of their territory to the north, named by them the Transvaal. The British had annexed it a few years back, claiming the territory to be now so impoverished and badly administered that it clearly needed the guiding hand of the British. The Union Jack had been hoisted in Pretoria, whereupon the Boer commandos – irregular mounted units, noted for their high mobility and shooting skills by those who had eyes to see and ears to listen – had begun to assemble. It seemed certain there would be war.

The 3rd/60th officers met in urgent conclave. Rumours told of a Natal Field Force to be formed to march against the Transvaal should the Boers not heed the British warning to de-militarise the territory, and the 3rd/60th would form part of this. The Field Force was to be commanded by the new Governor of Natal, Sir George Pomeroy Colley, said to be one of the brightest of the up and coming generals of the British Army, a protégée of that great soldier, General Wolseley. The officers thought this might be a campaign on which to advance their careers, while the rank and file eagerly anticipated something more befitting riflemen on active service than picket duty and barracks inspection.

Further news arrived in late December that year of 1880. It came as the 3rd/60th were enjoying what Christmas cheer they could muster up at their bleak Zululand outposts around Eshowe. Fortunately, the supply lines were good. They had beer and suckling pig, roasted in the sweltering sunshine over open spits. As was the custom, the officers served the men at outdoor tables set up at Fort Pearson in the shade of a great mahogany tree, one of the few trees in the area to survive the recent siege.

The news, brought by a despatch rider, told of the Boers' cutting up of a British column going to the relief of Pretoria: some 80 men of the 94th Regiment had been killed, one of whom was their colonel. Detachments of other British troops were now besieged by the Boers in various forts and settlements of the Transvaal. General Colley was already readying his response. The 3rd/60th was to march at once to Fort Amiel at the small town of Newcastle in Northern Natal, where Colley's field force was assembling.

The regiment, with its wagons and a screen of locally-raised cavalry, marched across country to Greytown, and so north to Fort Jones, then – the last part of the journey – upcountry to Fort Amiel. They reached there on 19th January 1881. Another regiment was already present – a regular foot regiment' (the 58th), with its red tunics and white pipe-clayed strapping and tropical helmets. Also there, having marched with the 58th, were a further 200 newly-recruited men of the 3rd/60th, sent out as reinforcements and only recently landed at Durban. George Maple now felt the experienced veteran alongside these new, raw lads, whom he could see staring about in some bewilderment at this strange new world they had taken the shilling for. It was raining heavily.

To the cheers and waved encouragement of Newcastle's scattered civilian settlers, four days later General Colley's improvised force of some 1200 men marched north towards the border of Natal with the disputed territory of Transvaal. General Colley rode with his staff – a stiffly remote figure, sitting up tall on his horse, staring ahead. His bearded face, George thought, seeing him pass close by, looked devoid of emotion.

A range of high hills occupied the horizon ahead of them, a northern spur of the Drakensberg mountains that ran through much of Natal. Many of these hills were flat-topped, but one stood out, taller than those about it, like a volcano with its top sliced off. It made a distinctive shape, which, after long marching that day and the next, George's eye kept returning to. He learnt from a native guide that in the Zulu language it was known as Amajuba – the 'hill of doves'. It was a place where many of the Natal Field Force were destined to die, including General Colley himself. But that was yet four weeks away. By then, two other battles would have been fought and lost by the British.

On the second morning, after further heavy rain in the night, it was very misty. They had slept under canvas by the Ingogo river, at least those who been able to: George had been on picquet duty half the night. The hills ahead were hidden under low rain cloud. Later, the sun came through, burning away the mist, bringing strength back into George's aching limbs, his body once more dripping with sweat.

General Colley ordered a camp to be set out on flat ground below the hills that made an enveloping curve here and marked the border with the Transvaal. The camp was named Mount Prospect after a farm nearby. While the camp lines were being laid out, the tents erected, the entrenchments dug, Colley stood with a group of his staff officers studying the hills in front through field glasses. The road – just a broad, stony track that weaved across the grassy plain – could be seen crossing the top of the ridge ahead at its lowest point, known as Laing's Nek. To the left, Majuba mountain rose steeply to its flat summit, its bare sides coursed by ravines.

Two days later, Colley put the plan he had devised into operation. He attacked the ridge to the right of Laing's Nek. It was a steep slope, seamed by gullies, many filled with spiky cactus plants. Artillery opened up, the shells exploding on the ridge top. The mounted squadron charged a detached hill on the right. At the centre, the 58th Regiment advanced in lines of red, with colours unfurled and hoisted high. Officers on horseback rode amongst them, flourishing swords.

The 3rd/60th were drawn up outside the camp, the gunners close to them. Rfn. George Maple in the front rank could see what was happening. Amongst the excitement at watching the battle unfolding before him was also a sense of incredulity –

that he, who so short a time ago had been fussing over pieces of pottery brought from the earth, touching his forelock to his lords and masters, should be present at such an event – a battle of the like the first Duke of Wellington would have known, the red lines advancing, horsemen wheeling, the guns booming out.

The red lines, broken in places now, figures bunched together, were climbing the slopes. They were approaching the ridge top. Distant rifle fire could be heard, individual shots at first, then volleys of firing, incessant, continuous. The red lines bent and fell, individuals rising, then falling again. Figures could be seen lying flat on the ground. A horse collapsed, then tried to rise again, riderless, before collapsing onto its side. The colours, held up so bravely, were visible no longer. A block of men appeared suddenly, without order, stumbling back from the ridge, some dragging comrades by their arms and legs.

George's company, and a second one, were ordered forward to cover the retreating 58th. They advanced halfway to the ridge. The only sign of the enemy was a body of mounted men seen on the skyline at the Nek itself, but they did not advance further. The Boers who had shot down the 58th remained under the cover of the trenches they had dug for themselves.

The survivors of the 58th were close to them now. George, his rifle pointing forward at the alert, saw bare-headed men with torn tunics hanging open, blood on heads and arms, blood jetting from one man in a spray. A medic ran towards him, already uncoiling his bandages. The sun rose to its peak, burning down at them. The firing died away.

Yells and groans and shouts filled George's ears. The dead lay all along the ridge top, together with the carcasses of horses. Two officers, their drawn swords still in their hands, their heads smashed open, were tumbled side by side. All about the slopes the red bodies lay, some in the gullies entangled with cactus bushes, their limbs still twitching under the fury of the sky. General Colley's attack had failed.

The next day George's company helped with the burials. Under a flag of truce they scooped holes on the flanks of the hills to bury the men. The officers' bodies were borne in solemn procession to the Mount Prospect Camp, where graves had been dug to receive them. They lay in a line of newly turned earth, scarce-covered, for the soil was thin and rock was close to the surface. A lone bugler played the last post, his call interrupted by a great crash of thunder as it began to pour again with rain, great bolts of lightning searing the sky. In the night, jackals got in amongst the graves, scraping at the soil, and had to be shot by sentries. The fusillade of fire woke most of the camp.

Ten days later, General Colley sent a column of the 3rd/60th south, together with some mounted men and four artillery pieces, to escort wagons carrying supplies from Fort Amiel to Mount Prospect Camp. The Boers had been cutting the road with their commandos, and Colley wanted to make sure his sole supply route was kept open. He determined on a demonstration in force. Unfortunately, after the column, commanded by the general himself, had crossed the Ingogo river and was climbing to the high plateau of Schuinshoogte, it began to be surrounded by Boers, riding on fast ponies, dismounting and taking up firing positions behind rocks. The British soldiers were outlined above them, and immediately began to fall. Colley flung out skirmishing lines of rifleman to try and forestall them, but they in turn were pinned down by the fast and accurate Boer fire. One of these was Rfn. George Maple.

It was midday on 8th February 1881, the sun at its zenith, burning from an unclouded sky. Rfn. Maple sheltered behind his rock. The Boer positions were less than a hundred yards away. Artillery shells were exploding there, but the Boers were still firing. George pulled down the wish-bone lever on his Martini-Henry rifle and pushed a lead-headed cartridge into the breech. He could see no target to fire at. Then he pulled his bayonet from its scabbard and twisted it onto the rifle. They would be certain to order a bayonet charge soon. How many times had he practised this on exercises on Hampshire commons, howling through the trees, stabbing at dangling sacks. But no order came. After a while he decided he did not want to die here in this lonely, miserable, burning place. The Boers were welcome to it. He thought about survival. It was water he wanted most of all. It was very hot.

26

Rfn. G. Maple was lifted with others into an ambulance and taken from the bloodied battlefield to a field hospital at Newcastle. When he reached there, he was falling in and out of consciousness. An army doctor hummed and hawed over him, cleaned and bandaged his head wound, and also his right arm – at least as well as he could, for the bone was clearly badly shattered. He realised he could not operate himself in the hope of saving the arm, but gave him some strong spirits and put him on a convoy with other wounded bound that same day for Durban. Three days later, George reached the hospital there, scarcely alive. Two others had died on the journey. A surgeon examined him, turning his head from the vile, putrifying smell of the wound, muttered that the arm should have been taken off in Newcastle, so he did so himself straightaway. The operation was successful. Neither gangrene or sepsis appeared. George slowly recovered, got back a measure of strength, and was discharged to be returned to England on the steamer 'Lapland'.

By mid May he was back in England, and was able to walk down the gangplank at Portsmouth Harbour. Taken with other of the seriously wounded, several with amputated legs hobbling on crutches, to the hospital at the Winchester Barracks, he spent a further six weeks there learning to dress himself and cope with having only one arm, and hiding the disfigurement to his ear by pulling down a loose woollen cap over that side of his head. Just until the flesh settles down and becomes a normal colour again, he told himself. At present where the ragged remnant of the ear hung was a mixture of mottled crimsons and purples: it looked like a ragged cabbage leaf, he thought – that is, when he was able to think.

His head was often full of pain, his memory blurred about what exactly had happened to him, and his speech at times uncertain. Then all would clear, and he felt himself again, whole and certain, his hopes of some sort of future returned. Only for the blurring and the doubt then to return the next day. He fought these awful feelings, but he was frightened for the future, he had to admit, even when his head was clear.

He was asked by the medical officer if he wanted to stay on with the regiment, provided some administrative task could be found for him in the Winchester Depot, but he said no, and so was registered for discharge. What would he do? He did not know. Then the Colonel of the Regiment, brought out of retirement to command the depot, one morning visited the hospital, with the walking patients in uniform lined up by their beds, as neatly as the many crutches and slings and other bandagings allowed. The Colonel seemed to signal out George, with his empty sleeve pinned across his chest, and talked in kindly tones to him, telling him he would ask around for him to see if there was any opportunity for a disabled man. The Colonel was a titled gentleman, elderly and much-whiskered, who seemed to move in high circles. However, George thought it unlikely he would hear from him again. Colonels did not often concern themselves with the affairs of private riflemen, particularly one who wished his discharge, despite the possible chance of a job at the depot.

One day, however, towards the end of his allotted six weeks of convalescence, when George was sitting in the hospital recreation room, trying to read 'The Times' and make sense of the news from South Africa, where the British government appeared to have chucked in the towel and allowed the Boers back their independence – 'for what purpose then, all those torn bodies of my comrades?' was George's thought – an orderly poked his head through the door.

'Rifleman Maple', he said. 'You're wanted in the Colonel's office. Serjeant Mathews is outside. He'll take you across.'

George buttoned up his tunic, practised now using his left hand, made sure his right sleeve was fastened at the correct angle, placed his glazed, peaked cap on his head, and followed him out. 'Good luck, George,' someone called after him. 'Don't let them send you back again.'

His mind blurred. Send me where? Then he realised. Turning his head, he saw that 'The 'Times' he had been reading was already opened out in other hands.

After crossing the square beside the serjeant – 'As well as you can now, lad, left, right, left right, keep your head up' – Mathews knocked on a heavy, brown-painted door, and pushed it open. A pause. George stood behind the serjeant's bulky body, wondering what was to come. His mind felt disordered. He did not really feel himself in his own body, as if he was only playing at being George Maple, and someone, or something, else was manipulating him.

'Rfn. Maple to see you, sir!' bellowed Mathews.

'Bring him in, Serjeant.'

'Smartly now, lad. As smart as you can.'

George obeyed instinctively. It was what he had been trained for, marching with one arm, saluting with his left hand. 'Rifleman Maple, sir.'

The Colonel, rising from behind his desk, raised his hand in acknowledgement of George's salute. A man in the room was also getting out of his chair. Despite the sense of unreality encompassing him, George recognised him at once. The shock served to sharpen the edges of his mind, as if he had suddenly emerged from shadows into light. He knew this man. It was Lord Selborne, more be-whiskered than he remembered, wearing a light grey coat with a high pointed collar and a necktie at his throat. He offered his hand, which George touched with his left, feeling the coldness of the white fingers.

'Very good to meet you again, George,' Lord Selborne intoned. 'Although, I am sure, we would both wish it to be under happier circumstances.'

'Please be seated,' the Colonel said. There was a cushioned chair next to Lord Selborne's. George fell back into it gratefully. His legs felt weak, his mind already blurring again. What did Lord Selborne wish with him now? A sense of the shame of his sacking returned to him, but it seemed such a long time ago, it did not matter. Did anything matter now?

The Colonel was holding up a buff-coloured file. He slapped it back on his desk, tapping it with a finger as if to ensure it would not jump up again. 'Reports tell me how well you have recovered, Maple. Do you feel ready to leave us?'

'Yes, sir.' He knew that was the expected answer, as with most things in the army.

'Do you know what you will do once you are discharged and where you will go?'

'No, sir. I expect I will mange, sir.'

He made an attempt at a weak grin, trying to turn his head away from the two men staring at him, so that they might not see so clearly his discoloured torn ear, of which he was more self-conscious than his missing arm.

Lord Selborne spoke. For a man, so used to moving with calm assurance amongst the great and powerful, an astute observer might have judged him to have an uncertain, almost diffident, look about him now. His voice too did not have those firm, decisive tones that had often set the Law Courts, and indeed Parliament itself, afire.

'If you will allow me, George, I can help you.'

'In what way, sir?'

George's response was instinctive. Lord Selborne had erupted from his past like a phantom intoning painful memory. He did not wish to look back to that former time. The trouble was he did not know what he *did want* now. The future was like a grey curtain before him, a curtain the colour of this man's coat. It gave him no warmth or pleasure to see it.

'I can employ you again. Give you a roof over your head. Food to eat. People about you, who care about you. You have served your country and suffered for it. It is the least I – we – can do.'

'I would be of little use to you, my Lord, with one arm.'

'You don't know that yet, I would judge there is much you could do. It is an arm you have lost, not your entire body. You are not paralysed, like some, or have lost your legs. What say you then? Lord Selborne was much bolder now. Then, in a softer tone, almost pleading. 'Let me help you, George.'

George looked up at him but said nothing

Lord Selborne thought: at least he has not cast my offer back at me at once, as I feared he might. He had come to realise how his summary dismissal of George had been far too draconian, lacking in that natural justice he had so often called for in legal cases that came before him – and the matter had caused him some considerable soul-searching since. Through the Reverend Mr. Joyce, he had followed the young man's progress with interest, and been shocked by his abrupt disappearance after the Reverend's untimely death. He had even made efforts to find out where he had gone to, but without success. It had been the merest coincidence that he had spotted the name, Rfn. G. Maple, in a list of the returning wounded of the 60th Rifles. As a patron of the regiment, he had donated large sums to their benevolent fund, in particular to its hospital at Winchester Barracks, which he made a point of visiting whenever he could

George did not know what to say. He had never once thought he might return to Blackmoor House. A memory of a girl on a ladder, impatient, complaining, came back to him, her body falling onto him in a tumble of fine-laced petticoat and white-stockinged legs.

Then he spoke, his voice a bit slurred, for the pains in his head had become suddenly much worse. 'What about Lady Sarah, my Lord? Would she not mind my presence at Blackmoor?' It was a surprise to him that he recalled the name of Lord Selborne's daughter.

Lord Selborne looked puzzled at first, then amused. 'No, indeed. She is not at Blackmoor very often, anyhow. She lives in London these days for much of the time. She writes books occasionally, I do believe. Her mother knows more'.

There was silence. George could see Lord Selborne exchanging glances with the Colonel.

'Would you then be agreeable to taking up a position with Lord Selborne?' the Colonel asked at length.

'Well...' George was still undecided. At times he did not wish to face the future at all, at others, when a calmer reason returned, he knew he had to. These pains in his head were dreadful. They were much worse than the loss of his arm.

'What would I be employed as?' he asked

'I will need a new porter soon,' Lord Selborne answered. 'At the main lodge. Mr. Catchpole and his wife are to retire to the south coast. You could learn the duties from him before he goes. They would not be very onerous, and you would not need to look after the lodge itself.'

'And also', he added hastily, as if he knew this would clinch his proposal, 'when you can write a good hand again with your left, you could come to the house some days, for the library catalogue still needs completing. But first, as I understand well, I assure you, you need to recover fully.'

The lodge? – George thought. He would be like a small pebble in that house, knocking his head on the walls. When darkness came he would be alone. He did not wish to admit this, but he was frightened of being by himself now; his thoughts could grow tumultuous and threaten to consume him. He needed to have someone to talk to.

Lord Selborne was smiling at him. Why was he smiling? What else was up his sleeve? Why did this man think he could hold him in the cup of his hand?

'Now, I need to tell you of something else that may help you to make up your mind. Another person will join my staff very soon; someone you know, and with whom, I understand on the best authority, you have been good friends. After the Reverend Mr. Joyce's sad death, so unexpected, his rectory passed, of course, to the new incumbent, and Mrs. Joyce, in any event, wanted to move away to live with friends. So this person, I speak of, a servant in that house, did not wish to stay. There were too many memories, she said, some happy, some very sad. So she went to work at Stratfield Saye House alongside her mother: his Grace was most gracious in making a position available for her. Yet, it appears, she has not been happy there either, a shame as she came with an excellent recommendation from Mrs. Joyce as a good worker. What is the reason for her unhappiness, I wonder? The housekeeper has brought several rumours to the Duke's ears. He is a man who pays attention to all things, great and small. He is particularly concerned for the welfare of all who work for him – unusually so perhaps these days, but the old type of paternal lord still abides.'

Lord Selborne leant forward in his chair, fingering his necktie as if it had suddenly become too tight. He continued,

'I had occasion to visit the Duke just two days ago. We talked of the late, sad war in South Africa, and I had cause to tell him your story, having only recently learnt of your presence amongst the wounded. Your name matched – remarkably indeed – with the rumours his Grace had heard. And so the rest of this story can be set in motion, if you are so willing, if you understand me.'

George's heart had started to beat faster. This couldn't be. He had not ceased to think about her, although in his present state she was the last person he would seek to find.

Lord Selborne's eyes were boring into his. 'You know of whom I speak, I think. Someone to whom – as those rumours tell us – you had become much attached.'

George did not dare to say the name in case he was wrong.

'Her name is Ivy Bedser. Her mother will come with her onto my staff as well: she comes with the reputation of being a most excellent cook. I had an interview with the Bedser ladies after I had spoken with the Duke, and told them of your service in the army, and that you had been wounded. They knew nothing of this, as you can imagine, and were astonished, possibly an understatement because at one moment I thought Miss Bedser had fainted right away. My proposal is that Mrs. Bedser live at the porter's lodge with you, so that she can keep an eye on you, and cook for you and keep the house clean. And to that she has agreed. Miss Bedser will, of course, be in our servants' quarters at the house.'

Against all his expectations, George was filled with a sudden great sense of joy, the first such emotion of warmth and comfort that had come to him, even remotely, for many long months.

'Thank you, my Lord,' was all he could think to say, but there were tears in his eyes.

Rfn. George Maple was discharged from the army three days later, wearing a suit of the Selborne livery, kindly sent to him by his Lordship's house steward. He pinned up his empty sleeve to this new uniform jacket, and from his left hand carried all he possessed in the world, wrapped up in one canvas bag. Checking the pockets of his army uniform, now discarded and to be returned to the quartermaster's stores, he found at the very last something he had long forgotten about, deep in the folds of a breast pocket – the coin of Allectus. He was tempted to throw it away, or perhaps give it as a curio to one of the other injured survivors from Ingogo, many in a far worse condition than he. His head ached trying to think over the matter. The polished bronze profile of Allectus stared up at him from his palm as if in reproach. Something deep within him told him he must keep the coin.

A cart had been sent into Winchester from Blackmoor to collect him. Seated up beside the driver, he came to the depot gates for the last time. There was no one to bid him farewell, just a rifleman on sentry duty who gave him a nod passing by.

27

Catchpole, the porter at the main (north) lodge of Blackmoor House, had long been nicknamed Scratchy by the other servants. George found him rather more fussy and pompous than irritable, eager to show him the multifarious jobs a porter's work involved, while George sensed he did very little of these himself, being content to sit in a chair in the July sunshine, awaiting the call of the bell pull at the gate, which would make a great clanging sound to be heard everywhere in house and garden. In fact, he was less troubled by the bell than the porter at the south lodge, for most of Lord Selborne's guests usually approached the house from that direction.

Most regular visitors, in any event, knew it was best to avoid the porters, both gates being invariably left open during the day. Lord Selborne was little concerned by the occasional unauthorised incomer, who would normally go through the arch to the kitchen courtyard, anyway. So there was little for the north gate porter to do, other than to ensure the gates were shut at night, and to take milk and other supplies, including the post, up to the house steward, when these were left for convenience at the gate.

Mrs. Catchpole did much of the work about the lodge, and she took George straightaway under her wing. 'Poor lamb, can you manage now?' was one of her sayings, every time she saw George appear from his most comfortable room, with its view over the park from the rear windows. He assured her that he could.

Three days passed, and he still had not gone up to the house. He longed to see Ivy again, and had made enquiries about her of Mrs. Catchpole, to be told that both she and her mother were yet to arrive to start work, although they had made one visit of inspection a while back. There were some affairs they had yet to settle in Stratfield Saye, Mrs. Bedser had told her. It was thought they would be returning to start their new employment at Blackmoor House very soon.

Then on the fourth day, a message was received from the house that Lord Selborne himself, just returned from London – George had seen his carriage sweep through the gates last evening – wished to interview him. And so he walked up the driveway, and made his entry into the well-remembered kitchens, where Mrs. Broughton, and some maids and footmen he had known, were present, looking at him in wonder as he entered. There had been only a rumour amongst them of his return – the north lodge was a separate domain to theirs and the Catchpoles not on the best of terms with the house staff, anyway – so no real information had come to them about what had happened to him. Seeing his pinned-up sleeve and the coloured mash of his ear, the purple stain spreading onto his cheek, they lapsed into a subdued, almost fearful, silence.

'So that's where you went?' said Mrs. Broughton. 'We had heard ye's was at Stratfield with the Reverend – God rest his soul – but nought since. The army, eh? And I would never have took yer for a private soldier, if I may say so.'

'I fought as one,' said George stiffly.

'Yes, I'm sure you did, and suffered too by the looks of it.'

'I did my duty.'

'Are you well enough now?'

George did not know what to answer. The life he had lead so recently seemed a million miles from here. These people had no idea of either Zulus or Boers, of the great heat and the fear and the pain; men, their bodies smashed, suffering and dying so the people back home could read about it in their newspapers, and feel pride at 'our gallant men' and of their flag waving over 'them foreign places'.

'Well enough,' he answered. But his head was throbbing. Something was telling him. I don't fit in here now. All he wanted to see was Ivy.

'When is Ivy Bedser to come here to work, do you know?'

'You knows her, do you? I heard some mention when she visited with 'er ma to see how things are done here that she had a soldier friend. So that is you?!'

She cackled, and turned away, pushing up her sleeves. George saw her hands were white with flour. Other faces at the familiar table looked up at him, moon-like and unspeaking She turned back. 'That mother of hers – Rose, 'er name. She's a great one at bakin'cakes. Shows me up, she does.'

George sensed there would be no love lost between Mrs. Broughton and the Bedser new arrivals. Would Ivy be able to fit in here then? He knew she would hate to be the focus of any ill-feeling. When was he to see her? When would she come? A type of desperation rose within him. His head swayed. He had to sit down.

'Yes, you sit. You look all in.'

And so George sat quietly, now ignored by the others, until the house steward – a new man he did not know – came to him. 'I'll take you through to Lord Selborne now.'

The meeting was of little consequence and of short duration, just a welcoming back by Lord Selborne, and a check to see if George was settling in alright. His lordship seemed distracted, which George thought unusual, as he remembered him giving his full attention to every matter in the past, however small. He did not look at all well either.

Indeed Lord Selborne was to become quite seriously ill, and advised to rest at home. 'Overwork' was the word whispered about the house. He was to be rarely seen outside his private quarters after this until early in the new year. By the spring of 1882 he had recovered his strength. He was created Earl of Selborne that same year.

But that is to jump ahead of our story. George has yet to have his reunion with Ivy, to whom he had promised one day to return. And he had done so now, even if he had to admit to himself it had not been his first intention. A couple of Boer rifle bullets, and Lord Selborne's intervention, had hastened fate along its way.

In fact, Ivy came running down the drive to the lodge the morning after his meeting with Lord Selborne. She had returned the night before with her mother, not knowing George was now at the lodge, but had learnt of his presence there from Mrs. Broughton, who gave her the news in her usual offhand manner. She made no mention of his wounds. When Ivy had asked how George was, she had but answered, 'You must see'.

It had been too late to make a visit to the lodge that evening, and so Ivy had spent a restless night filled with a mixture of joy and fear at how she would find him on the morrow.

George had been having his breakfast at the kitchen table, served by Mrs. Catchpole while her husband sat reading 'The Times' – then to be ironed out for the porter to take up to the house – when an urgent knocking came at the front door, repeated twice in quick succession. George himself rose to open the door, with a sudden premonition of who this caller might be.

There was Ivy on the step, her cheeks flushed, her hair wildly loose, her eyes wide with expectation. She fell against his chest, sobbing. He placed his one arm around her and nuzzled his face into her hair, eventually finding her lips with his own, seeing those dark eyes he remembered so well staring into his. He felt a great love for her. It was a feeling he had scarce known before. Seeing Mrs. Catchpole had come into the hallway they broke apart, standing awkwardly. It was then for the first time Ivy noted the purple stain on his face and his empty sleeve, and her hand came up to her mouth in shock.

'Go into the drawing room,' Mrs. Catchpole said kindly enough to Ivy. 'You can look after your man now.'

28

So it was done.

George was soon to meet Mrs. Bedser – Ivy's mother – too. He had come upon her several times when working in the winters at Stratfield Saye House, where she was employed in the kitchens, but he had never had much of a chance to talk with her. Ivy had told him once that her father had left home years ago, when she was very young, and not come back: the story was that he had gone out to Australia looking for gold, as he had often talked of doing. It was not a venture her mother had wished to make herself, particularly with a young child in tow. Was there such pain in everyone's life, George wondered?

After the Catchpoles had left, George found his new work was easily accomplished. He carried out his expected duties, but could not be concerned to seek out further tasks. It was enough to get through each day. He would feel extraordinarily weary at times, and the stump of his arm still pained him badly. When Ivy came off duty at the house in the evening, she would come to the lodge to see him. Her mother – a stout, buxom lady with permanently red cheeks – would be present at first, although she would retire to her room to allow them as much time together as she could. But there was little enough they could do those evenings, which were often, that late autumn of 1881, cloudy and wet, but sit and talk, holding hands, with a kiss and an endearment or two when it was time for Ivy to leave.

He tried to tell her of the army and of the battle, and how fortunate he had been that the bullet had scraped the side of his skull and not gone through his head, although it had made mincemeat of his ear. And he told of the loss of his arm, and how it had been sawn off in Durban by a surgeon with a cheroot in his mouth. She did not want to hear any more.

Ivy was worried about him. It was wonderful to see him returned, although quieter and stranger at times in his manner than she had known him before. At times, she wept over his injuries – not wishing for him to see her do so. She helped him re-bandage the sore stump of his arm, which showed signs of inflammation, shuddering to touch it.

With Lord Selborne's permission, a doctor was called, for they did not have the money to pay a professional man. This was Lord Selborne's own doctor, who was presently coming to the house, anyhow, to tend to his lordship's ills. He provided ointments to sooth the stump, and showed Ivy how best to apply a dressing. She hated doing this, but she tried not to show it. The doctor made no charge. He said he was happy to help one who had been injured in the service of his country.

He told her of the noises in his head that seemed to come out of his injured ear, and of the pains he had there too, and of how his mind was so jumbled at times he did not know what he truly thought. This was not what she wanted to hear. This was not the clear, bright George, full of new ambition, that she had once known.

'My head feels like a broken egg,' he said to her one evening, 'with bits sliding about all over the place. I have some of South Africa there, and the soldiers I see are ours, and then there are others, and they look like those ancient Romans I have told you about. I hear their trumpets: the sound blares out to me.'

She was very concerned at hearing him talk this way. It seemed nonsense to her, not like the way George had used to speak at all. Had the blow on his head sent his mind astray? Yet there were other times when he would laugh at himself, and apologise for any stupidities he might have said. And then, the old George with the laughter in his eyes came back – yet it did not last long.

It had been a long, hot summer. By September, the weather was cooling and the rains came – days of rain, spattering the lodge's windows, turning the paths to mud, creating pools on the gravelled driveway.

George's behaviour suddenly grew very much worse. He would drape himself in a large, waterproof cape left behind by the Catchpoles, and plunge out into the rain. Sometimes he would return only when it was getting dark. Ivy might have been waiting for him, gnawing her knuckles with worry, for an hour or so. There were several days, on the other hand, when he scarcely rose from his bed at all.

He seemed to lose all interest in the details of his job, performing his basic functions only very poorly, so that he had to be reminded of them, increasingly sharply, by the house steward, who had the daily responsibility for him. George would leave the lodge now during the mornings, and walk the lanes, without obvious purpose, as if he was trying to find something, but did not know what it was or where it would be.

On more than one occasion when she had a day off, Ivy would follow him to see what he did, not wishing him to know she followed, but greatly concerned when he eventually returned to the lodge, having apparently achieved nothing, but talking to himself, just as she imagined a madman would. Mrs. Bedser told her not to worry so much.

'He is just getting what happened to him out of his system,' she said. 'As soon as he's done that, I'm sure he'll be himself once more. It's a big blow for a man to be rendered disabled.

He has to get to grips with life again. If you can, help him. But he might be better left alone – at least for now.'

At first, Ivy thought her mother's words were wise, but then later she was not so sure. George seemed to be getting worse and worse each day. At this rate, he would put his porter's job in peril, despite Lord Selborne's patronage. She would like to be able to give his Lordship her fears, or express them to the chief steward, or someone else in the household perhaps, but she never seemed to have the chance. She had her own daily job to do, and she was usually very busy – in fact, quite worn out at times.

One day Lord Selborne sent a note addressed to George at the lodge. It took him two days to get around to opening the envelope. When he did so, he found two sheets of paper, one was his Lordship's note and the other a page of writing arranged neatly in groups of several lines, some words of which were crossed out and replaced above by others.

The note read: 'My dear Maple. Lord Tennyson has sent me a draft he has written of a poem on the late disastrous war in which you were so sadly wounded. I have told him I have a man on my staff who had fought in that war, and he was interested enough to request that you pass an expert eye over the poem he has composed to see if it represents correctly the spirit of the conflict, and the sentiments of our fighting men whose company you kept. Any comments you might have, he would be pleased to receive. You are honoured by such a great man's interest, I assure you. Yours truly. Selborne.'

George read the lines –
Amajuba's dark and sullen slopes
Upon which our brave soldiers fought,
Rise high above the grieving camp
Where now the laurelled fallen lie at rest:
Let no man say, to honour's shame,

> *Where shone such valour of the race –*
> *Our warriors who died so well*
> *For England, Home and Queen.*

And two stanzas further of this type.

George seemed lost in thought for a while, then wrote as neatly as his left hand would allow at the top of the poem in red crayon: 'I fear it was nothing like that. Over 70 were killed in my regiment alone, most in great fear and pain. And there were many Scots, Welsh and Irish too.'

He would have liked to have written more, but decided against it. He did not wish to be the cause of upset to anyone. Lord Tennyson was a great man, but he knew f--- all about war. He did add at the bottom of the page, however: 'No man I saw died well. We were badly led'.

He replaced the page of verse in the envelope and sent it back to the house, marked 'Att: Lord Selborne.' He never heard anything more about it.

As October came, and the leaves were beginning to fall in the woods around Blackmoor, Ivy became more and more worried about George. He would be gone for the best part of some days, only returning as the shortening days were growing dark, his work entirely neglected. Her mother had had to try and cover for him. It cannot go on like this, Ivy thought, increasingly desperately. She had hoped – oh, how she had hoped! – and now all was turning to poison. She pleaded illness, herself, one day mid-week, and she was allowed to rest in her room, for there was usually some consideration for staff, in particular the women.

She slipped out of the house that day, and followed George to see where he was going now. It was into the woodland, she saw, as she followed him at a distance, prepared to duck out of sight should he suddenly turn to look behind him. But he never did. Into the woods he went, and into the forbidden army land. At least the red flag was not flying that day. She waited an hour, and longer, behind a screen of evergreen bushes, then suddenly there he was returning. Surely he had seen her, but it did not seem he had. He was talking to himself. With a chill in her heart, she heard him muttering the name, 'Allectus'. She had heard him try to tell her of this man before – a Roman emperor, or general, or something of that sort – she knew not what really.

'I am doing what I can,' came to her clearly as he passed her, crouching behind the bushes. 'I will join you when I can, when I am well enough. I have already given you an arm. What more do you want, you bastard?'

Ivy was terrified by what she heard. George had gone mad. It was not now just a strangeness, but a real madness. So quickly it had come about. Dreadful! Terrible! A sense of panic filled her. Her dear George who had kissed her, and for whom her body had ached. Oh, why had she not given herself to him in that arena so long ago? If she had, he might never have gone to be a soldier, to be wounded, to have his brain overturned in this fearsome manner.

Who could help him now? Her mother could only provide his practical needs at the lodge. What about his mind, his soul? Should she try and let Lord Selborne know what was happening, or someone else at the house? They would be aware already, of course, of his inattention to his job. Oh, what should she do? What should she do?

She wanted to scream out in her agony and fear. But she knew that whatever George did now, whatever he said, perhaps to try and push her away, she would continue to care for him, to watch over him, to love him. She would stay with him to whatever ending might come.

Knowing she might be risking her own employment, the next day she left the house again without telling the housekeeper as soon as her morning work was done, coming into the lodge by its back door. Her mother was in the kitchen, busy washing pots and pans to be hung in bright rows from the white-tiled walls.

'That Mrs. Catchpole,' she was muttering, scarce looking up as Ivy came through the door, 'she let this house go to seed, I can tell you. As if I have not enough to do without having to get the whole place clean again.'

'How is he?' Ivy asked, breathlessly. Her face was flushed with worry, her hair, normally pinned up at this time under a white cap, hanging loose

'And what are you, on an afternoon off?' Mrs Bedser queried, then seeing the worry in her daughter's eyes and guessing the real reason for her visit, answered. 'He seems content enough this morning. He is up and shaved with his uniform on. He's even taken the post to the house, as he should.'

At that moment George came into the kitchen, and Ivy was happy to see how his face broke into a smile at the sight of her – the smile she had known so well in the past.

'What-ho,' Ivy,' he said cheerily. 'I didn't expect to see you today. Is there no work for you?'

'Oh, yes,' Ivy gabbled, pleased to see him looking so well. Her fears subsided. 'I must get back. I had just a message for my mother. I will come down tonight for an hour or so.'

She kissed him on the cheek, and he held her to him, tightly, his one arm fully about her, so her breasts were flattened against his chest. It was the embrace of a lover, of the sort she longed for, that he had so seldom shown – if not perhaps here at this moment in front of her mother. Mrs. Bedser, however, had coughed and turned discretely away.

'I look forward to it,' George said. 'We haven't talked properly for a while.'

'You are not going out for one of your walks?'

'Oh, no, you silly thing. I have my work to do. A man comes to mend the gate pillar where the brewer's cart struck it, and I must see to him.'

Perhaps, thought Ivy, he has got the madness out of himself now – I overheard the last of it – and he will return to me, as he used to be. She thought, with excitement thrilling her body, tonight I will let him love me. We will walk outside. There is a full moon. We shall have light enough to see, and the ground beneath the trees will be dry enough for... .

She could think no further. There was no experience, just imagination, her body longing for him. His wounds made no difference to her own devotion to him. She knew not why, when there were other men, their bodies whole, she might make eyes at. But only George would do. It was George she wanted, whatever problems might yet come.

'Goodbye, Ivy,' said George, smiling at her. But there was something about that smile, and his voice, that set her nerves trembling again, and her fears returned. Was it her imagination, or did she sense a tone of finality? But she had to go. She had the whole front hall to clean, and she was letting the other housemaids down. George would be alright now, she told herself determinedly. But her worries about him remained.

That mid-afternoon, when Ivy was cleaning her own small room at the top of the house, she chanced to look out of the small attic window, which faced north. From here she could just espy, beyond the Blackmoor House estate, a junction of lanes near the rectory. To her great surprise and shock, coming into view was the unmistakable figure of George Maple, with his great cape thrown over his shoulders, slouching by on the lane away from the village. What was he doing? Her fears for him returned in a rush. He had said he would not be going out. He had work to do, a builder to see. Why would he change his mind so suddenly. It was not a good day for a walk, anyhow. There was a light rain on the air, beneath a slate-grey sky.

She was so perturbed, her instincts telling her that something was now very wrong indeed, that she quickly pulled on her boots, wrapped a shawl about her shoulders, rushed down two flights of the back stairs, then came outside into the courtyard and through its archway onto the drive. The astonished calls behind her of other servants, the housekeeper too, she ignored; indeed, it might be said, she did not hear them.

She hurried as quickly as she could down the drive, past the lodge, and onto the lane, then to the north to the point where she had seen him passing by at the dividing of the lanes. Peering frantically ahead, her body bent forward like a sapling tree blown by the wind, she could see no sign of him. But she thought she knew where he would have gone. It would be the same journey she had followed him on yesterday, to a place he had clearly come often, by paths over the open moorland into the great forest trees at Holy Water. She knew he liked to stand there and look out at the view all around, although today there would not be much to see, as the greyness of the late afternoon was already weakening the light.

Taking a footpath from the lane, she squelched along the muddy track. Her best boots would be ruined, but that was the least of her concerns now. Passing from the open land into woods, she still could not see him, and she thought perhaps he had stopped and hidden, watching her go by. But why would he do that? Or perhaps he would. His brain was clearly unsettled. There had been something about that last farewell to her that she knew now to be wrong.

Then, coming out of woodland into an open area of fields, she spotted him ahead, his figure scrambling from one muddy side of the path to the other, his one arm thrust outwards, as if to give his damaged body better balance. Occasionally, he would stop, his head down, as if pondering what he should do next. At these times, Ivy shrank back. She did not wish him to turn and see her. But he never did.

He was climbing now to Holy Water Clump, where she could see the red flag drooping in the still, grey air. She tensed, seeking a place to hide herself as she had yesterday, because, with the red flag flying, he would surely turn and come back by the same path. Yet, this time she would confront him and let him know her concerns.

Then she saw him disappear into the woods despite the flag, and her fears for him returned. She hastened forward to follow him.

29

George walked quickly between the trees. His brain felt heavy once more, full of noise. It was as if he was being called forward to a destination long-awaited, where he would learn at last what was expected of him. The army of Allectus, he knew, were all about him. He would surely come to the tribunal soon, where Allectus would address the legions, and he would learn of his role too. Then the battle would begin against those forces that had begun once more to howl in his head.

Somewhere, far off, he began to hear the thuds of firing. Fear seized him. But also, excitement. The battle!

He thought he had survived the battle, but it was still going on. The battle of Allectus; the green riflemen falling, the blood jetting out. Had they then combined – the past and the present? Where was he? What day was this? His mind was splitting with his incomprehension. He only knew he must go on.

He heard a shout now, and saw a dark figure which waved its arms above its head, but he heeded it not and plunged on, the bushes and undergrowth pulling at his clothes, the rain dripping onto him. His right arm, it hurt now all down its length: he could feel it trying to grasp the hilt of his sword, but it fell away. If his sword arm had been injured, then Allectus would not want him, and he knew he was prepared to fight and die for that man.

Behind him, she hurried, hearing the same shouts and thuds as he. She knew they were trespassing here, and it was unsafe, but she could do nothing else but press on. She tried calling out to him, but he did not hear. Then he disappeared from her sight and she could not follow him anymore. She cast about fearfully. To where had he gone so suddenly?

More shouting behind her now and the sound of feet crashing through undergrowth. More thuds on the air, and the sudden clear call of a bugle sounding out. She came through a screen of trees and saw she was at the edge of the great Woolmer Pond, which stretched away veiled in a mist of rain, its far reaches hidden by an encroaching darkness. Away to the right, men were drawn up in rank. They wore dark-coloured tunics and trousers.

Then, lying amongst the rushes at her feet, she found him, face downward on the water, his cape like a dark ring about his shoulders, his body still and drifting outward, his one arm flung outwards as if to pull himself onward.

She screamed and screamed again, stumbling into the water to try and reach him, and then all of a sudden there were others about her, and many voices, and soldiers were in the water, seizing George's legs, pulling him in. They turned him over: his face was white, his eyes closed.

A soldier took her arm and tried to pull her back away from him, but she would not go. 'Oh, George, George!' she cried. 'Don't leave me, George. Don't go.'

A soldier was bent over George, wrenching his cape aside, thumping at his chest, breathing into his mouth; on and on, he went, but then slower now, more despairingly, looking round, looking into Ivy's eyes, perhaps to give up and say it's too late....when suddenly George coughed and retched and water spurted from his mouth. They turned him, and he coughed and spluttered more, and more water seeped up from his lungs. He tried to speak, but could make no sound.

'Sit up, if you can,' a voice commanded. It was a man in a blue jacket with gold braid on his chest. George did so, and then was sick, the spume rolling out his mouth onto his front.

'Serves you right, you stupid bastard,' the man said, turning his head. 'Where's that bloody stretcher?' he called.

Ivy's arms were about George. 'Oh, my dear. Oh, my love, what have you done? Why? Oh, why?'

A strange smile came to George's face, as if he was not seated here, soaked, half dead, saved by the merest chance, by the merest sliver of time, to bring breath into his lungs again, to reach his brain before it failed and died. He spluttered, and he coughed, able to speak now: Ivy had to bend forward to hear him.

'I saw him, you know The Roman, Allectus. He was as clear as day. It was hot and he beckoned me on. But you know...' – he coughed badly, as a blanket was brought and wrapped about him, and the stretcher was lowered to the grass at his feet.

'....You know, my Ivy, I did not want to go.'

And with that he turned his head away and he wept.

Little can be written now. This story is almost at its end. Yet a few more lines can be added, and it will be seen that out of near tragedy came happiness – which is good, for we all like a tale that ends well.

George spent some time recovering. After initial treatment at the infirmary of the army camp nearby, he was borne to Blackmoor House in one of their own wagons, the army being anxious to help when they learnt he was a discharged and wounded veteran who was still suffering great trauma. Lord Selborne, arising from his own sickbed, ensured George could stay on at the lodge, his duties suspended until he was better.

He paid for a hospital nurse to visit him regularly, while Ivy was released from her normal work to help nurse him.

And George did recover well. Whatever it was that had created the sickness in his head had been expelled now. He could never understand what had happened to him, and what had led him into trying to destroy himself. For he knew that when he had fallen into that pond, he had not simply stumbled; he had entered those waters because he had wanted to.

His headaches had gone now, and he slowly grew back into being the old, happy, hopeful George once more, still interested in the past – the Romans in particular – but now everything was in its place, as it should be. If that seems like a miracle, well, so be it. Miracles can indeed happen, as the observant may see every day, if he or she only looks around.

Ivy helped him, of course. It was she who found the coin of Allectus still in his pocket, and they decided to throw it away. In fact, it went off to the local blacksmith's furnace to be melted down, and she and George watched as the sharp-nosed profile bubbled away into a small pool of bronze.

Ivy was the most wonderful thing that ever happened to George, and, when he was fully recovered, and a little more time had passed for propriety's sake, the two were married at St. Matthew's Church in Blackmoor. The village children and many of the staff from Blackmoor House lined the churchyard path and threw rose petals upon the happy couple. The bride – as the papers recorded – looked a 'radiant vision of happiness', and George very dapper in a formal suit and top hat, a present to him from Lord Selborne, who attended the ceremony in person, with others of his family.

George resumed his job as lodge porter, which he did now to his fullest ability, and performed many services of great value to the family. He became a familiar figure to those calling at the house, with his empty right sleeve pinned across the jacket of his porter's uniform. He was later called back by Lord Selborne to take charge of that library from which he had once been so summarily dismissed, Mr. Whiteley having long moved on to a position in London. After some years, a vacancy having arisen, Ivy took up the position of housekeeper, and, a confident woman now – she had borne George two children, a boy and a girl – she ruled the house with a rod of steel, but a forgiving heart.

When a new period of excavations at *Calleva*, sponsored by the Society of Antiquaries began in 1890, financed once again by the Duke of Wellington, but now the 3rd Duke, his predecessor having died six years earlier of a heart attack at Brighton Station, George would visit as often as he could. He would talk to the excavators and tell them of his own days there and of some of the things they had discovered.

Before the new digging began, George wandered the site, marvelling at what they had achieved those years back under the wonderful Reverend Mr. Joyce, whose grave both Ivy and he would visit often to lay flowers upon. The evidence of the Reverend's work was still there at *Calleva*, having been left open to decay greatly, although some small amount of further work had been carried out in the Reverend's trenches, ending finally on the 2nd Duke of Wellington's death. The walls he had revealed were now tumbled down in places, and a debris of tile and stone, oyster shell and pottery fragments, was spread all around, left by those very last excavators. One of the first tasks of the new Society of Antiquaries' excavations was to tidy the place up once again.

While at *Calleva* – the digging there continued until 1909, having uncovered almost the entirety of the town – George would look into Silchester Church and gaze upon the painting of the crucifixion the Reverend Mr. Joyce had made, and reflect that he had known a most Christian man whose memory should never die – first in most of the many things he put his hand to, but his Christian calling was yet above all. George learnt that his son, Arthur, had entered the church as well, becoming rector in 1887 of a church in Winchester.

Both Ivy and George retired from service at Blackmoor House when old age called, but they were able to take a tied cottage not far from the church, where they lived out their lives in great contentment. George was the first to pass on at a good age shortly before the Second World War, but Ivy lived on to a very great age, living through that war, and eventually going to meet her maker one year short of her century. She died in 1956. As a young boy the author of this book knew her, and was able to hear her talk about those grand, old days she had seen.

And thus, are we able to reach back across the ages.

AFTERWORD

The Hampshire locations which are described in this book can be visited with relative ease. First and foremost, the Roman town of Silchester provides a most interesting day out, if armed with the English Heritage guidebook and, for those with a deeper interest, Professor Michael Fulford's recent publication, 'Silchester Revealed' – a most valuable resource. Silchester Church, hard by the Roman east gate, however, fails to reveal any sign of the Reverend J. G. Joyce's painting of the crucifixion, which he completed for its re-opening after restoration.

Reading Museum now holds the main collection of archaeological finds from Silchester, including those once in the possession of the 2nd and 3rd Dukes of Wellington, including the famed horse and eagle. The Museum also has in its library the three bound volumes of the Reverend Mr. Joyce's journal of his excavations from 1864-1877, which came most fortuitously into its possession in 1933. At Stratfield Saye House, which may be visited at certain times of the year (consult their web site), three of the Silchester mosaics are set into the floor of its front hall.

Mr. Joyce's church at Stratfield Saye can also be visited: there is a driveway there from the lane, the gates to which will open at the approach of a car. The Reverend is buried in a vault in the churchyard, but when I visited on a day of sweeping rain I could not locate the spot. There is no other memorial to him that I know of, other than for his journal and the published reports of his work.

Certain of the finds from the grounds of Blackmoor House, including the Roman enamelled jug, are on display at the excellent Curtis Museum in Alton.

St. Matthew's Church in Blackmoor is the legacy of the 1st Lord Selborne, whose Blackmoor House, now divided into apartments, can be viewed from the outside by a wander up the driveway. Do not, however, trespass further without permission! Nearby, Woolmer Pond, where George nearly met his end, may be visited by a walk, although not when the Army is in use of the area. Hogmoor Inclosure, further to the north, provides excellent walks and an adventure playground for children, most tempting for adults too. Along the 'Roman trail' here, various wooden figures have been set, which have a strange, melancholic appeal – sentinels of time, indeed. An information board also provides information about the battle that overcame Allectus, possibly fought over this very ground.

The Rifles Museum in Winchester will tell you all you wish to know about the 3rd/60th Rifles and its service in South Africa. I have had the opportunity of visiting all the battlefields where the battalion fought in the years 1879-1881.

If you seek the graves of Ivy and George in Blackmoor churchyard, you may be as unsuccessful as I was in locating the Reverend James Joyce's grave at Stratfield Saye. Yet, that they are there somewhere goes without doubt.

My thanks are to Jane Hurst of the Curtis Museum in Alton for providing me with information regarding that town, in particular its inns and public houses. Any errors in interpretation, however, are mine alone.

I would also like to thank Davina Hudson, church warden at St. Matthew's, Blackmoor for invaluable information about the church and village, as well as a colleague for pointing me towards Hogmoor Inclosure.

Much gratitude as well to the website of the British Newspaper Archive, without whose excellent resources many of my reconstructions would have been impossible to write.

Finally, Susie has endured this project for twelve months or so, and accompanied me to many places in the text, often in very wet weather, which she has borne with great fortitude.

July 2024